Praise for
Dark Water

"Linda Hall has done it again in this whale of a tale called *Dark Water*. Not only did I quickly engage with midlife May and her partner, Jake, as ship-owning, whale-watching, struggling-with-life private investigators; I learned things about jewelry making, whales, a young girl's longing, the power of people's pasts to hold them hostage, and what it takes to heal. *Dark Water* is a triumph, and best of all, it's the first in a series."

> —JANE KIRKPATRICK, award-winning author of *A Land of Sheltered Promise* and *A Clearing in the Wild* (April 2006)

"Linda Hall's *Dark Water* does what any good mystery does: it snags you with unforgettable characters and teases you with tantalizing clues. Don't start this book unless you have a long stretch of uninterrupted time in front of you. Once you begin reading, you won't be able to stop."

> —THOM LEMMONS, coauthor of the Christy Award–winning *King's Ransom* and author of *Sunday Clothes* and *Jabez: A Novel*

"*Dark Water* kept me in suspense from page one. Its lively setting among the whale watchers of Fog Point provides a cast of captivating and highly suspicious characters. Who to trust? Who to fear? I was caught in the intricacies of the plot until the very end. Such an unlikely—but thoroughly convincing—killer! Such a charming—but lethal—town!

> —ROSEMARY AUBERT, award-winning author of the Ellis Portal Mystery series

"A quality cast of gritty, memorable characters keeps Linda Hall's dark mystery *Dark Water* moving at lightning speed. I was ensnared by this story from the first page to the very end. *Highly recommended!*"

> —RANDY INGERMANSON, Christy Award–winning novelist and author of *Retribution* and *Double Vision*

"Written perceptively and with compassion for the sufferings of any and all, Linda Hall's *Dark Water* follows a trail of abuse and deceit across the human soul."

> —SALLY WRIGHT, Mystery Writers of America 2001 finalist and author of the Ben Reese Mystery series

"The flawed lives of Hall's characters create a riptide of excitement and suspense that will keep readers guessing to the very last page. *Dark Water* is aptly named."

> —JANET AND RON BENREY, authors of *Little White Lies, The Second Mile, Humble Pie, Dead as a Scone, The Final Crumpet,* and *Glory Be!*

DARK WATER

A NOVEL

DARK WATER

LINDA HALL

WATERBROOK
PRESS

Dark Water
Published by WaterBrook Press
12265 Oracle Boulevard, Suite 200
Colorado Springs, Colorado 80921
A division of Random House Inc.

ISBN 1-57856-954-0

Library of Congress Cataloging-in-Publication Data
Hall, Linda, 1950–
Dark water / Linda Hall.—1st ed.
     p. cm.
  ISBN 1-57856-954-0
  1. Private investigators—Fiction. 2. Stalking—Fiction. I. Title.
PS3558.A3698D37 2006
813'.54—dc22

                                                              2005032886

Printed in the United States of America
2006—First Edition

10 9 8 7 6 5 4 3 2 1

For Joshua

ACKNOWLEDGMENTS

There were so many people who helped me with the technical aspects of this book:

A special thank-you to Mark Sumner of Atlantic Jewels for an amazing tour of your studio and equipment and kilns. I never before realized how much went into this process. I was very impressed with your beautiful pieces.

To Tim Finley of Flight of the Eagle Jewelry Arts for a remarkable look at how silver strands are twisted to make gorgeous designs. You are truly an artisan.

Also, to biologist Dr. Chuck Schom of Surge Tours—thank you for an awesome ride aboard a fast, and I do mean fast, whale-watching boat, the *Noteworthy*. On that day in September, we saw every whale the Bay of Fundy has to give up: humpbacks, minkes, finbacks, and rights, including a basking shark that breached right in front of us. I will never forget it!

Thank you to Tim McDonald and Steph Whitson, who shared Harley information with me.

I also thank those who lent their support to make this book a better one: To my husband, Rik, who is always my brainstormer and patient first reader; to my agent, Danielle, for your support and constant encouragement; and to my editor, Shannon, for helping to whip this whole thing into shape.

PROLOGUE

To my mom,

My hands are all white. I've just broken apart a piece of the wall in my closet, and there's all this white stuff, like chalk. It's all over me now. Even in my hair.

I was looking for a way out, like in the Chronicles of Narnia; maybe a secret passage, a place I could go. Instead, I dug and dug until I had this perfect little square hole, this private place.

At first I was just ripping off little pieces of wallpaper. Then I pushed the sharp point of my pencil into a little crack and made it bigger. And then all these pieces started falling away like chalk. My hands are white and dirty, and there are dead bugs. Now there's a square hole in the wall that fits my diary book exactly.

My teacher, Mrs. McLaren, gave me the idea of doing this, not of breaking my wall (ha!), but of writing letters to you in this book. We're supposed to write in a journal book every day and then hand it in at the end of the week for her to grade. She told us we could write letters to someone we know and then not send them, or even make up a person to write to if we felt like it. So I decided to keep two journal books, one that I hand in for school and one that I write to you, my mother. My school journal will be about whales and how I want to be a marine biologist when I grow up, and this one, my letters to you, no one will ever see. Not even you.

Sometimes when I'm at my best friend Ashley's, I pretend that Ashley's mother is my mother and her brothers are my brothers and her sister is my sister. I'm never afraid when I'm at Ashley's for a sleepover. I'm afraid at home sometimes.

A few nights ago I was in my room reading my whales book, and you were on the phone. I could hear you swearing even through my closed door. You curse sometimes. Not in front of people, but when you're mad. This makes me afraid.

I crept out of my room in my bare feet and went to your bedroom door. It was open just a crack, and there you were, facing the window, still in your high heels. I don't know why you always have to wear high heels. Even on picnics. Once at a picnic you played softball in them, running around the bases in your short shorts and high-heeled sandals, your feet like Barbie feet. You tell me it's because you need the extra height. But even with your high heels, you're littler than everybody. Including me. My feet are already the same size as yours. I wish you were normal-sized.

That night you held the phone with both hands and stood first on one leg and then the other.

"I'll get a restraining order," you said. "That's what I'll do. If I'm forced to do that, I will. I'll even get a gun. I'll learn how to use it..." Then your voice became a whisper, and I couldn't hear the words anymore.

A few minutes later you slammed the phone down and rushed into your bathroom. I don't get to use your bathroom. I have to use the one in the hall. I like your bathroom best because you have so many little jars of makeup and different color hair gels and, of course, lots and lots of jewelry.

Once when you were out, Ashley and I sneaked in there. This red hair of mine is a color I hate in hair. You tell me it's the same color as my father's. You told me he died in a car accident when I was a baby. I don't know what he looked like. How come you don't have any pictures of him?

Anyway, when Ashley and I were in your bathroom, I had my eye on the blue hair gel, while Ashley decided on the green. Before long we were not only gelling our hair into weird shapes but trying on all of your makeup, drawing lines around our eyes, sponging pink blush onto our cheeks, and ringing our lips all around with red.

And then you were there! And you went totally ballistic! Swearing. Even in front of Ashley. I ended up grounded for a month, and Ashley was banned from our house for two. I still remember the way Ashley walked out of the house—the ends of her blond braids coated in red and red streaks in her bangs. I thought it looked nice.

But later you came to me crying and saying how sorry you were for yelling. You were mad at something else and just took it out on me. We sat in the rocking chair together for a long time under a blanket and watched Everybody Loves Raymond reruns. I like it when that happens.

I was remembering this when I heard you throwing up. I went into your closet and touched all your shoes. There is one pair I like with straps that can either go behind your heel or across the top of your foot. I put on one shoe with the strap around the heel and one with the strap over the top. On the other side of the wall you kept throwing up and throwing up. I put my hands over my ears. Awhile later I heard the toilet flush and the water come on, then off. Finally, you came out and stood and looked at me for a long time with your face all white and your ghost eyes and the whole place smelling like throw-up.

I ran away from you and into my room and hid under the covers. I half-expected you to follow me, but you didn't. I was afraid. I had seen your eyes, and I was afraid.

I woke several times to your loud cursing and stumbling in the living room below. I put my hands over my ears and my pillow over my head. I smelled cigarettes just as the sun was beginning to shine through my curtains. I looked out my window, and there you were down below on the patio, inhaling quickly, exhaling quickly, like this was something you wanted to get over with in a hurry.

Smoking is another thing you don't like anyone to know about. Once I found your cigarettes and took one to my room and smoked it by my window.

"Smoking will kill you!" You grabbed the cigarette from my hand and stubbed it out on the windowsill. "Smoking is bad for you. You should never start."

"But you smoke," I said.

"I smoke one cigarette a week. That's all. Just one a week. A person can smoke one a week and still be healthy."

In the morning when I woke up, there was fog. It was Saturday, and I went downstairs and sat at the kitchen table with my whales book. I was reading about the North Atlantic right whale and how there are only around 350 left. They are nearly extinct but are coming back.

In a little while you came down all dressed up in your high heels and dangly earrings.

"Well, my pumpkin, how about some nice french toast? How about I make some with powdered sugar and cinnamon and vanilla in the batter? Just the way you like it." Your voice was so bright and cheerful.

"Are you okay, Mom?"

You turned quickly, holding the carton of eggs. "Of course I'm okay!"

"But last night you were sick."

"This is a new day. Everything's going to be okay now."

And then you grinned and I saw all your teeth, even the sort of crooked one on the side. But instead of making me feel better, it made me feel afraid.

Your daughter,

Rachel St. Dennis

1

O n the day Wesley Stoller got out of jail, the phone at Elise
St. Dennis's house rang four times. But no one was there to
answer it. Elise was driving the fifty miles or so down the coast highway to Ridley Harbor to deliver an order of her jewelry to Misty Gifts
and Gallery. She was singing "Slip Slidin' Away" along with Paul
Simon on the radio.

Her daughter, Rachel, along with twenty other sixth graders, was
writing in her journal. Bent over, elbow pressed hard into the ruled
pages, forehead in her hand, she wrote in her tiny, careful script.

And on the day Wesley Stoller got out of jail, the minke whales,
which were making their way up to their summer feeding grounds, had
been spotted somewhere off Thunder Island. Two Fog Point fishermen also saw a small pod of endangered North Atlantic right whales
near the breakwater out by the lighthouse. They had seen the whales'
V-shaped blow in the distance and had investigated.

It would be a good season for whales, and Jake Rikker was scrubbing away at the transom of his boat and wondering if he could get
away with not repainting the words *The Purple Whale* for one more
season.

A day like today, this luscious late-spring day as warm as taffy, was enough to make even the most pessimistic person hopeful. Clusters of locals talked about the weather as they drank coffee down at Noonan's Café. The *Farmer's Almanac* predicted a long, hot summer with just enough rain to keep the farmers happy, but not enough to keep the vacationers away. It would be a good season for tourists.

~

And on this day Elise braked to a stop at a yellow light and steadied the cardboard carton on the passenger seat. Inside the carton three dozen tiny green boxes bore the name Elise's Creations scripted in gold beneath a stylized dragon—her trademark. The boxes held varieties of gemmed barrettes, brooches, earrings, necklaces, bracelets, or silver coiled snakes with emerald eyes.

She looked back to the road and thought about changing the name. She'd never particularly liked the name Elise's Creations, which, in her estimation, could refer to anything from cake decorating to teddy bears. Yet at this point, changing it would probably be more trouble than it was worth. She pondered that as the light turned green.

She'd been Elise's Creations for eight years, ever since that first Summer Solstice Craft Fair when she'd breezed in pulling a wooden wagon containing her two-year-old daughter and a few boxes of her handmade jewelry. She'd needed a name then, quick, for the program. (No one had told her that when she rented the booth.) Elise's Creations had been the first thing she could think of. She'd made enough money that first year to almost pay for the booth rental. It had been that way for a while. Waitressing by day at Noonan's Café in Fog

Point and, by night, bending over her wires and beads with her soldering iron.

She'd finally persuaded a Fog Point bank manager to believe in her. She secured a loan and rented a huge and expensive studio on the boardwalk. She covered the floors with lush deep-lavender carpet, the most expensive on the market, and set her pieces on faux-marble pedestals with backlighting. With Enya playing in the background, a little waterfall sculpture in the window, and displays of bracelets, Celtic crosses, and her dragons, the shop offered a bit of an oasis from the hot, loud music and skateboarders out front.

She marked up every single item, and all the tourists from California thought they were getting a bargain. It was starting to make Elise's single life with her daughter just a bit more bearable. Two years ago she'd doubled the prices for a second time. Life was beginning to be good.

She was one of the few Fog Pointers who was on a first-name basis with a lot of the rich and famous "summer people," as the locals referred to the summer residents. The summer people raved about her stuff to all their rich and famous friends, and Elise found herself busier than she had ever intended to be. She was slowly building a name for herself. All of her hard work was finally paying off.

She learned to dress the part too. No more hippie funk with gauzy brown skirts and clogs; her costume could now be described as bohemian chic with mismatched gold chandelier earrings and delicate lace-up-the-calf high heels. Two years ago she'd had her waist-length hair chopped to within an inch of her scalp. Sometimes she slicked it away from her face with gel, adding bits of color to the ends. Sometimes she wore it in spiky chunks all over her head, blue or green.

Odd punk shades they were, but coupled with the expensive clothes and her delicate footwear, she looked hip and endearing—an artiste.

Two years ago she hired a business manager who had just graduated at the top of her class in business and advertising. Jess was vivacious, spunky, and had a flair for marketing. Her personal goal was to take Elise's Creations to the next level. "The sky is the limit now," Jess said. "Harry Winston move over." These kinds of statements always made Elise just the teeniest bit uneasy.

And while the manager at Misty Gifts gushed over Elise's latest designs, Wesley Stoller walked free after serving only ten years of a life sentence for murder.

The telephone-message button was flashing when Elise finally arrived home much later. Two calls, one right after the other. Blocked numbers. No messages. Jess? No, Jess would've left a message. The school? Something to do with Rachel? She pressed the school's number into her phone but hung up before it could ring. If it was the school, if Rachel was having problems again, the caller would have left a message.

She poured herself a glass of water and stood beside the kitchen window. Across the backyard Lenore Featherjohn troweled up winter weeds, her red cotton shorts pulled high and taut across her white thighs as she dug. A pile of scrub lay beside her.

Elise watched until she finished her drink. Then she pulled on her jacket, got in her car, and headed down to her studio. She walked in the back door still humming "Slip Slidin' Away."

A man stood there.

"Oh!" She nearly fell but quickly righted herself and grabbed the doorjamb. She recognized him. Jake something-or-other who ran a whale-watching business and sporting-goods store. He kept shoving his hands into his pockets and taking them out again as he looked at her.

"I came in the front door. No one seemed to be there. So I came back here."

"My assistant's not here?" She blinked and tried to steady herself. Three years ago she had installed a state-of-the-art alarm system, which, when activated, notified the police department of any illegal entry. She was always careful about security. She had to be.

"You must be Elise. I'm sorry I startled you." He walked toward her. "I'm Jake Rikker. I know who you are, but I don't think we've ever formally met."

"I can't believe no one's around." Then she looked back at him. "I'm sorry. You'll have to forgive me." She forced herself to stay calm. "Is there something I can help you with?"

"I came to buy some jewelry." He grinned. He was a big man and wore a slouchy gray sweater, uneven at the bottom, and round wire-rim glasses. "For a couple of very special ladies."

"Two?" Elise struggled to regain her composure. "You have two special ladies? What a lucky man you are."

"My daughters."

"Ah, doubly lucky, then." She smiled up at him. "How old are your daughters?"

"Eleven and thirteen."

"How lovely! I have an eleven-year-old. A great age. Well, I've got some teddy-bear necklaces that I make especially for little girls. Plus there are my dragons. Follow me out to the front."

He followed her through the door to the showroom and to a display of charm bracelets. "Have I seen your daughters in town?" she asked. She steered him toward several display cases, still uncertain about the security breach, still wondering if there was something she should do about the unlocked door. Call the police? She scanned the place. Everything looked in order. When Jake left she'd have a good look around, especially in her workshop in the back where she kept gemstones, diamonds, gold, and chemicals she used in her work.

"I don't think you would've seen them. They spend most of the school year with their mother," he said, "and some of the summers with me." He picked up a box while Elise ducked behind the counter and unlocked a glass display case.

"Here, let me see what I can find," she said.

Jake turned over a box. "Whoa! Is that the price?"

She nodded. "My pieces are all handmade. Every one is different; every one unique. That's why they might seem expensive. Plus, I work exclusively in gold and silver now. I've got a similar piece in silver, and it's slightly less expensive."

She chose a few small barrettes and necklaces and bracelets and spread them out on a black cloth on the glass counter.

"I can see why movie stars like your stuff." He put the box down and continued to browse. He turned over another box and looked at the price. He turned over a lot of boxes, something her rich clientele never did.

"I have to ask you something," she said. "Did you happen to call earlier? My house?"

"Nope." He didn't look up.

"And the front door here was unlocked?"

"Yep."

"I got a call, but no one was there."

"That happens to me all the time. Telemarketers. I think I like these."

"What's nice about charm bracelets," she said, "is that you can add charms anytime. It makes Christmas giving easy. And I have charms for many occasions: birthdays, Valentine's Day, graduation, Christmas, even for a good report card. These are some I designed and cast. They're available in either gold or silver." She spread the charms out on the cloth.

He picked up one of the bracelets and jingled it in his hand. "Okay," he said finally. "These are nice. Two of these, in silver. Gold's a little beyond me."

"Would you like a special-occasion box? I have jewelry boxes for birthdays, special anniversaries, you name it. Or would you prefer an all-occasion box?"

"A regular box. No special occasion." He grinned at her. It was a nice grin, warm. He leaned over the counter. "Unless you have summer-vacation boxes."

She smiled up at him, perhaps for a moment longer than necessary. Then quickly, nervously, she looked back down at her boxes.

And while she was placing two silver charm bracelets into satin drawstring bags and then onto beds of tissue in the gift boxes, in another place Wesley Stoller was sitting at a window booth, drinking a large Pepsi, no ice, and relishing a steak—rare, with onions. He'd looked forward to this for ten years—a huge juicy steak with all the trimmings. Loaded. He licked his lips and then ordered dessert.

Two days later Elise stood outside the front door of a church that was entirely painted an impossible shade of purple. It was now home to Adventure Whale Tours and Outfitting, Salvage and Investigations. Churches were not her favorite places. Even churches that weren't churches anymore were not her favorite places. Although she allowed Rachel to attend every Sunday with her friend Ashley's family, Elise would not go. Could not go. "It's complicated," she told Rachel's Sunday-school teacher the year Rachel was chosen as Mary for the Christmas play. "I can't come. It's a personal thing. Rachel understands. We've talked about it."

The Purple Church's double doors were open, and Elise could imagine that at one time in its history, a minister would have stood on this very spot to shake hands with the faithful after morning services. Elise drew the ends of her cotton-lace shawl to her neck and walked up the steps.

In the two days since Jake Rikker had bought charm bracelets for his daughters, Elise had done her research. Buzz Noonan, who ran Noonan's Café, knew everyone in town, and if there was anyone who could tell her about Jake, it would be Buzz. Plus, for some reason Buzz and his wife, Nootie, liked her. She suspected that they always felt a bit sorry for the single mother who had shown up in Fog Point from out of nowhere, disheveled and desperately needing a job. For four years Elise had waited tables, washed dishes, and helped Nootie bake pies. Rachel grew up going there every day after school, watching *Veggie Tales* videos in the back room while she waited for her mother's shift to end.

A long time ago Jake had been a police officer, Buzz told her. He arrived about three years ago and, along with May Williams, bought the old condemned Congregational church. They sold the stained-glass window above the platform and got enough money to bring the building up to code, plus renovate the entire place and construct living accommodations in the basement for himself and the summer students they hired. Buzz laughed when he said, "If the Featherjohn brothers had any idea how much it was worth, they never would've sold it."

"The Featherjohn brothers owned the church?" Elise asked. She took a sip of the coffee Buzz poured for her and wrapped her legs around the stool.

It was a complicated story and went back to Fog Point's origins, Buzz explained. The church property had originally belonged to the faithful members, of which the Featherjohn brothers' grandfather had been their fire-and-brimstone preacher for fifty-five years. In a gesture of goodwill, the church building and parsonage were given to his widow when he died. When she died, the building was handed down to her only child, Lenore. It was expected that Lenore would marry a minister like her mother and grandmother before her. Instead, she married Harlan Featherjohn, who had never set foot in any church in his life. After her father died, the building sat vacant for many years, and most of the congregation migrated to Stone Church. In a moment of great weakness, Lenore signed the building over to her sons, who had great plans for tearing it down and building condos on the site because it overlooked the water. A decade of failed plans later, they finally sold it for a pittance to Jake and May, who saw the value in the stained glass.

"Tell me about Jake and May," Elise asked the Noonans. "What are they to each other?" She thought about the two of them. May was older than Jake, in her fifties, and she walked with a limp. Elise had heard that May's husband, a police officer, had died in the line of duty. That's all she knew.

"Business partners. She's the brain; he's the brawn. They've done well."

"Their sign says Investigations. What's that all about?"

Buzz cut her a piece of Nootie's raspberry sour pie and set it in front of her. "They're private investigators."

"Oh?"

"They specialize in finding things. Jake's a diver. So it's a lot of salvage work. Someone throws a gun out into the bay, and they hire Jake to find it."

Elise carefully cut into her slice of pie with a fork.

"You remember that fugitive who escaped prison and was living in the Browngreen shack out on the island?" he asked.

Elise nodded. She'd been extra cautious about her security then.

"He stole a dory and rowed over there at low tide. Jake and May found him. Well, May lives out there. Not on the island but over by The Shallows."

"So he works with the police then?" Elise asked.

"Sometimes. Yeah. I guess once a cop always a cop."

～

Once a cop always a cop, Elise mused.

"I did a stupid, stupid thing, and now I'm paying for it," she began. "I'm being stalked, and it's my own fault. I got involved with a crazy person—a psychopath. I need you to find him before he gets here, before he finds me…" She'd practiced the lines over and over in front of the bathroom mirror. Would Jake believe her? Could she trust Jake with this?

She stood in front of the open door of the church now and put a hand to her throat. She swallowed several times before stepping inside. It was quiet. It even smelled like a church. But instead of rows of wooden pews with ornately carved ends, stained-glass saints looked down on metal racks of plastic kayaks, life jackets, camp stoves, and packages of freeze-dried macaroni and cheese. Posters of whales filled the wall spaces between the saints.

A wooden kayak on a stand sat on a raised chancel at the front. Long, sleek, and glossy, the kayak picked up points of light as the sun shone through the clear glass window behind it. She walked toward it, her three-inch heels clacking on the wooden floor, the only sound in the place.

The whole thing was crazy. She should just turn around right now and go home. Pretend everything was the way it had been. *Go back, go back.* But of course things weren't the way they had been; things never would be the same again.

She heard voices at the back. Elise tried visibly to calm herself, uncrinkle the fingers that held tightly to her shawl, breathe deeply.

Breathe. Breathe. Like her friend Norah had taught her. *In. Out. In. Out. Cleansing breath. There.*

A door at the back of the church opened, and out came Jake and May. May was wearing a baseball cap with "Squirrels" written on it in shiny script and a red sweatshirt with a whale on it. She leaned on a wooden cane.

"Hey. Hi." Jake stopped. "Nice to see you again."

"Now it's my turn to ask the question. Are you open?"

"Of course we're open." He turned to May. "We're always open, aren't we, May?"

"Always open." May extended her hand. "And you're Elise from the jewelry store."

"May, May. She's more than the girl from the jewelry store. This lady makes all her own jewelry. Now to what do we owe the honor? You interested in a kayak? Some freeze-dried hot dogs?" Again, his face broke into that crazy grin.

She put a hand to her neck and said quietly, "I need a private investigator. Buzz told me you do that sort of work."

Jake raised his eyebrows, and May said, "How 'bout we go into the office?"

Much of the furniture in the back office bespoke its former era as a sacristy. A small laptop computer sat on a dark, sturdy wooden table, ornate with crosses. Brochures, posters, and newspapers lay in piles on the other sideboards and tables. Elise sat along with Jake and May on collapsible wooden folding chairs.

"Coffee?" May asked.

"Thank you." She was nervous. She hadn't expected to be this nervous. Maybe it was the church or maybe it was Jake. Maybe both.

May poured three cups from a small electric coffeepot that sat on a wooden table.

Elise swallowed several times. "I need a detective..." She couldn't continue. The words weren't there.

"Tell us what you need," May said gently.

Elise bit her lip and began. "My daughter and I are in danger from a man who has just been released from prison." Jake seemed to study her, and she felt suddenly shy.

"Tell us about it," he urged.

She did. A number of years ago, she was watching a TV program about prisons, specifically about inmates and their daily lives. "I've always felt sorry for prisoners," she said. "The program gave an address and said if we wanted to write to them, we could." She stopped, looked at May and Jake, bit her lip.

Jake shook his head ever so slightly. "Go on," he said.

Elise explained that she found a Web site that explained how to e-mail prisoners, and she began an e-mail correspondence with several of them. "I just wanted to be friendly. I even sent some jewelry to a couple of them and suggested they give it to their mothers. I never had any trouble. Everything was fine, until...until I e-mailed this one guy..." She paused.

"What happened?" May asked.

She told them about a prisoner who seemed friendly enough at first, but whose e-mails had gradually become more and more intense.

"Intense?"

"He wanted a relationship with me. He wanted me to visit him in prison. I told him no. I just wanted to be friends, but then he began writing lots of e-mails. Sometimes there would be four and five a day.

I used a Yahoo! mail account that I've since canceled. At least I was smart enough not to use my regular e-mail address. I thought I was safe. He was in there; I was out here. He didn't know where I lived. How could he? Eventually I wrote to him and said I didn't think we should e-mail anymore. Well, that's when he started getting weird. Threatening. Writing things like if he couldn't have me, no one would have me. In his last e-mail he described in great detail what he was going to do to me and to Rachel when he found us. Rachel's my daughter." Her hands shook when she said her daughter's name. She was aware of Jake's face as she talked. It was an expressive face, large-featured and sun-brown. He looked kind. She addressed her comments to him, looking at him rather than May.

"Was it e-mail correspondence only? Were there any letters?" Jake asked.

"Just e-mail."

"So he doesn't have your street address?"

"No." She looked past them at a whale poster on the wall—the tail fin of a monstrous creature surfacing on rough, black water.

May asked, "How long has he been out?"

"Just a couple days."

"How do you know this?"

"He sent me an e-mail. He told me he was getting out. I didn't respond. I canceled that Yahoo! account then." Elise closed her eyes briefly.

"What about the jewelry you sent him?" Jake asked. "Did you have your business name on it anywhere? Did you send it in one of your boxes?"

She shook her head. "I was pretty careful with that."

"Well, that's good, then," May said. "This may be a stupid question, but why don't you go to the police?"

"I can't."

"Why not?"

Elise shook her head. "It's complicated."

"How complicated could it be?" May asked. "Surely they must know about this guy. Where is he now? Some halfway house somewhere?"

"I don't know where he is! That's the whole thing. I don't know. But what if he finds out where I live?" She ran a hand through her spiky hair.

"Then don't waste your time with us. Call the police." Jake leaned forward. "We've got a friend on the force here. Name's Bill. Maybe you've seen him around town. He's a good friend."

"No police. I can't. The police, they won't believe me. It's a long story."

"We're listening," May said.

"My family..." She paused and looked down at her hands, small and white, her red polished fingernails like little dots of blood. "It's why I'm here. Why I came to Fog Point in the first place. Why I wanted to start over. My father is...was...incarcerated. He died in prison a few years ago. I used to bug the police all the time about my father and the treatment he was getting. Maybe that's why I'm so concerned about prisoners, which is probably why I started writing to Wesley Stoller in the first place. A family connection." She looked at another poster on the wall behind Jake that showed several kayakers paddling side by side on a diamond-sparkled sea. "How many people can say they have a family connection with prison?" she added quietly.

May set down her coffee. "How long have you two been e-mailing?"

"Seven years." Elise looked down at her feet, tiny toes in stiletto sandals.

"Seven years of e-mails. And you would have these on your computer?" May asked.

"No."

"No?"

"That's the thing." A thread had worked its way loose in her shawl, and she pulled at it. If she pulled it long enough, her whole shawl would unravel. "I trashed them. Then I emptied the trash."

"That should be no problem," May said. "We can take your hard drive and have them recovered."

"No, that's just it; you can't. I took my computer to this computer place in Ridley Harbor where they totally cleared it. I did it yesterday. I didn't want any trace. I didn't want him to be able to find me..."

May frowned. "What about the Web site where you found him?"

"I can't remember which one it was. I went to several. You've got to understand that I was trying to forget. I wanted him out of my life and off my computer."

Jake put his hands on his knees and looked over at May. Elise noticed a hole in the right knee of his khaki pants. His fingernails looked as if he'd been painting.

"That wasn't very smart," May said.

"I know, I know. You don't have to tell me. The whole *thing* wasn't very smart! It's my daughter... I know you have daughters, Jake, so I know you'll understand. She's only eleven. She's been through so much already. How could I have gotten her into something like this? How could I have put her in danger like this again?"

"Again?"

"I…" She looked down. "My father. Her grandfather. I wanted to keep her from all of that. Even though I loved him. Even though he was unfairly treated. I didn't want her to know… Don't want her to know that her grandfather…" She paused. "How would kids at school treat her if they knew her grandfather was…that he was a convict?"

They were quiet for a while. Finally May asked, "What is it that you want us to do exactly?"

"Find out where Wesley Stoller is and make sure he doesn't find out where I live. And please, please…this service, what you do…it's confidential, right?"

"Very much so," Jake said.

"We're good at keeping people's secrets," May added.

3

M orning sun had turned to lunchtime drizzle, which had turned to relentless rain. Persistent rain always made Jake restless. It made him feel sad and tired and as weak as an old man. Days like this made him wonder why he'd ever left the Caribbean. Right now he could be leaning against the bulkhead in the cockpit of the *Constant,* his thirty-seven-foot Hunter sailboat, a nice rum punch in his hand, watching the girls in bikinis.

With the information Elise had given them, Jake was easily able to make a few calls and locate Wesley Stoller. He learned that Stoller had served ten years of a life sentence for first-degree murder and had been released on parole three days ago. It'd been a little more difficult finding out where Stoller lived, but not impossible. Jake called an old DA friend, who contacted someone in New York State, who got hold of another friend at the maximum-security prison, who told him that Wesley was now living not in a halfway house but in an apartment building in Buffalo, New York, more than five hundred miles away from Fog Point. The building was owned by someone named Troy Davenborn and managed by someone named Moon, no first name given. Jake called Stoller's number and let the phone ring seven times before hanging up. No answering machine. It was the middle of the day, and he was probably at work.

He'd found out the name of Stoller's parole officer, so Jake called him and left a message. Next he called Mr. Moon. No answer there either. He left his business number, his home number, and his cell. *You've got to like voice mail in this business.*

May promised to research the guy on the Web, but right now she was in the sanctuary of the Purple Church organizing their floor displays and getting their summer students—Lyndsey, Matt, and Ethan—squared away on their work schedules. May was the resident Web expert. Jake just used the Internet to e-mail his daughters and a few old sailing buddies. Even though the word *Investigations* was on his business cards, he seldom used a computer for any true investigating. Mostly he did salvage work. People paid him to find things: evidence of crimes from the bottom of the bay, stolen jewelry and other expensive items, misplaced wills and legal documents, stolen artwork—mostly things people didn't want to go to the police about. And even though he used to be a police officer, he didn't usually ask a lot of questions about what he was looking for or why.

He got up and extracted a clean notebook from the cupboard. When he was able to get ahold of people, he would need to take a few notes. He saw that the closet was well supplied. May kept it that way. When they first bought the place, this cupboard was overfilled with dusty artifacts, moldy clerical garments, a stack of prayer books, a bunch of mildewed red hymn books, and a few old King James Bibles. A month after clearing everything out, they donated most of it to the Fog Point Historical Society. Some of it was on display in the museum downtown. Now the cupboards were used for their junk, including brochures, legal pads, small spiral notebooks, computer paper, fax paper, toilet paper, and whale posters. Lots of whale posters.

He grabbed his pen and sat down. Laughter floated from the sanctuary. Maybe they had customers. He wrote "Elise St. Dennis" on the top of a lined page.

He knew a little about her, but only a little. She'd come to this town ten years ago with her baby daughter and now made expensive jewelry that the summer people snapped up. She seemed to be doing all right for herself by the look of her clothes. And she certainly seemed sophisticated enough, with those high-heeled shoes and earrings that looked like something people hang on a Christmas tree.

Rain pelted his office window like buckshot. He checked his e-mail. While he waited for the messages to download, he thought about Elise. He was surprised that she had come to them. Didn't she have rich Hollywood contacts? Movie stars who had PI contacts? Why them?

His in-box showed an e-mail from his thirteen-year-old daughter, Jana:

Hi Dad,

How're you doing? I'm supposed to be doing homework now, and if Keith came in and knew I was e-mailing you, he'd be upset and tell me to get to my homework. Mom is out at Weight Watchers. Only two more weeks of school and then just a couple more weeks after that and I'll be out there. Bye for now. I have to get my math homework done. You would NOT believe the amount of work all at the end of the year! You should get on chat, Dad. I'd put you on my list of friends.

Can Alex and I work in the store when we get there?

Love,

Jana

Keith. Even after six years, the name still rankled.

Six years ago his wife had run off with Keith, the chairman of the church board, the church where they—he and Connie and Jana and Alexandra—had faithfully attended Sunday after Sunday. After she left, Jake fell into a downward spiral of craziness and depression, getting arrested for assault, quitting his job with the police department, and moving aboard the *Constant*—derived from his wife's name.

Connie and Keith and his daughters now lived in Jake's old house and went to his old church, ate food out of his refrigerator, blew snow from his driveway, mowed his lawn, and slept in his bed. The two of them. In *his* bed.

Keith was still a deacon, of course, while Jake, whose wife had left him and trampled over him, ended up being the bad guy in the whole scenario. He ended up being the one everyone prayed for on Wednesday nights. How *that* happened was something Jake still couldn't figure out. *Was it bad luck to change a boat's name? Well, how much worse could it get?* he wondered.

After everything happened, Jake moved aboard the *Constant* and sailed to the Caribbean. On Grand Bahama Island he met a French woman named Ghislaine, who'd captained a one-hundred-foot boat across the ocean for its owners, an old and grumpy and very rich fashion designer and his much younger wife. When Ghislaine's boss was sent home to France after a massive stroke, Ghislaine was basically out of a job. She moved aboard Jake's boat. For a year they sailed from the Bahamas to Venezuela and back again. In St. Lucia, by mutual consent, she hired on another sailboat and left him. It was just as well. She was convenient. She was nice enough. She was someone to pass the time with. She was someone to help at the helm in rough weather. She was someone to share his V-berth with. Every once in a while he still got an e-mail from her.

When Ghislaine left, he gradually brought his boat north up the Grenadines to the Bahamas and finally into American waters. He missed his daughters. His daughters deserved more of him than this deadbeat boat bum of a father. He slowly made his way up the coast until, with his diesel engine smoking and fuming and complaining, he limped into Fog Point.

A few months later he met the recently widowed May Williams. Fifteen years older than him, she was looking to settle in Fog Point, the first place she and her husband had been posted. The town had happy memories for her, she said. Plus, she was looking to invest her money in a Fog Point business. Jake was looking for something to settle him down here. They forged a partnership. It had worked well for three years.

He took off his glasses and wiped his face with his hands. Now he was trying to reforge a relationship with his daughters, daughters he had effectively ignored when he was on his boat in the Caribbean. He hit Reply.

Hi Jana,

How're you doing? I'm looking forward to seeing you! Boy, yesterday I could have used your help. I spent the whole day painting the Purple Whale. It goes in the water in a couple of weeks. Yes, I certainly will have something for you and Alex to do in the store. We're already getting lots of people signing up

for whale tours. Would you like to go out on the boat or stay in
the store with Lyndsey, Matt, and Ethan?

I love you,

Dad

The business line was ringing.

"Adventure Whale Tours and Outfitting. Jake Rikker."

"My name is Moon. You left a message."

Jake grabbed the notebook, turned to the first page. "Thank you
for calling back. I'm looking for information on a Wesley Stoller."

"New tenant. Been here just a few days. What's up?"

"Is he staying put, Mr. Moon, do you know?"

"The name's Moon. Not Mr. Moon. And I don't know too much
about him. I don't make it my business to go around prying into my
tenants' lives. Are you his parole officer?"

"So you know he has a parole officer?"

"I know he's been in prison," Moon said. "But so far he seems to
just go to work and then come home again. Goes to AA at night, that
I do know. I see him get his mail in the lobby, that sort of thing. And
then I hear his television at night. He doesn't seem to go out much.
He's right below me."

"Does he have a computer?" Jake asked.

"How should I know?"

"Just thought you may have seen him move one in when he
came, or something."

"I could find out."

"You happen to know where he works?" Jake asked.

"A car wash, I think."

"You happen to know which one?"

"Aybeez Car Wash on Third and Peabody here in Buffalo."

Jake rapidly jotted down the information. For a guy who didn't make it his business to pry into his tenants' lives, Moon seemed to know an awful lot.

"Thanks, Moon, you've been a big help. Just one thing…you see him leave, take off anywhere, can you call me right away? You've got my number."

"Will do."

4

M onday morning Elise phoned Jake. "Have you found out anything yet?"

"You don't need to worry," he said. "I know where he lives, and for now the guy seems to be staying put. He works at a car wash. He goes to work and then back home. He goes to AA or watches TV."

Silence. Then she said, "AA...well."

"I haven't talked to him, though. I'll keep trying. He doesn't seem to have an answering machine, so I have to catch him when he's home. So far we haven't been able to connect."

Jake heard a sharp intake of breath. "If it's possible, I want you to keep tabs on him without him knowing. I should've made myself clear on that."

"You don't want me to *talk* to him?"

"I don't want him picking up on anything. I just can't take any chances."

"Elise, have you received any more e-mails or letters from him?"

"No. I haven't."

"Let me know right away if you do."

"I will, but I shouldn't get any e-mails because I canceled that account."

While Jake was on the phone, May had walked in with the mail and was going through it. She shook her head while she leafed through a magazine. The magazine in question, Jake could see now, was the premier issue of *Fog Point Summer*. A brand-new venture by the Fog Point Tourism Association, the monthly magazine would run five full-color glossy issues from May through September. The magazine featured historical articles, points of interest, ads, coupons, and a listing of area events, including a two-page spread on the annual Fog Point Blueberry Days coming up in mid-July. Jake could see the cover montage of businesses, faces, and tourists.

May opened it and laid it down in front of Jake, flattening the seam with the heel of her hand. He found himself looking down at their own half-page ad. There they were, in full color, their purple church in the center, their sign prominently displayed at the bottom. Along the sides ran various shots of people kayaking and people leaning over the stern of the boat looking at whales. Big smiles. And, of course, a mention of their money-back guarantee: "If you don't see whales, you don't pay for the cruise." Everything looked fine to him, but May's growl told him something was obviously wrong. As soon as he was off the phone, he was sure he would hear about it.

"Do you think…" Elise paused and sighed gently. "Could we have lunch sometime…today, maybe?"

"Lunch?" His intake of breath surprised even himself.

May stopped and looked at him.

"Oh," Elise said. "I'm sorry. I just thought maybe we could meet again. I could tell you more about him or something. But if you don't think lunch is necessary, it could be someplace else…" Her voice caught. Jake tried to picture her, so small, maybe curled up on the corner of her couch, her tiny feet tucked underneath her, a fleece blanket around her on this cool, rainy day. But, of course, that wouldn't be the case. She would be calling him from Elise's Creations. She was at work, as he was. She was probably standing behind a counter in sandals that tied up around her calves.

"Lunch would work. We'll look forward to it. I'll see if May's free."

"Jake…um…I know this is going to sound really strange, and I apologize, but could it just be you? It took so much out of me to just walk into your place yesterday. I guess—I don't know—I guess I have this acute fear combined with this intense embarrassment; fear that he might actually come here, and embarrassment that you'd think I was so desperate that I had to e-mail prisoners…"

"No one thinks that. May doesn't. I don't."

"But could it be just you? For today?" she asked.

"I'll come by myself. Lunch would be nice."

Across the room May fumbled through their file cabinet and retrieved a legal-sized file folder.

After he hung up she asked, "Lunch, Jake?"

He nodded.

"Just the two of you?"

"It's what she wanted for now."

"You're not lunching with Ben today?"

"Ben!" Jake sat back. "Today is Monday, isn't it?"

"It's Monday. All day."

Jake had a standing lunch date every Monday with his friend Ben McLaren, who was minister of Stone Church. "I'll have to call him. I'll call him. He'll understand."

But May muttered and grumbled. Was she *that* upset that Elise wanted to meet with him alone?

"What's wrong, May? Did we get up on the wrong side of the bed? Did we pour our orange juice in our cornflakes this morning?"

"It's that." She pointed at the ad in *Fog Point Summer* open in front of him on the desk. "And this." She placed the ad copy they had approved and finalized next to the ad in the magazine. Jake compared the two, could see no discernible difference, but he kept looking and still saw nothing.

May said, "We specifically asked for a coupon with a font different from the regular ad. This was not in the copy we were given to approve."

Yes, okay, there it was. A magnifying glass might show the difference. "It looks okay to me," Jake said.

"The fonts, Jake. Look at the font in the coupon. And you tell me if the font in the magazine is the same as the font we approved."

Jake looked carefully.

May jabbed the paper with their ad copy and kept muttering. "A simple thing like matching the fonts, and they mess it up. We specifically asked for a friendly font. Is it too much to ask for a *friendly* font? We paid enough for this." She grabbed the magazine and flipped through it. "Oh, and would you look at the ad the Featherjohn brothers came up with. They got the whole inside back cover. Man, that must've cost them a pretty penny. Mama probably footed the bill on that one." She slapped the magazine on the desk.

He looked down at the Featherjohns' ad. Carl and Earl Featherjohn were Jake and May's main competition. The brothers had recently purchased an old schooner and planned to take groups of tourists out on it to watch whales. Their ad filled the whole inside back cover with splashes of color and more smiling faces. It even included a generous population of bikini-clad women and hunky guys.

"Do we tell everyone that their schooner is nothing but a leaky rust bucket with rags for sails?" May asked.

"Nah, I go for letting them find out for themselves, and then when the boat sinks and they have to swim ashore, we offer them a tour on a real boat."

She frowned, picked up *Fog Point Summer* yet again, and flipped through it page by page. "Well, isn't this strange," she muttered.

Jake looked up.

"Okay then. This is interesting. It looks like Elise's Creations isn't even in here. And we thought everyone had to be in here. We were told every single business *had* to be represented. Unless I'm missing something, Jake, she doesn't look to be here."

"And this is significant because…?"

May shrugged. "I don't know. Maybe nothing. Probably nothing."

He spent the rest of the morning helping May with the displays. He called Ben. His friend understood. "Business," Jake said.

But as he unpacked boxes of backpacks and underwater flashlights, he found himself looking forward to lunch with Elise.

5

M oon took off his wraparound mirrored sunglasses and laid them on the counter. Then he put two double Quarter Pounders with cheese into his microwave and set it for two minutes. From his fridge he grabbed a two-liter Pepsi and drank it right out of the bottle.

About twice a week he went to McDonald's and came home with two huge bags of hamburgers, cheeseburgers, Big N' Tastys with cheese, McNuggets, double cheeseburgers, Hot 'n Spicy McChickens, sausage-and-egg McMuffins, and lots of those little containers of fries. For lunch and supper he just opened his refrigerator and made a choice. Today felt like two double burgers.

Moon liked his job. Even though this was definitely a low-end apartment building, he liked it here. He'd worked here three years now; took this job right out of high school. It gave him a place to stay and money while he went to college part time. Plus, the part he liked best was that he was his own boss. All it required was a bit of expertise in plumbing and wiring—skills he'd always been pretty good at, having grown up reading *Popular Mechanics*.

But first the job required that he make people happy, a skill

Moon learned and constantly perfected. A smile, a friendly word, a "Hello, how're you doing?" had his people raving about their building super. He'd read this in one of those pop psychology books for managers: *Make your no sound like a yes.* That had become his mantra. And most of his tenants were a few fries short of a Happy Meal anyway.

His microwave dinged. He grabbed his burgers, sat at his kitchen table, and ate. Nothing fancy here, just a square box of twelve apartments, six up, six down, three on either side of the hall. And no fancy decks for barbecues and those white plastic lawn chairs. These people were lucky to get windows that worked. He lived in the middle on the second floor, which was a good place to watch his charges.

Moon called his tenants "charges," and he had nicknames for all of them. The pug-nosed, pig-faced single mother in 1A was Miss Piggy, and all her children were the piglets. The tall, spooky guy who looked out of his apartment window with the telescope in 1B was Ebenezer. The lesbian couple who lived next door to him were Tweedledum and Tweedledee. Oh, no one had come right out and told him that the couple were lesbians, but what's with two women rooming together? No, those two were lesbians.

Then there was Pierre the French guy who worked at Wal-Mart and spoke with an accent. His name wasn't really Pierre, but Moon called all French guys Pierre. Barbie and Ken, the perfect-looking couple, lived in 2C right next to him. He was a six-pack ab guy, and she was a real looker. They both worked in a gym, and Barbie had all that hair and the black makeup around her eyes. But the thing nobody knew was how Ken shoved her around when no one was looking. Moon had seen it. It was better than television.

Then there was the little library lady, Miss Bookworm. Every night she soaked her feet in one of those plastic foot things while she read. She didn't even have a television. What kind of person doesn't have a television?

And his name for his newest charge? His best nickname of all: Cain. Because he'd killed his own brother.

6

W hile Jake was at lunch, May unpacked boxes and set up displays in the sanctuary of the Purple Church. Who knew there were so many kinds of sunscreen? They had one for noses, another kind just for ears, and yet another kind for lips. Plus, they were getting e-mails almost daily from people wanting to sign up for kayak adventures and whale tours. *Now we just need the rain to stop,* she thought.

This ocean kayak thing was new. A year ago they'd hired Ethan, a recent graduate from some fancy outdoor PE program who was all gung-ho about ocean kayaks. He had three of his own and talked May and Jake into offering day adventures that would include lunch. By the end of that summer, they were offering overnight camping tours. They'd hired a few other college students to work with the weekend groups. So far it was going okay, even though they'd had to double their insurance coverage. May wondered if it was worth it. Jake drove the *Purple Whale* on the whale-watching tours, and May generally stayed in the office and did the paperwork and answered the phones and e-mails. With her lame leg and bum knee, it would be fun trying to climb down into one of those kayak things now, wouldn't it?

Taking on an investigation at this point seemed ludicrous. They were far too busy, she thought as she pulled out yet another type of sunscreen. This one for hands. But on the face of it, the investigation looked simple enough. Find out where this guy was, talk to his parole officer, and give Elise a stern warning about getting involved with shady characters. Like psychopaths who've been convicted of major crimes.

May knew this Elise St. Dennis a little. She'd been an established jewelry maker way before May arrived in Fog Point five years ago. Her jewelry seemed to be doing well, even though her Web site wasn't much to write home about. Well, it was sophisticated enough, with photos of necklaces and bracelets. But there was just something about it that bothered May. She would have to think about it for a while.

The display set up to May's satisfaction, she returned to the back office and the computer and opened up the Elise's Creations Web site again. What was it about the site that bothered her? May took off her glasses and let them hang around her neck. She stared at the screen. No, she couldn't see a great deal without her glasses, but sometimes when she looked at blurred images, out-of-focus images, the big picture became clearer.

She put her glasses back on and clicked through the links. Professional, yes, but generic. Plain. That's the problem. It was too professional. It had none of the homey touches that other businesses tried for, that she and Jake aimed for on their own site, such as staff photos and pictures of people on the whaleboats. Elise just had product photos, but her name—Elise St. Dennis—was nowhere to be found, not even on any of the links. *Well, isn't that strange,* May thought. Plus, the address was listed as an office suite in Ridley Harbor. Ridley? They had an office in Ridley?

An e-mail came in while May was browsing. A family from the Midwest wanted to reserve two two-person kayaks for mother, father, son, and daughter. "We hope you give lessons. We've never done this before, but the pictures on the Web site look so nice we thought we'd try. We were able to get a couple of rooms at Featherjohn's B&B. We hope that's a nice place." They included the dates they would be in town, and May added them to the growing summer calendar and e-mailed back that those dates would work and that Featherjohn's B&B was a fine place.

That is, if Lenore's two do-nothing sons aren't there. She didn't add that last sentence.

That's what you did, thought May as she wrote the names on the calendar and saved the e-mail. *You stayed in business by having a Web site with homey pictures of people having fun, by listing your e-mail and address on the Tourism Association Web site, by communicating via e-mail, and by advertising in* Fog Point Summer.

She tried something else. She plunked Elise's Creations into several of her favorite search engines and was directed to the Web site. She entered Elise St. Dennis's name on Google and came up with exactly nothing resembling the Elise St. Dennis of Fog Point.

She did a casual search using her own name and, of course, was directed to hundreds of archived articles about the Allentown Gas Station sniper. She didn't click on them; she knew what they said. She did a search for Jake Rikker and was directed to their Web site as well as to a short press release in his hometown paper about his resignation from the police force. They both had their demons. All she had to do was google far enough back, and she'd find most anyone's bad luck and bad choices leaving their jelly-slug trails in cyberspace. So how did Elise St. Dennis manage to stay so free of this?

"So Paul, what do *you* think is going on?" she said aloud. Sometimes she did that, talked to her dead husband. "How come she isn't listed multiple times? Why only once? Or does she just have an inept Web master?"

She was puzzling over this when Ben, the minister, appeared at the door. "Knock, knock," he said. He carried a book.

"Hey, Ben."

"So Jake's here after all?" He peered around the office.

"Nope, he's not."

"Oh, I heard you talking."

"To myself. I was talking to myself. Didn't Jake call you? He's having lunch with a business client today."

"Ah, I heard about that. I just came by to drop off a book for his daughter." He placed it on a stack of boxes near the door.

"Don't put it there. Unless you want it to end up with a display of Croakies out in the sanctuary." She looked at the book. "What is this? Fantasy?"

"It's for Jana," he said, picking it up. "She and I have Tolkien in common." He put it next to a box of whale posters. "I also came by to tell him I'm free if he wants to bottom paint. Do you know his plans?"

"He's heading down to Pop's after lunch to paint. Maybe you can catch him there."

Pop Maynard ran the best and only marina in Fog Point. If there was boat work to do—painting, engine repairs, or needed parts—Pop was the guy to do it.

"So is this a budding romance or what?"

She looked at him. Ben leaned against a carved wooden pulpit, furniture May and Jake hadn't found a good use for in the whale-watching business. Ben looked at home among the church things in his black turtleneck sweater and skinny glasses. "Is *what* a budding romance?"

"Between Jake and that young jewelry designer."

May stared at him. "He told you who he was having lunch with?"

"He did, indeed."

May was mildly annoyed. They usually kept their client names confidential.

"I told him her prices are…" He pointed to the ceiling.

"Heavenly?" May offered.

"No. Through the roof. I wanted to get something for Amy there. For Mother's Day. I ended up not buying anything."

"I'm surprised he told you who he was having lunch with," May said.

"He wanted my opinion of her. Her daughter comes to church quite regularly."

"And what did you tell him?"

"That she's a bit of a strange one," Ben said.

"How so?"

"Her daughter comes to church. She doesn't. Amy and I have tried to be friendly, inviting her to the house. But she seems to rebuff all overtures of friendship."

"Obviously, Jake is having better luck," May added.

~

7

J ake and Elise had ended up going to Mags and Hermans Café on the boardwalk for sandwiches and coffee.

"I like it here," Elise said.

"Here? Mags and Hermans?" Jake bit into his ham-and-sauerkraut sandwich.

"No, here. Fog Point. This has been a good place for my daughter and me." But then she frowned into her coffee. Jake waited. "But now there's this." Elise had ordered a cream-cheese bagel and was busy scraping off most of the cream cheese and smearing the gobs on her plate. "It's been a good place. I don't…"—she looked up—"I don't want to move. Rachel loves it here."

Jake kept watching her scrape off the cream cheese.

"They always put too much on," she said by way of explanation. "Rachel, if she were here, she'd be taking my leftovers and putting them on her bagel. She's such a precocious little girl." Her eyes lost that empty look when she mentioned her daughter.

"What's she like?" Jake asked.

Elise described Rachel as smart and athletic. "And her face lights up whenever she talks about her love for whales."

"She loves whales?"

"She's doing some sort of school project. Been working on it all year. And yes, she loves whales. I'd love for you to meet her."

"I would like that too," Jake said.

Elise paid, which was awkward for Jake, who kept insisting on paying. Elise kept saying no, this was a business lunch and she should pay. Finally Jake acquiesced, saying, "Okay, then, but next time I'll pay, only to feel instantly stupid. *Assuming there would be a next time?*

Now it was afternoon, and Jake and Ben were at Pop Maynard's sanding and scrubbing the bottom of the *Purple Whale*. It was one of those jobs that needed to get done, rain or shine. They rolled on the bottom paint, working in companionable silence. Clouds were moving in, all the more reason to talk little and work fast.

By the time Jake got back to the Purple Church at four-thirty, the drizzle had moved into the realm of outright rain.

"A real downpour out there," May said without looking up. She was wearing her computer glasses, clunky, black frames hooked by a chain around her neck.

"You're right about that," he said.

"Cats and dogs."

"Right again."

People around here never called it rain. Today it's a downpour. Another day and the sky would be spitting. On other days that looked no different to Jake's unpracticed eye, locals would pronounce it a drizzle, a spring shower, a sprinkle, a torrent, a mizzle, or a Scotch mist, which sounded to him more like a drink than a kind of precipitation. It sometimes surprised Jake that he lived in a place that had all these names for rain.

"How's the boat coming along?" May asked him.

"A couple of inside things to fiddle with, and she's set to go."

"And how was lunch?"

"Fine." He flipped through the morning's mail.

"That's it? Just fine?"

"Fine."

She eyed him.

"Okay," he said. "What she wanted was to clarify business procedures. How and when she pays us—that sort of thing."

May took off her glasses.

"You're giving me your look, May."

"Why'd you tell Ben you were having lunch with Elise?"

"He asked."

"He *asked?* Jake, we're supposed to be running a confidential PI service here," May said.

"May, we had lunch at Mags and Hermans. Everyone in the vicinity of the boardwalk saw us eating together. We just talked."

"You just talked."

That part was true. They had spent a full hour talking. Rachel had been their first topic of conversation, and then they'd moved into Elise's lifelong love of jewelry. "I've always loved the feel of it," she'd told him. "The cool feel of beads in a jar. The way they roll around in your hands."

Elise had doodled on the napkin while they talked, and even her doodlings were artistic.

But, curiously, they hadn't talked about Wesley Stoller.

"We need to go to the police with this," May said. "When Paul was alive he had a case similar to this. Innocent little farm girl from Iowa e-mails poor, trod upon, misunderstood serial killer in prison. He e-mails back. She hops on a bus. Goes to visit. Then goes to visit again. And again. They get married in prison. The newspapers take pictures. They have trailers set up with kitchens and rooms, the whole bit. And guess what? The next morning she shows up dead. And the guy's sitting there, 'I didn't do it. I didn't do it.' If Paul were alive, he'd be scolding you by now, Jake. If this woman is really in danger, she needs to go to the police. I hope you told her that at your little lunch."

"Stoller's only been out of prison a few days," Jake said, "but he's going to work and AA meetings and then comes home. So far he seems harmless."

"Yeah, and maybe Charles Manson is really Mother Teresa. Do you know how many women fall prey to this kind of thing? Every lonely little woman writing to a prisoner is going to be the one who finally changes him, who turns his life around. Here, let me show you something."

She opened up the home page for E-mail-a-Prisoner. "Look at this. All these male and female prisoners who want to connect with that special someone. Look at this young woman. Doesn't she look sweet? Lists her age, twenty-six, and her hobbies"—May clicked on a link—"butterflies, scrapbooking, and collecting birdhouses. 'I like long walks on the beach and writing poetry.' And you know what she's in for?" May scrolled down. "Voilà! Armed robbery." She clicked on another link. "Here's another one. Oh, look, how exciting. This one likes drama, and she's studying to be a clown. Oh, and what's she in for? Second-degree murder."

Jake looked over her shoulder. "Show me the guys."

She scrolled. Wesley Stoller's name was not among them.

"Have you found his name on any of those sites?"

"Not so far, but I'm still looking. I find it odd that she can't remember the Web site where she got his name. But there's something else I want to show you." She pointed to *Fog Point Summer.* "Our client is not in there. So I made a few calls. I called the company in Ridley that produces the magazine." She aimed the back of her pen to the magazine. "All these faces? The boardwalk? I found out that she asked specifically that her business not be photographed for the cover."

"Maybe she's the smart one. You remember how outrageously expensive those ads were."

"The cover thing was free, Jake. And the fact that she would specifically make that request? I find that odd."

"I don't see what this has to do with Wesley Stoller, May."

May clicked her pen. "I also called the Fog Point Tourism Association. She's not a member."

"I don't know what this has to do with anything. Noonan's Café opted out, if you recall."

"They did not." May opened to a business-card-sized ad on the last page.

Jake grinned. "So, old Buzz caved after all. He wasn't going to, remember? He was dead set against it." He looked up. "Maybe she can't afford it. And obviously she's hiding out from Stoller."

"Wrong on both counts. Let me tell you where she *does* advertise. I spoke with Jess, her business manager, and guess where she *does* advertise?"

"I give up. Where?"

"The *New Yorker.* The *Boston Globe.* Do you realize how much an ad costs in one of those? It would be our payroll for a month. No, make that two months. Probably three."

"So she's doing well. So what?"

May seemed not to hear the irritation in Jake's voice, or if she did, she chose to ignore it. "It's not just that." She swiveled her chair around and accessed another Web site. "Here's her mailing address. An office suite in Ridley Harbor. What's that all about?"

"Well, at least we know our checks won't bounce." He sat down and pushed his glasses up on his nose. "May, she's our client. I don't understand what all of this has to do with Wesley Stoller. She's a single mother. She made a mistake, May. Give her the benefit of the doubt. So what if she has money? What does that have to do with anything?"

May just scowled at the computer.

~

Lonely Orcas
By Rachel St. Dennis, Future Marine Biologist

The orca whale's family ties are very strong. Their families are called clans, and they're not like our families with a mother and a father and children. Orca clans are all related to each other; aunts and uncles and grandmothers and nieces and nephews and children all live together.

Occasionally, scientists have found orcas living by themselves or in very small groups of a dozen, or even one or two. No one knows how these "lone wolves" got to be like this, broken away from their real family, but it happens. These small whale pods travel hundreds of miles compared to the family whales that stay together in one place and travel maybe only fifty or sixty miles their whole lives.

I feel sorry for these lonely orcas. I'd like for them to get back with their families. When I get to be a marine biologist, I'm going to see if I can take them back and find a family that wants them.

~

8

A path along the beach wound its way from May's cottage up toward Pop Maynard's boatyard. From there she could either turn right and head on up to the Purple Church or go straight a hundred yards and climb the wooden steps that led to the boardwalk. On good days, if her knee allowed it, May walked.

She had always been athletic. As a young woman she ran marathons, hiked, and played competitive softball. Those days were long over now, but she still walked as much as she could. Her doctor said it was fine, if she didn't overdo it and if she didn't experience pain. *Good luck on the not-experiencing-pain thing,* she thought. May walked in spite of it. There was no way on God's green earth that she was ever, ever going to get one of those motorized carts. If she ever did, if she was ever reduced to that, she'd attach a skull-and-crossbones flag to the back.

Her knee was iffy, but today, on this foggy morning, she walked with her cane. The fog was moving in like a misty hand that covered and smothered everything, until suddenly all she could taste was fog on her tongue, and it became part of the air she breathed. She breathed it in and continued her slow walk.

To her left was the public wharf, a dock built on strong pilings, wide enough to drive on. A series of floating finger docks along the sides rose and fell with the tide. Visiting yachtsmen and fishermen tied up here, although a lot of the lobstermen used a dock near Pop's.

Her walk was slowed as she endeavored to keep her cane out of the cracks in the boardwalk. The water was on her left, and Fog Point Lighthouse stood beyond it in the distance. Businesses lined the boardwalk to her right. In the summer, when it was hot and sunny, this place was alive with color and outdoor displays and people eating ice-cream cones and hot dogs and wearing new Fog Point T-shirts.

But today it was quiet, except for the sound of the foghorn, which droned its mournful song every thirty seconds. The storefronts looked muted, partially smudged out by the fog.

A few years ago the Fog Point Tourism Association had hired a huge public-relations firm from New York to put this hitherto struggling fishing town on the map. One of the many suggestions was that the business owners who catered to tourists paint their establishments bright colors. No dull whites or creams or pale blues. Instead the PR firm advocated purples and hot pinks and even shiny black. Murals were encouraged, and three summers ago art students up and down the coast spruced up the sides of buildings with paintings of old-fashioned seacoast villages complete with square-riggers out in the bay.

She and Jake had painted their entire building a vibrant shade of purple and had commissioned a giant whale mural on the side facing the boardwalk.

Elise's Creations was the last building on the boardwalk and the largest by far. She really had the best location. Steps led from her studio down to the beach. Beyond Elise's the boardwalk ended and became a path that wound upward to a lookout point that included a couple of park benches and a gazebo. Because of her knee, May hadn't been up there in years. Beyond that path, one finally came to the houses of the summer people.

Elise wasn't in, a tall young woman in heels informed May. Like Elise, Jess wore lots of jewelry, but whereas Elise wore layers of dainty necklaces and filigree earrings, Jess's choice was clunkier and bigger.

It had been awhile since May had been in here, and she was struck with the elegance and silence of the place, with its thick pale purple carpet and waterfalls. Nice.

"You're May," Jess said smiling widely. They shook hands. "Elise should be here soon. It sometimes takes her awhile to get Rachel off to school. I man the fort for the first little while, usually. Did you need to see her?"

Actually, May didn't. Her mission today was to find out about Elise, get a feel for the woman they were working for. It was better if Elise wasn't there.

"Does she go to Ridley every day?" May asked.

"Every day? No. Not hardly. Only when she has a delivery. And it's usually me who ends up driving."

"Don't you have an office in Ridley?" May asked. She was circumspect. She didn't know how much Elise had shared with her assistant about her extracurricular activities with prisoners.

Jess laughed. "No, we don't. It's just a mail drop. Elise doesn't want to use a street address. She wants to keep her private life private. Her words. And the only box numbers in Fog Point are post office box numbers. And they don't look professional, she says. But you can get these boxes in Ridley that make it look like you have a suite. That's all that is."

Jess was a very pretty girl with an animated face. When she smiled, her eyebrows raised, the sides of her cheeks went up, and a vein appeared from the top of an eyebrow to the top of her forehead.

"Business must be pretty good, then," May said.

"Not bad," Jess said, grinning. "Not bad. Let's just say we have good bankers. I'm just trying to get Elise's Creations out there more. She's been kind of resistant to that in the past."

"Resistant how?"

"Here's what I think. I think Elise is basically shy. And I'm so *not* shy! So maybe we complement each other in this business."

"How long have you been with her?"

"Two years. Ever since I graduated." She grinned again, her expressive face ever in motion as she talked. Then she started drumming her fingers on the glass counter and shifting her weight from foot to foot. May got the idea that the girl was never still for more than a second. She was probably one of those people who, when forced to sit down, crossed her legs and swung the top leg up and down, up and down, driving everyone around her crazy.

"Marketing is my specialty, although my major was in advertising. I even applied to be on Donald Trump's show. You know, the reality one? Sent in a video and everything. But my application wasn't accepted, and so here I was, wandering around the coast on vacation. So I came in here, and the next thing I knew I was talking to the manager—that would be Elise—and then she hired me. On the spot." She kept smiling, grinning. "And you know something? I love it here. I've surprised myself. I've never regretted it for a minute!"

The whole lower half of her face was teeth and mouth, May noticed. "Isn't that something," she said.

"I would love to do more for Elise. I have all these ideas." She waved one of her hands in a circle. "I'm one of those people who's really out there, ya know? And Elise, well, she's quite private…shy, really, I think."

"When she comes in, tell her I dropped by," May said.

Back out on the boardwalk, the fog was even denser than before. *If that's possible,* May thought.

Absently, she touched her knee. It felt swollen and hurt a bit. It was a pain she was never very far from. Even with Advil and all the anti-inflams she took.

She tested it, bending it forward and back a few times before setting out the few steps to Mags and Hermans Café. Maybe they knew Elise. Maybe they'd have something to say about her. There were only two other patrons at the café. Norah Waterman of Inner Healing Books and Gifts was at the counter pouring cream in her coffee-to-go. On this day of fog and chill, she wore a brown knitted poncho and leather boots. The other patron was a guy in ragged pants who sat by the window, his big hands around a mug of coffee.

From behind the counter Mags said, "Nice to see you, May." Today her ample body was covered in a cotton print dress. Over the dress she wore an L.L.Bean fleece vest. Her long grayish brown hair was drawn back in a ponytail at her neck.

"Nice weather, isn't it?" May responded.

"It'll get better."

"Ever the optimist."

"It better get better. That's all I can say."

"It will," Norah piped up.

"You have psychic ability?" said the guy from his window perch.

"No, but I just know it will. The energy's too good this year for it to stay foggy for long."

"What, is the moon aligned with Venus or something like that?" he asked.

"Something like that," Norah said.

"So what're you doing in this neck of the woods?" Mags asked.

"I was just at Elise's," May answered. "Nice place she has there."

"It is at that."

"You guys know her at all?"

"She comes in for coffee now and again."

"Now and again?" Norah said laughing. "She's a regular. We both are."

"She and that Jake of yours were in here yesterday for lunch," Mags said.

"So I heard. I'm just wondering who her friends are," May said.

"Why? You worried Jake will get into something he can't handle?"

May thought about that. "For starters, yeah." She chose her words carefully. "Single mother. It must be hard on her and her daughter here all by themselves. Rachel growing up without a father."

"Rachel is growing up with lots of good female energy and a good support system," Norah said. "She'll be fine. She'll be more than fine. That little girl is an indigo child."

"That sounds like mumbo jumbo to me," said the man who had been sitting by the window. As he approached the counter, he asked for a muffin.

"Well, it's good she has friends, then," May said. "I mean, you don't see her around town much. Like at those blasted Tourism Association meetings, for example."

"Elise does fine without them," Norah said.

"I suppose she does. Still…" May wasn't ready to let this go. "A woman like that here. No family."

"She's had a difficult life," Norah said. "But she has family here. The Noonans, for example."

"She's related to the Noonans?"

"Not by blood, but there is a closeness between them. Which has always been somewhat confusing to me, because the Noonans are Protestant Christians, and Elise is like me. She worked there before opening up her shop. Nootie's always treated her like a daughter."

And then Norah turned and walked out of the coffee shop, waggling her fingers over her head as a good-bye gesture.

Interesting.

9

Moon received two checks and a money order in the mail. He drove to his bank machine and deposited the money. That's how he did business, with faceless ATMs and on the Web. Better that way. A guy like him couldn't be too careful.

Then he repaired a leaky pipe in the basement, went to one class at the college, and was back in his apartment by the time his charges came home from work. He ate two Big N' Tastys while he sat at his window and watched.

Barbie and Ken were the first to arrive home from the health club. Then one half of the Tweedles. Yesterday Cain had come home with a computer. Moon knew this because he had helped Cain carry in three huge boxes. Moon took the steps two at a time to get down there before Cain made it in the front door.

"Hey Mr. Stoller! Need some help with those packages there?"

"Oh sure. Thanks."

Moon grabbed the box that housed the monitor.

"You got yourself a computer, I see."

"Yup."

"A big one."

"Yup."

"Why not a laptop?"

Cain shrugged. "I got this off a friend. It's not new, but the price was right."

"You going to get Internet?"

"Of course. That's the main reason I got this."

"High speed?" Moon asked.

"If I can afford it."

"Pretty soon," Moon said, "apartments are going to have Internet connections built into the price. Like cable. Plus, it'll all be wireless then."

"Could be."

"Hey, you want me to come down later?" Moon asked. "Help you hook it up and all? I'm pretty good at stuff like that."

"I got a guy from my Bible study coming to help me."

His *Bible study*. "Well, if he doesn't show up, you just give me a shout."

"I got a bunch of disks with my stuff on 'em," Cain said. "I need to get it all installed."

"Well, hey, I'm good at that, too."

"I'll let you know if I need you."

"Hey, anytime you want to go grab a beer, let me know," Moon said.

"Thanks, but I don't drink anymore." Cain shuffled a bit with the packages.

"Yeah…well…okay, a Coke, then."

"Sure, okay."

Soon, maybe tomorrow or the day after at the latest, Moon would get into Cain's room and onto that computer of his.

10

B ecause Noonan's wasn't on the boardwalk, the locals hung out there more than at Mags and Hermans. With metal napkin dispensers and a worn oilcloth covering each table and stapled underneath, the café certainly didn't attract the yuppies who frequented the cafés in Ridley Harbor that sold designer coffee for three bucks a pop. Buzz served regular coffee, which he bought in big metal canisters down at the Shop 'N Save. And the cream was poured from a carton. He didn't even stock those little creamers of varying, nauseating flavors. Plus Jake could get home-cooked meals at Noonan's, like meatloaf or pot roast and potatoes. He could also buy foil casseroles of lasagna to take home and heat up in the oven. Nootie was famous for her pies, her specialty being raspberry sour pie, a recipe she had invented and so far had shared with no one. And on this cheerless morning, Jake decided to grab a coffee and a homemade donut. When he got there, May was already seated at the counter, sipping tea and talking with Buzz.

"Mornin', Jake," Buzz said, wiping the counter. "Coffee?"

"Please." He sat down next to May. "Didn't expect to see you here, May."

"Well, I am."

"And you're drinking tea?"

"Already had my coffee quota for the day."

From the kitchen, laughter and high voices carried over from some morning television talk show. Nootie watched a lot of television while she worked.

"Take out or a mug?" Buzz asked him.

"Mug," Jake said. "I hate coffee in paper."

"Don't blame you." He frowned at the coffee. "This is old. Let me make a fresh pot." Then to May, "You were asking about Elise? Well, a person couldn't want a better employee. Four years she worked here, and she was never late once, never even called in sick."

May and Buzz were talking about Elise? Jake mused.

Buzz dumped out the old grounds and added scoops of fresh coffee. "Picture this. She comes traipsing in here with this little baby. I thought they were sisters. Like she was an older sister or something."

"Where'd she come from?" May asked.

Buzz shook his head as he wiped the front of the coffeepot. The thing began dripping. "Don't know. Never asked. She needed a job; I gave her one."

"So you don't know where she came from?"

"Nootie thought New Jersey."

"New Jersey?"

"Because of her accent."

"I don't detect an accent," May said.

"Not anymore. She had one once."

"Did you look up her references?"

"May," Jake said quietly, "why all the questions?"

Buzz laughed and made the rounds with a new pot of coffee.

"Because," May whispered to Jake out of earshot of Buzz, "there's something funny about her. That's all."

He shook his head. He and Elise had talked the previous night. He'd called her. They'd talked and talked. She said she felt so foolish about the whole thing. If she had to do it all over again, she'd run away from that E-mail-a-Prisoner Web site and not look back. And she was so sorry for laying all this on Jake. He told her it was okay. He kept telling her it was okay. She was vulnerable. She'd made a mistake, just a mistake. People make mistakes. Look at him. So why was May grilling Buzz about her?

May repeated, "Did you call her references?"

"Didn't need to."

"You hired her without references?"

"Why should I ask for references? If she didn't work out, I would've fired her. No need for references. We're not some fancy place in Ridley Harbor. If a person doesn't work out, I let them go. Like I said, she needed a job, so I gave her one."

"She worked out fine for you?" May asked.

"She was a hard worker. We still think of her as a daughter. She and Rachel spend Christmas with us. Did you know that? Have from the first year they arrived."

"So she has no family then, no blood family?"

"None that she's ever talked about."

Jake took a drink of his coffee and thought about that.

11

O kay, so what is it about Elise that you, as you put it, find funny?" Jake asked. They were in his pickup driving to Ridley Harbor, she to visit the doctor and he to get a few marine supplies. He needed more bottom paint as well as a few shackles and some rope. The dock lines for the *Purple Whale* probably should've been replaced a year ago.

"Do you know she does jewelry consultation?" May asked, ignoring his question.

"So what's wrong with that? Whatever jewelry consulting is."

"Why are you defending her?" May took off her Squirrels baseball cap, smoothed her hair, and put the cap back on again.

"And why are you so intent on nitpicking every single thing in her life?"

"She hasn't told us everything. I just question her story, that's all." She looked out the window. "I'm entitled to my opinion."

Neither said anything for a while as they sped along the highway, trees zipping past. May's hands lay folded on her lap. She still wore her wedding ring, a thin silver band, even though her husband had been dead six years.

After a while she said, "I have a theory about Elise."

"Okay," Jake said.

"Elise is pretty fancy. You have to admit that. Her place on the boardwalk is fancy and urban and definitely *not* Fog Point, if you know what I mean. She's in a different class. I mean, who do you know who can advertise in the *New Yorker*? No one on my planet. And she, for whatever reason, gets involved with a *prisoner?* A guy in for first-degree murder? So she writes to him using a different e-mail address, which she doesn't have anymore, by the way, because she canceled it. Convenient. And so little Miss Sophisticate gets involved with a shady character. And she ends up writing some pretty embarrassing stuff, stuff she doesn't want anyone else to know about. Which is why she had her computer completely reformatted so no one can retrieve anything, which is why we don't have the hard drive. Which is why she doesn't want to involve the police. You get the police involved, and all of a sudden it's a matter of public record. So she comes to us. She's afraid Wesley Stoller might have embarrassing stuff on his prison computer, and she wants it destroyed somehow."

"And that's your theory?"

She nodded. "I've been thinking about it. That's why she emptied her computer and emptied the cache and got a new e-mail. So even *we* wouldn't be able to read the stuff she wrote. You wait. Her next request is going to be to retrieve Stoller's e-mails somehow. I don't know what she expects us to do—go get the prison computer he wrote them from?"

Jake shook his head. "I don't know. I just don't see her that way." Rain started pelting the windshield and he turned the wipers on. "I think she's just lonely."

"So she's lonely. Everybody's lonely. I'm lonely; you're lonely. We're all lonely. Plus, she's got you snookered, Jake."

He turned suddenly as he pulled into the lot of May's doctor's office. "May…"

"I just don't trust her, that's all," she said as she opened her door.

"You've made that abundantly clear."

But May was already out the door. Despite her somewhat crusty temperament and the fact that her glass was usually half empty, he adored her. He watched her make her way into the medical clinic, limping slightly as she plowed through the rain. They'd made a good pair ever since she approached him at Noonan's three and a half years ago and told him he was going about his whale-watching business all wrong.

At that point he hadn't even called his little whale-watching venture a business. He'd merely been trying to pay for his new diesel engine by taking tourists out on the *Constant* to see the whales.

"If you want to make a go of it, first of all you need better signage," she'd pointed out. Up to that point, he'd been running his business out of a rundown shed attached to Pop's boatyard. But moving to a more prestigious location required cash, something in short supply for him. But not for May. She had a lifetime of savings as well as her husband's death benefits and pension. And she wanted a reason to stay in Fog Point. So they joined forces.

Since she was studying to be a PI, they added that to their dance card. Because of his history, Jake didn't think he'd ever be able to get a PI's license, but May was confident. Two years later he got his license.

She was like a sister to him, a sister with good instincts. Yet in this case she was wrong. Elise was just a lonely young woman who'd made a dreadful mistake. He knew about mistakes.

He drove to the Ridley Harbor police station, an imposing old stone building with Justice Department engraved along the top. He entered the structure and bypassed the receptionist. Frank was a friend from his cop days, who'd recently been transferred to Ridley Harbor.

When Jake walked in, Frank was hunched in a telephone conversation behind a square desk strewn with papers. He looked up, grinned in surprise, and pointed at a chair. Jake sat. It was a cubbyhole of an office, smaller even than the space the two had shared when they were officers. Three children and a dog smiled out of a small metal frame that had toppled onto a stack of dog-eared file folders.

Back in the old days, Jake and Connie got together quite regularly with Frank and his wife, Louise, for barbecues on their back deck. They went to the same church back then, their kids were about the same age, and they even took a vacation together—a trip around Cape Breton, Nova Scotia, with all the kids and two dogs.

During the time when everything was falling apart, Connie and Louise were fast friends. Jake always wondered how much garbage Frank had learned about him from Louise, who'd heard it from Connie. It had become easier to just not talk to anyone anymore. So he didn't.

When he learned that Frank had taken a posting at Ridley Harbor, he kept meaning to look him up.

"Jake!" Frank said when he hung up the phone and stood. "Is this Jake Rikker in the flesh?"

They hugged each other briefly. "Great to see you, man. You're looking good," Frank said. "The salt air must agree with you. How goes it?"

"I'm fine. I run a whale-watching business over in Fog Point."

"I heard that."

"I also do a little PI work on the side."

"PI work? Man, I should join you, get out from under all this paperwork. With this homeland security, you wouldn't believe how much our work load has increased. And stupidly so."

"How're Louise and the kids?"

"You didn't hear? We split. My divorce just came through."

"You and Louise?"

"Yeah, well. This job…" he smiled sheepishly. "You know. We should have a club."

Frank had gained weight since Jake had seen him last. He looked smaller and rounder, even downtrodden. They chatted some more, asked after each other's children, and then Jake said, "It's my PI work that brings me here." And he told him about Wesley Stoller. "I know it's not in your jurisdiction, but I'd like to know stuff in his background, particularly any charges related to stalking, threatening behaviors, computer stalking, that sort of thing."

"You want his rap sheet."

"Yeah, if you can get it. And this has to be confidential. My client doesn't want any police involvement."

"I don't know, Jake."

"You can try, though, right?"

"I'll see what I can do."

After that they chatted about work, the state of the police department, and the state of the government. They promised to get together for a beer sometime, but Jake suspected that each man knew it probably wouldn't happen.

Just before Jake walked out the door, Frank said, "Just want you to know something, Jake. I never believed all that stuff about you"—he made circular motions with his finger—"you know, from before."

"Thank you, Frank."

After he bought boat supplies at the marine store, it was time to pick up May. His time with Frank had left him strangely sad. He wondered if there were any happily married police officers in the world. He wondered if there were any happily married people in the world. He and May were quiet on the way home. He was glad, at least, that May was off her Elise soapbox for a while.

Halfway to Fog Point, May said, "Do you know what an indigo child is?" She held a package on her lap.

"I have absolutely no idea what you're talking about."

Ahead of him, a truck loaded with logs inched its way up the hill. The yellow lines down the middle of the road were annoyingly solid.

"Norah said Elise's daughter is an indigo child."

Elise again. Jake grunted. "Probably some astrological thingy whatsit that Norah's thought up."

Up ahead, Jake saw a glint of broken lines and gunned the engine to pass. The thing in May's lap fell to the floor. She picked it up. It was some sort of knee brace.

"Got something new for the knee?"

"Yeah."

"You're not wearing it."

"No."

Ten minutes before they reached the town limits of Fog Point, Jake's cell phone chirped. He reached into his shirt pocket and looked at the caller ID before he answered it.

"Hey, Ben."

"I found another book for Jana. On the making of one of the Lord of the Rings movies. I'll bring it by tomorrow."

"Great. I'm on my way home from Ridley. Just picked up three more quarts of bottom paint. At fifty bucks a quart."

"Ouch."

"Thought I'd strip and paint the *Constant* as well." Jake stared at the road.

"She still on the hard?"

"Yep, she is. As we speak, she is still balanced unhappily on jack stands down at Pop's."

"Won't be long though."

"Gotta get the bottom done before I launch her."

"Well, buddy, we better get her done. Club races are coming up. We gotta get a few shakedown races under our belts if we have any hope of beating Doc in that famous J/29 of his. I'll help paint. You just name the time and place."

"Monday?"

"Monday it is."

Ben and Jake raced Jake's Hunter sailboat in the Fog Point Yacht Club races. Jake thought about the upcoming race as he took the Fog Point exit. He wondered whether Elise liked sailing. He tried to imagine her navigating the decks in heels. His cell phone chirped again. Ben must've forgotten something. But it wasn't Ben. *Blocked number,* Jake read.

"Jake? Jake?" It was Elise, and she sounded frantic.

"Elise? What is it?" Beside him May looked up sharply.

"He's here! Wesley Stoller is here, Jake! He's here!"

"What do you mean he's here?"

"At my house!"

"He's there now?"

"Yes. No. I don't *know!* He was here. I don't know. I..." Her words were a jumble.

"Elise, get off the phone and call 911 right now."

"NO!" She fairly screamed it. "No, please. I can't do that. Please…" Tiny muffled sobs. "Oh, Jake, I'm so afraid."

"Then I'll call 911."

May turned and faced him.

"No, please don't. You don't understand. I can't have the police. I can't have them here and everything. I can't… I'm so sorry. I've made such a mess of things."

"You haven't. Okay, listen, May and I will be right there. We're on our way into Fog Point right now. We can be there in five."

"No!" Elise was emphatic. "I mean no," she repeated, her voice sounding small now. "Can it just be you, Jake? I just don't think I can handle a lot of people right now."

12

M oon crouched in his closet and looked through a peephole to the apartment below, into Cain's crummy little box of a place. Moon expected another check today for two thousand dollars and more checks at the end of the following week. His little business venture was beginning to pay off big time. Well, not big time yet, but soon enough.

Shortly after he took this job, Moon installed peepholes into all the apartments. From his closet he had access to two of them, Cain's and Miss Piggy's. He could access the others through peepholes in broom closets all over the building. He'd even installed cameras in most of them so that he would have a recording to go over later, if necessary. Actually, camera film was really the best idea; then he had proof. Most of the time he didn't need it, though. Nine times out of ten, people didn't need to see pictures. Didn't need to be shown things. They knew what they'd done.

Yes, he would lose this job if Davenborn, the apartment complex owner, ever discovered his peephole activity. It was a chance he was willing to take, though. Chalk it up to the cost of doing business. No, he didn't look through peepholes to get his jollies. That wasn't even a small part of the equation. Who would willingly stay in this cramped, hot closet, face pressed against a filthy baseboard, just to watch Miss Piggy scratch herself and yell at her little piglets. Or watch Ebenezer in his droopy old man's underwear yelling out the answers to *Jeopardy!* Or Barbie getting her face punched in again by Ken, or the Tweedles sitting on their couch eating ice cream out of a shared carton and watching reruns of *Will and Grace*? Would people willingly put themselves through stiff legs and sweat just to watch strangers grunt and eat and belch in their apartments? No, his goals were higher. He had *plans.*

And Cain was of utmost importance to him now. With the others it was money. With Cain it was something else, something more important to him than money. Earlier Moon had been scouting out PI cameras on eBay. He found one and figured he could get it easily enough using a stolen credit card he'd recently acquired.

Moon watched Cain scrunch his head toward the computer screen, as if he needed glasses or the writing on the monitor was too small. Then he leaned back on the legs of the chair and reached into the chip bag that had been there all night. When nothing was immediately forthcoming, Cain picked up the bag and shook its contents into his hand. Then he shoveled the pieces into his mouth and licked his hand. *Remind me not to shake your hand,* Moon thought.

The peephole gave a complete view of the one-room apartment, except for the bathroom. None of Moon's peepholes were quite that invasive. Maybe that would come, but in Moon's detecting theory, which came from PI listservs and chat rooms he frequented and from experience, people usually didn't hide things in bathrooms. Despite what television showed, people actually put things in drawers and bookcases. People generally hide like things with like things. If people are hiding shampoo, well, they might put it in the bathroom, but most people hiding papers will hide them in places where papers are normally kept: desk drawers and bookshelves. Most people aren't very creative that way. They like to think they are, but when it comes right down to it, they're not.

Cain wiped his hands on his jeans, took a swig of Pepsi, and turned back to his computer. From this distance Moon couldn't tell what Cain was working on.

Moon needed to get into Cain's computer. He'd gone into Cain's apartment the previous day, his leather tool belt slung around his hips. He was standing in front of the computer and was just about to jiggle it to life when Cain was suddenly there. He hadn't even heard him! Not a good sign.

"Hey," Moon had said, scrambling to put on the sunglasses he'd hooked into the neck of his T-shirt.

Cain had just looked at him.

Moon pointed to the ceiling. "I was afraid your computer might be getting wet here."

"Wet?"

"Leak in the apartment above. I've been working on it all morning. Your computer—it's right underneath. I was just checking it."

Cain looked up at the ceiling. "I don't see anything," he said. His eyes were dark, sort of deep set and brooding.

"We got lucky this time," Moon retorted. "Friggin' water pipes in this old building." Moon was pretty quick with the comebacks. It was something he'd learned by studying self-help books on public speaking and dramatic improvisation. It hadn't come naturally, though. Just ask anyone who knew him when he was a bucktoothed, geeky kid.

Cain was eyeing the Glock on Moon's belt. Moon saw this and patted the gun. "I'm licensed to carry. It's for the job. For protection.

Trust me, you want a superintendent who packs. Hey, you're home from work? This time of day?"

"I had to be somewhere."

Moon peered at him through the mirrored shades. Then he turned to leave. In the doorway he said, "You let me know if you see any drips, any water spots up there." Then he made a gesture like cocking a gun and aimed his forefinger at Cain before he left.

Stupid, stupid! Moon usually didn't make mistakes like that, having a charge suddenly walk in like that. What he should've done, what he normally did, was to call his charge's place of employment before he went traipsing in anywhere. He wouldn't make that mistake again.

Moon wiped the bubbles of sweat from his upper lip as he crouched in the closet. Cain's phone rang, and Moon was instantly alert, his eye pressed against the peephole, keeping himself perfectly still so he could hear. Drat. Just dribs and drabs of words. *Do I buy more cameras with my next paycheck,* Moon thought, *or do I buy some sort of audio magnification system?* Maybe he'd put a bug in the guy's phone.

Cain hung up the phone, pushed back from the computer, and stood up. Then he sneezed. Sneezed again. Blew his nose into a tissue. Threw the tissue at a corner wastebasket. Missed. Left the tissue on the floor. Wiped his hands on his jeans. Another little-known fact: People are quite gross about personal cleanliness when they think no one's looking. Even beauty queens like Barbie. Moon could tell stories.

Then Cain moved into the bathroom. A few minutes later he was back out again. Moon watched him pull on his Aybeez Car Wash golf shirt and a pair of khakis. Then he took his Bible from the kitchen table, sat down, opened it, and read for a couple of minutes. Moon recognized it as a Bible from the time he was in the apartment. Well,

Cain wouldn't be the first person who got religion in prison. *A place where you either got religion or you died,* he thought.

When Cain left, Moon changed into his work clothes: black jeans, black T-shirt, black sneakers. And, of course, he put on his tool belt, attaching his holstered gun on one side, his knife on the other. Time to get into that computer.

13

E lise lived in a two-story house at the end of a street of imposing old homes covered in ivy. Hers was one of the smallest. She'd told Jake at lunch that they'd lived there for two years and that Rachel still missed the old place, an upstairs apartment only a block from her best friend from school.

The double door had an old-fashioned knocker, but before Jake could lift it or ring the bell, the door opened.

A red-haired little girl scooted under his arm and out the door, muttering, "I'm glad you came. She's upset." She nodded her head toward the house. "I have to go. I can't stay with her. I have papers to deliver."

While Elise was tiny and pale, with a waist, Jake thought, that he could span his hands around, this daughter of hers was chunky and sturdy with a mass of red curls for hair. Except for the hair, Rachel reminded him of his own daughter Alex: strong, athletic, and independent.

He stepped through the door. The house seemed oddly quiet. "Elise?"

"Jake?" A muffled call came from the back of the house. He moved quickly toward the sound and found himself in a large kitchen. She was sitting on a chair and staring through french doors, her face in profile.

"He knows where I live," she said. "He just got out of prison, and he came right here. How could he do that so quickly?"

"Elise." He moved toward her.

"Don't step on the glass."

He looked around him. The kitchen was large with an island and pots hanging overhead. It looked like the type of place meant for gatherings and dinner parties. He wondered if she ever entertained. Behind the island, shards of blue glass lay scattered on the floor like a scattering of gemstones.

"Did he do this?" Jake asked.

She shook her head, opened her mouth to say something, then closed it again.

"Did he hurt you?"

She shook her head again and said quietly, "He knows where I live. How can he know where I live?"

She hugged her arms. Jake spotted a throw blanket on a wicker couch in the corner. He placed it over her shoulders and knelt beside her. "What happened?"

"I need a coffee first," she said. "I was getting some when I saw... It's there. It's all made."

He found two mugs in the cupboard and poured the coffee. There was something wrong with this room. It was large. It had pots, an island, and matching appliances and hardwood floor, yet it seemed empty. It was as if someone else lived here and Elise was only boarding and hadn't gotten around to putting up her own things yet. The front of the refrigerator was bare. There were no pictures on it, no report cards of Rachel's, no notices of swim meets or gymnastics classes or appointments or art drawings. Nothing. When he was married his family fridge was a repository of announcements and pictures. Plus, it was completely covered with little magnets advertising everything from banks to florists. Even the fridge in the kitchen of the Purple Church was a notice board of staff announcements. Elise's was smooth and clean.

Elise hadn't moved from where she sat. He followed her gaze. The deck was large but, like the kitchen, empty. Several flowerpots were devoid of the blooms and colors meant to be there. *Hollow* came to mind. *Vacant.* The place a lifeless showroom.

He put the mugs on the table and sat down next to Elise. "Now tell me what happened."

"I saw him there." She pointed toward the french doors. "He tried the door, but it was locked, and when I screamed, he ran." Her voice caught. "Rachel had just gotten home from school. She was getting her papers ready to deliver."

Elise further explained that Rachel delivered newspapers after school, the evening edition of the *Ridley Harbor Post.* "She was out in the garage getting the papers together, and I was in here. Something felt wrong. I couldn't put my finger on it, but something wasn't right. Do you ever get that feeling? You know there's something, but you don't know what? Like when someone's watching you. Sort of this skin-crawly feeling. I felt that when I was in here." She rubbed her arms as she talked. She tried to shake it off, she explained, but the feeling had only intensified.

"What did you do then?"

"What could I do? I thought it was this whole craziness manifesting itself, so I decided to put away some of the dishes from breakfast. The bowl… When I climbed onto the kitchen stool to put the bowl away, I heard a noise at the door and turned around and…there he was! At the door right there." She pointed. "His face was big and pressed in against the glass. And he was looking in at me with this horrible expression on his face. Then he tried the door. Put his hand right on the doorknob. Then I screamed; I couldn't help it. I screamed and dropped the bowl."

"And you're absolutely sure it was him?"

She nodded. "I know his face. He e-mailed lots of pictures to me. I would know that face anywhere."

"Where was Rachel at this time?"

"Still in the garage."

"Do you think she saw him?"

Elise shook her head. "I don't see how. There are no windows on that side of the garage. I don't want to involve her in this. She's been through enough as it is."

"Elise, we really need to call the police. You know that, don't you?"

"I can't. I really can't. Please don't ask me to call the police. It's something… I just…" She was visibly shaking and her face was pale.

He walked to the door. Using a dishtowel, he carefully opened it. There would be fingerprints. There would be something. There would be lots of somethings. The place would be crawling with evidence. A good CSI would find everything. Jake had been out of law enforcement for six years, and forensics had never been his strong suit. He stood at the door looking out. The late afternoon sun was casting horizontal rays across the deck. He stepped outside. It was a hexagonal wooden deck with two steps down on all sides. *There should be deck furniture out here,* he thought. *There should be wooden-slatted deck chairs in bright, shiny colors around a table with an umbrella.* Elise followed him and stood beside him.

"That's Featherjohn's B&B, right?" he pointed straight through the trees.

"Yes."

"And next to it, that's the Nation's place?"

"I think so, yes. I don't know my neighbors too well."

"We need to have the police come and check for fingerprints on the door handle. You said he pressed his face against the glass."

She nodded. He knelt down and checked from all angles, but he could see no smudge marks. "You sure you saw his face pressed against this?"

"I thought I did. Maybe I was wrong."

He walked to the edge where the deck met the side of the house. A narrow strip of garden ran along the back of the house. He looked down.

"Elise, do you have a camera?"

"Yes."

"Can you get it right now?"

"What do you see?"

"Look."

In the dirt right under the window was a fresh, clear boot print. It was parallel to the house, as if its owner had jumped off the deck and run along the back of the house.

Elise was back within minutes with a 35-millimeter camera, and Jake began photographing the boot print from different angles. Again, a good CSI would already be making casts of it for comparison with the thousands of boot treads in their database. "Elise, you need to call the police. They could get this guy. Find out who it is. This boot print would tell them a lot. I know you don't want the publicity, but Elise, this man could be dangerous now."

She kept looking at the boot print, not saying anything.

"We've all done stupid things at some point. I've done my share, let me tell you. And let's face it, writing to this Wesley Stoller character was a stupid thing. But you're going about it all wrong. The police will do their job. They'll keep this thing as quiet as possible. I have friends there…"

He could feel her body shudder. She moved away from him. "I can't," she said. "I know you think I'm being ridiculous, it's just…" She sniffled into a Kleenex. "I don't like being so afraid."

"I know."

"Can we please not phone the police?"

He relented. *What can I do?* "Okay. For now we won't."

She gave him a half smile. "Thank you. I should…"—she got up and found a broom—"I need to clean this up before someone gets hurt. I've made such a mess of things. I just…"

"Elise, I'll do that. You just sit down."

He reached for the broom, and in doing so covered her hand with his own. Her hand felt small, like a child's. "You're cold," he said.

"I'm okay." But she sat back down in the chair, covered herself with the throw, and drank her coffee while he swept her floor.

"I've got an idea," he said when he finished. "When Rachel gets back from her paper route, why don't I take the two of you to supper?"

She smiled. "That would be so nice. Except it will have to be just me. Rachel's eating at her best friend's house. They're working on some sort of project for school. She won't be home until eight. So if you can have me back by eight, I'd love to go with you."

"It's a deal."

"I look forward to it."

"I do too." And he did.

14

H e wasn't going to be so stupid this time. So Moon called Aybeez Car Wash just to make sure the guy had shown up. Cain was there, so Moon headed downstairs and unlocked the door to Cain's apartment. *Do things right this time,* he told himself. *Do things right. Don't just run over to the computer and start hacking like the half-frigged way you did it last time. Inhale the guy. Get to know your mark. It's the first rule.*

So he stood just inside Cain's doorway and looked around.

Wesley hadn't changed his décor much from his previous address. The whole thing looked prison issue. All that was needed was the chrome toilet with no seat in the corner, and Cain would be right back in jail. Moon was careful not to touch anything without his gloves on. He knew he was leaving fibers and skin cells behind, even just walking through.

The faded red linoleum of the kitchen area was neatly swept, and an old straw broom leaned against the wall in the corner by the door. Every so often the ancient fridge hummed noisily like fans at a baseball game. With his gloved fingers he opened it. One container of milk, one of orange juice, some sliced sandwich meat, a loaf of bread, mayo, mustard, half a pizza from a takeout place around the corner, a small jar of instant coffee, about a dozen plastic containers of pancake mix, syrup, a couple of cardboard cups of those little Chinese soups. Even sugar. Stoller kept everything in the fridge. The guy was weird.

Next Moon checked the kitchen cupboards. Not much there—a few plates, bowls, two coffee mugs, and a plastic cup that said Coca-Cola on the side. Outside, crows cawed at each other.

A small couch with blue flecks on it nearly filled the living area of the one-room dump. A small television sat on top of a cheap TV stand, and next to that, on a cheesy kid's desk with stickers of Spider-Man on the side, sat the famous new computer. He wondered whether Cain's Bible-study friends had footed the bill for the furniture.

Moon carefully felt his way through the desk. Aside from a few receipts for pizza and fast food and an envelope of grocery receipts, there wasn't much. *Who keeps grocery receipts?* Moon leafed through a couple of magazines sitting nearby. They looked religious. He put them back.

Now to the bedroom corner. What he should do is get some of those TV makeover gay guys in here. Wouldn't they have fun? No. On second thought, they'd take one look and run for cover, their hands over their prissy little heads.

The double bed was saggy and old and came with the place. Cain had covered it with a brown bedspread that looked like it used to be some old man's bathrobe. A Bible lay on the nightstand. What looked like a softcover notebook was stuffed inside it. Moon removed the notebook and skimmed through it. It was some sort of workbook with questions and answers.

"What does this passage say about giving?" he read, and there was Wesley's answer written in gel pen, looking like a child had scrawled it. "I should give and forgive."

Outside the crows cawed louder. Moon walked over to the window, got out his Glock, and aimed it at the birds. "Kapowee," he mimicked, then put the gun back in its holster. He hated birds.

There was one garage-sale-issue dresser in the room, and Moon went through it drawer by drawer. The drawers held neatly folded T-shirts and neatly folded jeans and neatly folded underwear and neatly folded socks. When police went through people's drawers on television, everything always seemed so neat and orderly. But when he'd done this in real life—which was every time a person moved into his apartment—most often people's drawers were scattered and messy. T-shirts stashed in with loose and mismatched socks, old underwear all crumpled up with Visa receipts, and broken sunglasses and pens with the tops off. People always kept a lot of crappy pens in their drawers.

Cain seemed to favor plain T-shirts from Kmart and cheap jeans and Joe Boxer undershorts.

It was warm in the room, but Moon dared not open a window. He swept his gloved hand over his bald head to wipe up the sweat. That was another thing he did. If he didn't have any hair, at least he couldn't shed it. So he shaved his head once a week.

The only interesting find in the entire place was in the cheap TV stand. Moon almost missed noticing a DVD compartment in the bottom. No DVDs there, but at the bottom lay a small Ziploc bag, and inside wrapped in Kleenex was a ring. Moon held it up. A man's silver wedding ring. Moon spun it around a few times. Then he snapped a picture of it with his tiny digital camera and put it back.

Now to the real work. He placed a paper bag he brought with him on Cain's computer chair and sat down. Unfortunately, the idiot had turned the computer off. *Why do people do that?* Moon grumbled.

He switched it on, waited for it to boot up, and then discovered that Cain had password-protected the whole thing.

What kind of dimwit password-protects his computer in his own apartment? From his tool kit Moon took out a CD of software he'd recently purchased from a PI Web site. He inserted it, listened to it go through its various inner workings. This was the first time he had used it on the job. He'd tried it on his own computer and it seemed to work. A few minutes later, the password popped up. A single name. *Fiona.*

Moon smiled. He smiled bigger. Then he chuckled. Then he laughed at the stupidity of Cain. Then he laughed at the crows that were cawing even louder now. And he laughed at all the stupid people in the world. *Fiona!*

He went into Cain's Word files. Not a lot there. A couple of attempts at poetry.

Poetry. The guy's writing poetry. A guy's in jail for ten years for murdering his brother in cold blood and comes out and starts in with roses are red? Moon almost laughed out loud.

He went into Cain's Web cache history. Lots of hits on the AA site, but he'd also visited a few of those people-search places. He'd even paid money. Moron. There were easier ways to find people. Stoller was looking for people. He had five names on his list. Sarah McCarthy was one. Fiona was another.

15

After he checked and double-checked all of her doors and windows, Jake left. Elise felt better now, she told him. And in an hour, as soon as the Purple Church closed for the day, he'd come back and pick her up. They'd go out for a nice dinner at that new restaurant on the highway. He'd have her home in plenty of time for Rachel.

Back at the Purple Church, May and Lyndsey were in the sanctuary waiting on customers. Jake busied himself checking the e-mail.

"Well," May said when she came in. "What's going on with Elise?"

"She thought she saw Stoller on her back deck."

"She's mistaken, of course."

"I'm not so sure, May. She seemed pretty positive. There was a boot print under the window. I got a picture of it."

"Let's see it," May said.

"It's on Elise's camera." He paused. "I'm planning on getting it from her later."

"It's not digital?" May picked up her notebook.

"Apparently not."

May said, "You should've used our camera."

"I know, May, but I didn't have it with me."

She opened to a clean page in her notebook. "She may have seen someone. I'm not disputing that. But the person she most definitely did not see was Wesley Stoller. I called his work while you were out. He's been there all day. And how's he going to get all the way down here anyway?"

So it wasn't Stoller. Which was good news and bad news. Good news because Wesley Stoller wasn't stalking Elise. Bad news because someone else obviously was.

Forty-five minutes later, when Jake emerged from his apartment to go pick up Elise, he did a double take when he noticed her standing in the hallway in the basement of the Purple Church.

"Elise!"

"Jake, I'm so sorry. I know I said I was fine. And I am, but I didn't want to go back to my studio. So I decided to come here. One of your young men let me in."

"Did you see May?"

"No."

Why did he feel relieved? Yet he did. What he didn't need now were May's looks, her comments. He was a grown man, and what business was it of hers who he took to dinner?

"The front door was locked. I guessed you were closed, so I came to the back door. It was locked, but this nice guy opened it and said you were downstairs. I'm sorry. Should I not have come here?"

"This is fine. Probably Ethan or Matt let you in?"

Elise nodded.

"Well, welcome to my home."

"You *live* down here?"

"I do."

"But this is a church basement."

"It is."

"Wow." She looked around her.

"Would you like a tour?"

"I'd love one."

Jake led her first into the large kitchen where Ethan and Matt were eating microwave pizzas.

Ethan rose when they entered. "Hi, Elise. I see you found Jake."

"I did."

"So you two going out or something?"

"Something like that," Jake said.

Ethan made a point of looking from Elise to Jake and back to Elise. He nodded in appreciation.

Matt, the more reserved of the two, merely raised his hand in greeting when Elise came in and went on eating his pizza.

"I'm giving her a tour of the place," Jake said.

"Just don't show her my room," Ethan said. "I've got junk all over the place. Show her Lyndsey's room. She's not here. She's out getting groceries. Her place is always clean."

"I won't invade any of your rooms," Jake said.

Elise said, "This is a nice kitchen."

"It suits us. If everyone does the dishes like they're supposed to," he said loudly and grinned in Ethan and Matt's direction.

A washer and dryer flanked the far end of the kitchen, and a ladies' room and a men's room with showers adjoined the eating area.

There were a total of five apartments in the basement, including Jake's, which was the biggest. His was actually two rooms, a bedroom and a living room, where his girls slept when they visited.

All of the apartments used to be Sunday-school classrooms. Jake showed Elise the one vacant apartment at the end of the hall. Next to it was a larger classroom complete with a fireplace, a television, a stereo, and shelves and shelves of books.

"This probably served as a church lounge at some point in its history," Jake said. "Now it's our communal living room."

"You like to read," she said.

He did like to read and kept books for the cruisers, he explained. Having lived on his boat for a number of years, he knew a lot of cruisers, and he'd offered them a standing invitation to shower, do laundry, and trade paperbacks when they sailed into Fog Point. "You leave one, you pick up one," he told her. "Or if you don't have one to trade, you could pick up one anyway. Or you can take two if you want."

She laughed and picked through the books: Tom Clancy, Dick Francis, Stephen King, Clive Cussler, Elizabeth George, Nora Roberts. "You've got a regular library down here."

"I think people who cruise read more paperbacks per capita than anyone else on the planet."

"Not much else to do when you're out there fending off hurricanes, I guess," she said.

Elise had a sense of humor. He liked that. He showed her his apartment—the living room where his daughters stayed, the Hide-a-Bed, and a shelf of books.

"That door goes to your bedroom?" She pointed to an adjoining door.

"Yep."

"Can I see it, too? I'm sure it's nice."

"My cleaning staff and butlers haven't made it in today." He chuckled. Nevertheless, he opened the door to his bedroom. She brushed past him and walked right in. He had no choice but to follow and look at the place through her eyes: half-made bed, quilt pulled up slapdash, dirty clothes piled in a corner, the Ian Rankin he was reading opened facedown on his nightstand, and pictures of his girls in frames next to receipts and papers and more books on his dresser.

She stood in the center of the room grinning, hands on hips. "This is nice. You've done such a great job down here. I never would have thought you could do this to a church. I like it."

"Thank you."

"I like the colors." She stood next to the windows fingering the curtains, which were nothing special, just something he'd picked out of a Sears catalog.

~

Halfway to Ridley Harbor, Elise turned to Jake. "I have an awful, awful confession to make."

"What is it?"

"I ruined the film. All of the pictures you took of the footprints? I ruined them. I don't know how it happened. I guess I was terrified about seeing Wesley, so before we left, when I went up to get my jacket, I was shaking so much that the camera came open, and I accidentally exposed the film. I was so shaky and nervous. I'm not very good with cameras, I suppose. I should've just given it to you."

She seemed so small, so afraid, like a child really. Yet, he wondered, why did things keep going wrong around her to sabotage the investigation?

16

Y ou know what I think?" May said while retrieving sheets from the fax machine the next morning. "I think she's deluded. And I don't mean that in an entirely bad way. She's just so afraid of this Stoller fellow actually showing up with incriminating stuff about her that she *thought* she saw him. She probably did see something. It just wasn't Stoller. Did you get that film developed?"

He turned away from her. "It didn't turn out."

"What do you mean?"

"There was some difficulty getting the film out of the camera. I'm planning on going over there this morning and retake them."

"Some difficulty?"

He nodded. "I should've taken our camera. Elise was so nervous that she accidentally exposed the film."

"Take the digital."

He nodded.

"Okay, then, give me the lay of the land, Jake." She wheeled the computer chair away from the computer and handed him a piece of paper. "Draw me a picture of the house."

He obliged. Then she moved the paper this way and that and said, "Pretend you're a Peeping Tom. You're looking in a window, and then this woman screams at you. You decide to run away before you're caught. Tell me, would you run along the back of the house, as this direction indicates? Or would you just turn tail and run out through the backyard?"

"I don't know."

She frowned and looked at the paper this way and that.

"What are you saying?" Jake asked.

"I think this print belongs to someone who was sneaking along the back of the house—a classic Peeping Tom. He tried one window and then the next. We need to go to the police. This guy could be looking in other windows."

"She won't go to the police."

"I don't think she has a choice now, Jake."

"She told me last night that if we go to the police, she would deny that anything happened."

May adjusted her computer glasses, jiggled the sleeping machine awake, and said, "What *is* the matter with her?"

Jake shrugged. *She had said those words, hadn't she, that she would deny it?* Saying it aloud to May now sounded ludicrous, but last night it had sounded all right. Even sane.

"I have my daughter to consider," she'd said. "She's all I think about. If this goes to the police, I'll have to deny that it ever happened."

Even when he told her that Stoller had been at work all day, she wasn't satisfied. "You don't know what he's capable of. I'm sure he could have flown here. He has the resources; people he met in prison."

It was an eight-hour drive from here to where Stoller now lived, but a mere hour by air. That's what Elise had said, that he could've gotten here by air. She'd even pointed out the flights that would have put him in Fog Point at precisely the right time.

"Look at these." May handed him the faxed sheets. On the top page was a scrawled note: "Jake, let's not wait too long for that beer. Frank." The fax showed a ten-year-old black-and-white mug shot of Wesley Stoller, along with a two-page rap sheet.

"Look at that face," May said. "What a bright ray of sunshine this boy is."

He looked down at the photo of Stoller. Curly dark hair, full mouth, lips twisted into a snarl. He looked tough and hardened, but underneath shone a look of surprise, as if he were an innocent trying to look like a tough guy. The picture wasn't a great reproduction, but Jake thought Stoller might also have freckles.

Jake said. "I can see the girls going for this one on that write-to-a-prisoner Web site."

"Yeah, he looks like a charmer, that's for sure. A real Dennis the Menace," May said.

"'Life in prison, out now on parole after ten years,'" Jake read from the fax.

"Gotta love the justice system."

His rap sheet featured petty crimes: robberies, drug possession and trafficking, a number of driving while impaireds. And one little robbery he committed with his brother, David Stoller, the brother he'd been convicted of murdering. The two brothers had held up a convenience store at knifepoint for a case of beer.

"One case of beer?" Jake asked looking up.

"Yep, a case of beer. I suppose you gotta start somewhere." May turned back to the computer. "But I still can't find him on any of these pen-pal sites, and it's driving me buggy."

"He probably got his name and particulars removed from the Web site when he got out, or when he started e-mailing Elise."

"I can't imagine these Web sites are that up to date." She clicked on a few more links.

"Is this important, the Web site?" he asked.

May shrugged. "It's just interesting, that's all. It might help us get a handle on who this guy really is."

Ethan entered the office carrying a box. "This came," he said. "More sunscreen. Should I unpack it or what?"

"Who ordered all this sunscreen?" May grumbled. "What are we, Palm Beach? We're lucky to have three days when we actually need the stuff. Take it to the stock room, Ethan. I'll be right there."

When May left, Jake checked his personal e-mail. Another message from Jana. He wrote to both his daughters but seldom heard from Alex. They were two different girls. Jana, bookish and studious, and loving all things Tolkien and Lord of the Rings; Alexandra, the younger daughter, on a different sports team each season.

A momentary pang struck as he realized just how removed he was from their lives. Every once in a while, he thought about moving south to be closer to them, closer than a two-day drive. Other divorced fathers he knew lived closer to their children.

Frank was right; they should have a club. As he thought about Frank, Jake wondered how he worked out visitation.

Hi Dad!

Do you know what? I saw some people kayaking in the bay yesterday, and it got me really excited to try it again! I can hardly wait! Did Mom talk to you? Alex doesn't want to come right away. She made softball camp, but she'll come after that.

It's a Christian camp. Keith will be there. He's a coach, you know. Mom will probably call you about it. You know how Alex is! LOL! Of course, if you tell her she can go on a kayak camp-out, maybe that'll change things!

Love,

Jana

PS: I'm attaching a chapter of my report on The Hobbit. Can you maybe get your minister friend to check it out? I can't remember his name. Our pastor's so out of it, he doesn't even know who Tolkien is! What a dweeb!

PPS: I love you.

For a moment he forgot about Elise and chasing after footprints and thought about Deacon Keith raising his girls. After six years the rage and anger had transformed itself into a quiet hate, a dark piece of himself that he couldn't shed.

17

To my mom,

There is blood all over my hands. When I was reaching in for my book, I cut my finger on a nail that was sticking out of the wall. Now there's blood on this book. I tried wiping it on my shirt, but it didn't all come off. I'm not going to tell you about it, because if I do I might have to tell you about what I did to the wall and about this book. So when my finger got caught on the nail, I went into the bathroom and ran the water over it and put on a Band-Aid. It doesn't hurt too much. I don't think it's very bad.

After school Jake the Whale Guy came over. I call him the Whale Guy because he has a whaleboat.

Here's what happened:

After school I don't do anything else until I get my papers delivered. And that includes going to Ashley's. So I came home in a hurry because Ashley and I have all this whale stuff to work on. I was going to have supper at her house and everything. So I was in the garage putting the papers in my sack and getting my bike ready when I hear this screaming.

And I do mean screaming! I wondered what was going on, and I didn't think it was you right away because you're usually at work when I come home from school.

So I dropped my papers bag and ran around the back, and who did I see but that ick ball Carl Featherjohn running away toward his house. I ran into the kitchen, and you were screaming and yelling and there was this broken dish on the floor. Your face was all white, and you yelled, "He's come, Rachel! He's come! He's here!"

And I said, "Who? Carl Featherjohn?"

And you said, "No, it's wasn't Carl. It was him!"

"Who's him?" I asked, but you didn't answer.

So then I looked out the window and said, "Mom, you don't have to be afraid. There's no one there."

But you made me wait to deliver my papers. And you were all shaky and sort of weird, and I was afraid again. And I'm worried about you, Mom.

There is blood showing through my Band-Aid now, and it hurts a little. Maybe I should put ointment on it.

Your daughter,

Rachel

~~

Whale Mothers
By Rachel St. Dennis

Whale mothers are very important. The mother is the most important figure in the killer whale's life. Females travel around with their babies their whole lives. A whale mother's family is called a matriline. I learned that from this whales book I got from Ashley. When a bunch of these matriline families swim through the water together, it's called a pod.

Here's what it's sort of like: Me and my mother would be a matriline, and Fog Point would be a pod.

Whale watchers can often spot mothers and their calves. In fact, if you see a big whale, you can almost be sure that a calf is nearby. I hope I can go out with Jake the Whale Guy sometime this summer.

Whale fathers aren't important at all. No one even talks about whale fathers.

18

The sun was short-lived, and by the time Jake got to Elise's with his digital camera, drops of rain pockmarked the sidewalk. He knocked on the door. She wasn't there, but he hadn't expected her to be.

He punched in the number of her studio again on his cell while he made his way to the side of her house. Jess answered and told him Elise was in Ridley Harbor picking up a few things.

"Do you have a cell-phone number for her or a number where I can reach her?"

"You can try, but Elise has a bad habit of leaving her cell phone off."

"Can you have her call me as soon as she gets in, then? I've got my cell with me." He wanted to tell Elise that he was off to retake the pictures with his own digital camera and not to worry.

"No problem."

In the back he glanced across the yard to the Featherjohn house. A light shone out of the window he presumed to be the kitchen. Lights also glowed from several of the basement windows. The rain fell harder, big drops that landed on his head, his nose. He pulled his sweatshirt hood up and let himself into the backyard through a black wrought-iron gate. Very nice, he thought. The whole place was very nice. At the window he pulled his camera out of his pocket and knelt down to take a picture.

But the boot print was gone. Jake puzzled for a moment. He had seen it, hadn't he? It was right here. He bent down to examine the ground more closely, still puzzled. It looked as if water might have been poured directly on the print. He looked curiously at the spot. Had the rain done this? He looked up and noticed a break, a hole in the eaves trough, directly above where the print had been. Had that been there yesterday? He couldn't remember.

The boot print had been destroyed. Well, almost. Jake peered closer. In the upper right corner, a half inch of tread hadn't been sloshed clean by the water. He took a picture. Then he snapped a shot of the eaves trough, the wall under the window, the window.

His cell phone rang as he headed back toward his pickup.

"Elise?"

"Elise? Who's Elise?"

Jake recognized his ex's voice. "Connie?"

"Yeah, it's Connie. Who's Elise?"

"A business associate."

"I have the girls' flight numbers if you want to jot them down."

"Can you e-mail them to me?"

"You can't grab a piece of paper right now and write them down?"

"I'm not near any paper."

"Can't you get near some paper?"

"No."

He heard an exasperated sigh. "Okay, I'll e-mail them to you. Oh, and Alex won't be coming until two weeks after Jana gets there. But I have her flight information ready anyway."

Jake reached his pickup and climbed behind the steering wheel. One of Elise's next-door neighbors was standing on his porch peering intently at Jake. A little baldheaded, chubby guy. Jake grinned and waved at him.

"I thought they were both coming for five weeks. That was the arrangement, wasn't it?"

"No, Jake, just three this summer for Alex."

"It was supposed to be five weeks." Rain splatted against the windshield. He started the car and turned on the wipers.

"This can't be helped. She'll be at softball camp. It's a Christian camp, so it's a great opportunity for her. Keith and I hate to have her miss this chance. Keith is actually one of the coaches this year. We wanted Jana to stay too, so the whole family could be together at the camp. Mickey and I will be going too, but Jana's so intent on this whaleboat of yours…"

Mickey was Keith and Connie's four-year-old son, a half-brother to Jana and Alex. *The whole family.* It probably wouldn't do any good to remind her that *he* was Jana and Alex's family.

"I thought it would be five weeks." Even as Jake repeated the words, he knew it sounded like whining. He recognized Connie's pronouncement for what it was, though—another dig, another assertion that he had no right to his girls, not after what he'd done. Not after leaving them. Not after losing it and running off. Deadbeat Caribbean boat-bum dad. That's what he was, and she would not let him forget. Getting the girls for even two weeks a year was a gift. Connie had the upper hand, and she used it all the time. She and Keith had total custody of the girls. A few years ago Keith even petitioned the courts to adopt them.

Over my dead body, Jake thought.

"What's that noise?" Connie asked.

"I'm driving."

"I thought I called you at work."

"I forwarded my phone."

"Do you drive holding the cell phone when the girls are with you?"

"Never."

There were days when he wondered how things had gotten so off track. In the second drawer of his dresser, way in the back, he kept a photo of him and Connie on their honeymoon. They stood next to a huge tree in Redwood National Park with greenery all around. They were snuggled very close together, and she looked up at him as if he were the only person she ever wanted to see in her life, ever again.

There is no sure thing in this life. Nothing.

"'Bye, Connie."

When Jake got to Pop Maynard's boatyard, Pop wasn't there, so he unlocked the gate and went inside. Because Jake kept two boats there—the *Constant* and the *Purple Whale*—he had his own key. The *Constant* was on the hard in the boatyard, and the *Purple Whale* was in what locals fondly called Pop's boat barn. Jake stepped over salt-rusted engine parts, buckets, old rope, chains, and pieces of lumber that Pop kept because "You never know when you might need something."

The *Purple Whale* was a forty-foot reconditioned lobster boat with an extended back roof section for people to shelter under in bad weather. When he bought the boat, it had a head, a small galley, and two berths for sleeping. The sale of another stained-glass window provided May and him with enough money to remodel the boat. They took out the sleeping berths to expand the galley and added more seating area both inside and outside the cabin.

Today he planned to do that most wonderful of all tasks: over-hauling the head. It was sort of fitting, he thought, that he'd just come from a conversation with his ex-wife.

The head had started to leak at the end of last season, and Jake knew that no room was more important to passengers. He changed into a pair of grimy shorts and a grimier T-shirt that he kept onboard, then he got out the tools he needed and the head kit he'd bought when he was in town. With Jimmy Buffett on his CD player, he climbed down into the cabin, whistling along to "Son of a Son of a Sailor." The head needed new gaskets and all-around tightening. Plus, there was a leak in the holding tank, and one thing that doesn't belong inside a boat is a leak in the holding-tank line.

Ben had told Jake that he needed to forgive Keith, that he would find no happiness until he did.

"Keith steadfastly doesn't think he needs forgiveness," Jake had said. "He will go to his grave believing that he rescued poor Connie from the likes of me."

"So let him," Ben countered. "Is it Keith's fault you ran away from your girls for two years?"

Jake hadn't answered his friend but looked away. Ben was the only person in Jake's life, with the possible exception of May, who could speak to him so frankly and still remain a friend.

Just as Jake finished disassembling the entire head, and bolts and screws and pins lay scattered, he heard a thumping on the deck above him, then a woman's voice. "Permission to come aboard, Captain?" He climbed out of the cabin and saw Pop's daughter, Carrie, standing at the top of his ladder holding out a white box that said Noonan's Café. She set it down on a seat that ran along the stern.

"Nootie gave me some rum cake. You want a piece?"

"*Rum* cake?"

"I know, I know. At *this* time of the morning? But as Jimmy Buffett always says, 'It's five o'clock somewhere.' Plus, I've got two hands, and I can help you if you want. May told me you guys are really swamped, and I don't have a lot to do today," she said.

"You don't have to."

"I know I don't have to. It's not a case of have to; it's a case of want to. My family is driving me bananas, and I need some hands-on work to get my mind off everything in my life. Besides, I like Jimmy Buffett."

"Come on board, then," he said.

Jake had first met Carrie a year and a half earlier when she'd moved back to Fog Point. He knew she'd been a news reporter in Detroit, and Jake always figured it had been hard for her to leave such a hotshot city job to come back to manage her father's business.

During that first year, at the urging of May—who thought they were *perfect* for each other—he and Carrie had dated for a couple of months. *Do people still use the term* date *these days?* Jake didn't know what to call it; the term was *dating* when he was younger. But whatever it was, he and Carrie spent a lot of time together for two months.

May had told him, "You can't do much better that Carrie. She's one of those genuinely nice people."

In the end, maybe that was the problem. Her goodness. Her kindness. Even the fact that she was a Christian. And Jake assumed that a time would have come when she'd want him to come back to faith and go to church with him. And if he stayed away from church, he knew there would come a time when she'd break off the relationship. So Jake found himself imperceptibly moving away from her.

Maybe he wasn't ready. Maybe she wasn't ready. He stopped calling her. He quit returning her calls. She quit coming by. Thing was, he didn't know what was the matter with him. He genuinely liked her. And he knew that, if given half a chance, whatever they shared could develop into something more. He couldn't manage goodness in his life, though. When he tried to explain that later to May, she told him he was crazy to let Carrie go. Plus, he had broken her heart. Those had been May's words: "You broke her heart, Jake."

"Better to break it off now than later," he had replied.

"I don't know what's the matter with you," May had said, shaking her head. "I love you like a brother, but you're being a jerk. You know that, don't you? A total class-A jerk."

But Carrie needed someone better than a failed boat bum who'd been to hell and back and made a whole lot of wrongheaded choices and lost just about everything along the way.

"You've got to talk to her at least. You owe her that much."

"Things never work out for me," Jake had lamented.

May had shaken her head again. "You know, you think you have the corner on misery. Right now you know where I'm supposed to be? Where Paul and I are supposed to be? We should be sitting on our cabin cruiser somewhere along the Intracoastal Waterway, drinking iced tea and admiring the scenery."

Jake knew about this boat of theirs. May had told him many times that a week prior to her husband's death, May and Paul had taken delivery on a Bayliner 42. Brand new. Real luxury. With a huge master stateroom and, according to May, a galley bigger than her kitchen at home, with refrigeration and a freezer and furniture nicer than the furniture in her house. And it had all the bells and whistles for Paul too: GPS, chart plotter, radar, the works. It was to be their retirement home.

They never even had it in the water, and she sold it a month after Paul was buried.

May said, "It was for two cents, Jake. I don't know if I ever told you that part. I saw the sign for gas, and it was two cents cheaper than we'd paid in the city. I said, 'Paul, we should get some gas.' He said, 'We don't need gas, babe. We have half a tank.' But I argued. And he gave in. And he died, shot by a sniper. And so, for two cents, Paul died. So Jake, don't tell me you have the corner on misery, because you don't. Carrie's a good woman. She's kind, and for some reason that only heaven understands, she likes you."

She had pulled her ball cap down, hiding her eyes, and mumbled something Jake couldn't hear. Then, "What I'm saying, Jake, is this. If you have a chance for happiness, you grab hold of it with both hands and give it everything you've got. It's too late for me, Jake, but it's not too late for you."

In the end he hadn't. He and Carrie had parted, but not without a certain amount of regret on his part. It had been only lately, in the past few months, that he and Carrie had begun renewing their friendship, slowly by inches, as friends only.

Carrie was now cutting two pieces of cake and licking her fingers. Jake looked at her. Bigger, sturdier, more solid than Elise, her face sunburned and freckled, someone who never wore high heels unless forced. Why, he wondered, was he comparing her to Elise?

He washed his hands with hot water from a thermos, dried them on a rag, and then took a piece of cake. It was good. Anything Nootie made was good. He sat down across from Carrie, and they ate rum cake and drank tea out of her thermos and listened to Jimmy Buffett.

When they finished eating, she hefted up a bucket of sudsy water and scrubbed out the deck while singing along with "Margaritaville."

Jake went below to finish the head repair. He was surprised she knew this song and told her so.

"Oh, there's a lot about me you don't know," she said.

At lunchtime Jake said he'd go buy takeout burgers. It was on him. Buzz Burgers from Noonan's. Did she want something to drink?

"Iced tea's fine," she said.

He washed up properly in Pop's bathroom next to the office and then headed out the gate to his pickup. Just as he started the truck, he saw a flicker of something down by the boardwalk. He almost ignored it until that something moved from behind a tree, and he saw it was Elise in an animated conversation with someone still hidden behind the tree. With one hand she held a cigarette, and the other made thrusting motions as she spoke. Her entire body looked stiff with rage. He couldn't see who she was talking to, so he sat in his car and waited.

Finally the person moved from behind the tree and gave her a dismissive wave as he walked away. Her last gesture to the man was the third-finger salute. The small man with the camera around his neck looked a lot like the neighbor Jake had waved to earlier. Who was he? Jake watched until Elise stomped off back down the boardwalk toward her studio—stomping as much as one can stomp in heels. The little man walked toward his VW, got in, and drove away.

⁓

19

The whole thing was very odd. May looked at the computer screen, blinked, then took off her glasses, rubbed her eyes, and put them on again. May was sure, she was absolutely positive, that the last time she had looked at the Elise's Creations Web site there had been no pictures of Elise. A week ago there had been no pictures of the studio or the boardwalk. There had been only images of her jewelry. She'd even commented on it to Jake, hadn't she?

In the days since Elise had seen the face in her window, nothing new had surfaced. Elise still refused to go to the police and told May and Jake this over and over. May went back to organizing their summer tours, once again hiring Nootie to make pots of chowder for the whale watchers and greeting customers in the sanctuary of the Purple Church. In a spare moment for herself, she'd decided to visit Elise's Web site. She called Elise's Web designer and was put on hold.

And now, there was Elise, and not just one picture but lots and lots of pictures. The "Meet Elise" clickable link opened up a whole scrapbook of pictures. There was a full-face shot of Elise that looked professionally taken. There was one of Jess, of the shop, of Elise in coveralls and goggles bending over a worktable with something that looked like a soldering iron. There was another of her and Jess standing behind a display stand, captioned "Here in Fog Point where it all happens."

She studied the full-face photo of Elise. Her features were too fine, too sharp to be called beautiful. She had a thin nose that was slightly turned down at the end. Even though she was tiny, she couldn't be described as cute. Cute would be an upturned nose and freckles. Beautiful would be full lips and high cheekbones. Elise had neither. Yet the result was somehow striking.

The mailing address, May noted, was still the office suite in Ridley. She looked along the bottom of the Web site and saw that it had been created by the same firm that met with the Fog Point Tourism Association and told them all to paint their businesses in bright colors with murals on the sides.

May recognized the name of the photographer as the yuppie ponytailed guy who told them, in his New York accent, that his company could put Fog Point on the map. The firm was based in New York, with an office in Ridley. Or so they said. She wondered if it was really a Ridley office with an office in Ridley.

She got out the Ridley phone book, found the ponytailed Web designer's name, and dialed the number. She was put on hold briefly. While she waited, she surfed the Web for St. Dennises. Elise's father had died in prison. But St. Dennis might not even be his name. It could be her married name.

A picture, though, was beginning to form in May's mind of a woman on her way up, but a woman with a past, with a father perhaps, who had committed a crime she didn't want the world to know about.

She did a search for Elise St. Dennis, expecting again to find nothing. Instead, she was directed to a number of online articles mostly in the *Ridley Harbor Post.*

Jewelry Workshop Offered.

Popular local jewelry designer Elise St. Dennis will give a seminar on working with gemstones at the College of Craft and Design Monday...

May skimmed the rest of the article, then looked at the next article:

The Excellence in Jewelry Award recently went to Fog Point jewelry artist Elise St. Dennis...

There was one other one: *Award-winning designer Elise St. Dennis was recently honored...*

Interesting, May thought, especially since none of these articles had been here when she was last on the site.

"Jon Masters here."

"Oh, hello." May directed her attention to the speakerphone. She said she was interested in the Web site of Elise St. Dennis.

"That's been recently redone," the fellow said.

"I'm noticing that. It's quite nice."

"Are you looking for a Web site?"

"Oh, just shopping around, you know. I was on her site a week ago, and it was a bit different."

"She wanted a whole new look, which we delivered."

"I'll say. So did she say why she wanted a whole new look?"

"Who did you say you were?"

"Actually, I didn't. I run a business in Fog Point. So...uh...how soon can you deliver this...uh...whole new look?"

"Depends how soon you want it. In Elise's case, she wanted it in days. We delivered."

"Hmm. I wonder why she wanted it in days."

"Who did you say you were?"

She hung up and went back to the articles.

"Hey, May."

May turned and her cane, which had been leaning against her computer table, clattered to the floor.

Carrie entered the office. She bent down, picked up the cane, and leaned it against the table. "Sorry I startled you. I just came by to see if you want to go for a walk, maybe end up at Noonan's for coffee."

"I'd love to. I'm almost done here."

Carrie sat down in a chair. May really looked at her then, at the deep circles under her eyes.

"You okay?"

"It shows? I'm here because I have to get away from Pop. He's so cranky this morning. Worrying about summer. He's always worrying about something. I guess I should understand that. With Mom gone. Makes me feel so old, having to do all this—the bookwork and taking care of Stuart."

Carrie's brother, Stuart, was in his midtwenties and suffered from schizophrenia.

"You're not old. You're definitely not old."

"I'm thirty-seven. Some people would say that's old."

"If you're old then I'm in my dotage." May rose and grabbed her cane and then put it down again.

"No cane?" Carrie asked.

"I'm trying a new thing. An experiment."

She was only fifty-seven. She wasn't an old woman. Only old women used canes and knee braces. So far she had not even tried the knee brace.

They took the path that led from the Purple Church to the boardwalk. It was slightly overgrown, and May made a mental note to get Lyndsey or Ethan to weed whack it into submission before the tourists came en masse.

Even though the rain had stopped, fragments of it clung to the tall grass along the edge of the path, wetting the bottom of May's jeans. Smart Carrie was wearing boots, while May wore her ugly, brown supportive shoes with the corrective insoles. For all the money she paid for them, she should be able to dance a jig.

By the time they reached the boardwalk, the sun was sparkling through the water and their feet clacked on the now-dry boards. The boardwalk was empty. A lot of the businesses opened only in the summer: the fudge and ice-cream parlors, the french-fry stands, the places that sold T-shirts and cheap coffee mugs with *Fog Point* stenciled across them. But a few shops remained in business all year. Whole Foods Convenience Shop was open, as well as Owl Books, Norah's Inner Healing Books and Gifts, Fit You Footwear, Mags and Hermans Café, and finally, at the very end occupying the largest space, Elise's Creations.

Carrie told May about her father and how he wasn't listening to anything she said. Any change she suggested in the running of the boatyard met with a shrug of his shoulders and a raising of his eyebrows. "I told him we should think about cleaning up the yard and getting rid of some of the junk, and do you know what he said to me? 'Your mother liked it the way it is.' Like my mother would want to see a dirty yard. She would have a fit, my mother would."

Pop had done all the boat repairs while Daisy, his wife, had managed the books and organized the business. It had been a pretty good setup until Daisy had a stroke two years ago and died. Now Carrie was home and trying to fit into her mother's shoes. And they weren't fitting.

May listened. She never felt she was very good at comforting people. She just listened a lot and most times didn't say much. She had begun to realize that Carrie, like Jake, looked to her as some sort of wiser, older sister. May thought that was quite funny. An only child, she wasn't anyone's sister. Plus, she wasn't wise, and because she and Paul had never been able to have children of their own, she couldn't even claim to be maternal. Yet Carrie had latched onto May as her best friend. Jake pointed out that most of the women Carrie's age were mothers with young children, so in that sense she would have more in common with May, both single women trying to make a life for themselves.

And then there was the story of Carrie and Jake. May always thought they'd be perfect together and still did, but *that* little match-making venture was filling her with nothing but frustration, so she vowed to stay out of Jake's love life forever. He'd been spending a lot of time with Elise lately. Even though she distrusted Elise, even though Elise was, in her opinion, too young for Jake, she would try to hold her tongue.

"...So I told Pop that Stuart has to take his meds. It's not an option. And Pop said, 'Oh, your mother handled things so much better.' What am I supposed to do when he says that? I can't be as good as my mom. No one can be. Stuart *did* always listen to Mom, and he never listens to me. But then, why should he? I'm just his spinster older sister. What do I know about schizophrenia? I'm learning, though. I'm getting a crash course, let me tell you."

They were opposite Mags and Hermans now, where a few people braved the cool weather to sit outside at café tables, drinking coffee and reading newspapers. An empty bulletin board on the outside wall would soon be filled with notices of concerts, kittens to be given away, boats for sale, and the improv comedy coffee nights sponsored by Mags and Hermans.

Then they arrived at Elise's Creations. Through the front display window, they could see Jess in a very short, tight skirt and spiked heels, wiping one of the display cases with a cloth. She saw them and smiled and waved, then motioned for them to come in.

Carrie raised her eyebrows at May, and the two turned to go in. May whispered, "Get out your checkbook." But she was glad Jess was there. This would be a good opportunity to talk about the renovated Web site.

"Ladies, ladies, hello! I saw you out there walking. I'm glad you stopped in. Nice out, isn't it?"

May nodded. "It is, yeah."

"It's about time we had some nice days around here. Oh, I have to show you two something."

They followed her to the far back corner of the store where a pedestal stood with a kind of sculpture on it that looked roughly like a set of hands, palms toward each other, fingers up. The right hand was raised slightly higher than the left, but the fingers on both were grossly elongated, ridiculously so. It seemed to be made of wire and bits of metal welded or soldered together. The praying hands reached toward heaven but didn't quite meet in prayer. *Either that or it is an alien space creature just about to catch a volleyball,* May thought.

"Do you like it?" Jess asked.

"It's really something," May said.

"I think it's sad but beautiful," Carrie said.

"Elise made it. She's not only good in jewelry, she also does this wonderful free-form sculpture. She calls this one *Reaching*. I keep telling her she needs to do more than just jewelry. She's very talented, you know."

Carrie traced her fingers over the wire fingers and down to the wrists.

"Hmm," May said.

"I'm so glad you feel this way." Jess grinned, her hands in constant motion as she talked. "I'm going to tell Elise this. She was so nervous about putting it in here, but when I saw it I knew immediately that it had to go right here. I think it's really marvelous..."

"Sad."

"You could put a picture on the Web site," May ventured.

Jess beamed. "Have you seen our new Web site? I'd been after Elise forever to redo it. I told her we needed pictures of her and the studio. She's been so resistant for so long, and then last week, just out of the blue, she says, 'Jess, we do it today!' The new site's been up for a few days now."

"I wonder what changed her mind," May said.

"I don't know, but whatever it was, it's a good thing. I'm almost having to rein her in!"

"Is that right?"

Later, when Carrie and May were out on the boardwalk, May said, "You thought that hand thing was sad?"

"It spoke to me," Carrie said. "Reaching, reaching, reaching, but never quite getting what you want; reaching until your fingers become long like that, and still not touching anything that's real. Elise is a sad person."

"You think so?"

Carrie nodded. "I don't know her really well, but yes, she seems sad to me. She doesn't seem to have many friends." She paused, then added, "Did you hear about Carl looking in her window the other day?"

May stopped. "What did you say?"

"What I heard was that Carl Featherjohn was making googly faces at her through her window. Oh, this would've been maybe a week ago now. Maybe less."

May blinked and looked at her friend. "Where did you hear *that?*"

"Rachel, her daughter, is my papergirl. It was the middle of last week, and the papers were just a bit late. I was out there checking for it at the same time Rachel came trotting up my driveway. And she told me that she was late because Carl Featherjohn had been at the kitchen window making, in her words, 'googly faces.' And then her mother screamed, dropped a dish, and it broke into a million pieces."

"She told you *Carl Featherjohn* came to her window?"

"Door. The kitchen door. The patio door, I think is what she said."

"Rachel *said* this?"

"You look like you've seen a ghost, May."

May shook her head but didn't say anything. "I'm going to have to get a rain check on that coffee, Carrie. There's something I need to attend to."

"Tomorrow, then?"

"Tomorrow will be great."

Carl Featherjohn?

20

E lise stood at the entrance of Melon's Gun Shop. She had never been inside a gun shop before. She had never owned a gun. She had promised herself that she would never own a gun; there would never be a gun in her home. It was something she would simply not allow.

Because sometimes at night, the dream would come, and she'd remember the gun aimed at Rachel as she stood holding on to the sides of her playpen, laughing, giggling, babbling to the gunman as if he were a friend. Standing like that was new for her. She'd just learned to pull herself up and would giggle at her triumph. She was always a happy baby. And even when the gun was aimed right at her, she smiled up and reached for it, thinking it was a toy, a plaything, not understanding that not everyone loved her back.

Sometimes at night the dream would come, and Elise would remember screaming, sobbing, grabbing the baby, fleeing, the ends of Rachel's blanket trailing in the blood. And running, running, almost slipping, like on water, like on ice. The slipperiness of the blood surprised her. Then Sarah begging her to stay. "Everything will be all right now," Sarah had said. "Just wait, everything will be all right now.

I'll make everything all right. Like always. I will do anything for you. Anything."

The other day Elise found blood on a shirt of Rachel's. The sight of it unnerved her, and she sat down on a chair and looked at it but couldn't touch it. For a moment. Only a moment. And then when she tried to get the blood out, not all of it came out. That's the trouble with blood. It never all comes out.

She hadn't been quite truthful with Jake and May. Not really. She hadn't told them she was still getting e-mails. Exactly one per week. Yes, she'd reformatted her computer; yes, she'd changed her e-mail account. But he'd still managed to find her. Often the message was just one line: *I'm coming for you.* And then the next week it would be *I'm coming for the both of you.* Sometimes there was nothing in the text box and only *You won't get away from me* in the subject line. This would be followed the next week with *No matter how hard you try.* They all came from different e-mail addresses.

Elise didn't know why she'd started printing off the e-mails, but she had. One page for each, every week. Maybe someday she'd need proof. And when that day came, she would have a box full of proof. She kept the printouts in a box in her closet, along with all the magazine articles about serial killers and wife beaters.

Melon's Gun Shop was on her way to Ridley Harbor. The name always made her think of shooting melons on top of fence posts, of melons exploding like faces. Metal bars crisscrossed Melon's front door. Jingle bells sounded when she opened it. It was a quaint sound reminiscent of yarn stores rather than places that sold guns.

The store smelled like metal and leather and sleeping bags and new canvas. Shelf after shelf held holsters and camouflage jackets and orange vests and boots and knives. A man was holding a duck decoy, staring at it as if it would speak to him. A father and son were examining duck whistles and moose calls. The boy kept trying them out, and their sad sound tugged at her heart. A fattish man and a slim woman were at the counter looking at handguns on a piece of black cloth. On the whole she'd expected the place to be a bit sleazier.

A young man approached her. "Can I help you?"

"Um…"—she didn't look him in the eyes—"I'm looking to purchase a handgun."

She waited for the snide remarks. Like "Why's a pretty lady like you looking for a handgun?" She watched for the raised eyebrows, the leaning forward, the flirting. She was used to that. She had developed a kind of armor, a whole list of snide comebacks of her own. But this young man with short blond hair and glasses could have been a computer programmer or a loan officer.

"Come with me, then. We keep them under lock and key."

She followed him. The two people at the counter made room for her. She looked through the glass counter as one might look at jewelry, the way she set up her most expensive pieces. Under glass. Precious stones set on a black cloth.

"Are you interested in a revolver? I've got a five-shot Smith and Wesson revolver that might suit you just fine. Or here's a Colt. Is this for target practice? protection?"

Elise looked down at the array. "Protection. I don't know much about guns. I've never owned one in my life. I just…" she paused. Could she actually pick up one of those things, hold it, and shoot it? Could she actually do this? She had to.

He nodded. "I understand. I understand perfectly. A lot of young women purchase guns these days. It's always good to be prepared." He arranged a display of guns on the counter as he talked. "As I always say, it's better to have a gun and not need one, than need one and not have one."

She had brought a wallet full of cash. It was best if she didn't use a credit card and if there was no record of this purchase.

"Do you have classes of some sort? I've never used a gun before," she told him.

"We do. We're a member of the local gun club, and you can get lessons through them. We encourage it, as a matter of fact."

She picked up the revolver, held it for the first time. "If I got this today, when would the next class be?"

The young man put up his hand. "The whole process takes a bit longer than that I'm afraid."

"What whole process?"

"The process of purchasing a handgun. At most it's ten days but usually no more than a day or two. We type your name in the computer, do a quick background check, need some ID, a driver's license will work…"

Background check? She began backing away. She had forgotten about this. But of course there would be a background check. How had she expected to just walk into the store and take a gun home, like you would a bottle of shampoo? "I don't know. I was hoping I could just come in here and buy a gun and then walk out with it today."

"It's actually quite simple. We just type in your name and look for outstanding felonies. If nothing pops up, you get to take the gun home…"

It wouldn't be simple. She needed a gun, but this clearly was not the way to do it. "I'm sorry," she said. "I don't think so. Maybe I'll get a better security system. Or a dog…" She continued backing away, but she was thinking of something else. Another plan was already formulating in her mind. She backed out of the store, nearly knocking over a display of duck decoys.

~

21

It was drizzling when May found Carl Featherjohn down at the town wharf aboard *Freesia,* the schooner he and his brother, Earl, were fixing up to offer whale-watching tours. Wearing rubber boots, Carl was lugging a plastic bucket of what looked like engine oil or fish slop across his teak deck. A bit of the bucket's contents spilled and landed in drops on the deck. May cringed. Guys like the Featherjohn brothers didn't deserve boats like the *Edith Emma,* as the *Freesia* was originally called. This grand old schooner built in 1926 in Bridgeport, Connecticut, had spent her first twenty-eight years fishing the abundant North Atlantic cod and haddock. In the 1950s it was refitted and restored and became the flagship schooner in the Windjammer fleet. After providing people nearly thirty years of cruising enjoyment, it was dry-docked again, this time in Fog Point. It leaked, the teak had cracked in many places, and it needed total restoration. Unfortunately, that season of being dry-docked lasted nearly twenty years, until the Featherjohns bought the schooner for a song last year, put it back in the water, and changed the name to *Freesia. Probably in honor of some old girlfriend of Carl's or Earl's,* May thought.

It still needed a lot of TLC, and May and Jake both doubted whether the Featherjohn brothers were the ones to provide it. Now the boat listed against the wharf, one mast seriously askew and rust lines worming down from the portholes along the side. In short, the thing was a mess.

Plus, the Featherjohn brothers had even taken away its grand name.

Today Carl wore a New Jersey Devils T-shirt several sizes too small and torn in one long rip across his belly.

"Hey, May," he called. "My favorite old lady." He paused and more of what May could now identify as bilge water slopped from the bucket onto the teak.

"You're going to wreck that bright work even more," she pointed out.

He smirked. "That's what you don't know, darlin'. I'm getting it all sanded off tomorrow. This thing's gonna shine. I hired a professional crew from Ridley. We already got a lot of people signed up for whale tours. They log onto the Web site, they see what a great old boat this is, they sign up."

"Do they know it might sink?"

He laughed. "You wish. And in case you're interested, we got JoMarie Jardine as chef. We're going to do overnighters. Just like the Windjammers, but without the Windjammer price."

And without the Windjammer quality, she wanted to add, but how they got JoMarie Jardine was a puzzle. JoMarie was well known in crewing circles worldwide. Jake had met her in the Caribbean and had introduced May to her when a yacht she was cooking on sailed into Fog Point.

"How much you paying her?" May asked.

"Enough. Enough to get her." Carl dumped the bucket overboard.

"What are you doing?" May yelled. "You can't dump your dirty engine water into the harbor! There are laws against that!"

"There's laws against commercial ships discharging their bilge in the harbor, not for individual people dumping a bucket or two over-board, darlin'. No law against that. It's the old principle of the cedar bucket."

May scowled. He was right, of course, and it galled her. The principle of the cedar bucket stated that it was illegal to have a head that discharged directly into the sea, but it was not illegal to use a cedar bucket as a toilet and then manually dump that overboard. The thinking being that not many people took the trouble to maintain a cedar bucket onboard or dump the thing overboard by hand in full view of everybody in the harbor.

"What're you down here for, May? Come to admire the *Freesia*? Upset that you didn't recognize her beauty?"

"I came here to talk about Elise and specifically where you were Wednesday of last week."

"*Last* Wednesday?"

She nodded.

"How am I supposed to remember last Wednesday?"

"Think. Did you go to Elise St. Dennis's house last Wednesday afternoon around three and look in her windows?"

He guffawed. "What? What are you accusing me of?"

"Of looking in her windows. A witness puts you at the scene then."

"And what's your interest in all this, darlin'?"

"Let's just say it's professional. Jake and I are looking into a Peeping Tom incident that occurred at her home. And a witness puts you there. A witness who just came forward, I might add."

"Let's see, last Wednesday? Three?" He counted on his fingers. "Last Wednesday you say? I was down in Ridley at a meeting with JoMarie. We had a long lunch. I didn't get back here until evening."

"And you can verify this?"

"I can, but I don't know why I would need to."

"Where's Earl? He on the boat today?" May asked.

"Earl? He's home. Working. He does the real work."

"He *works,* does he?"

"Yeah, don't say it like that. Earl, he's the man. Everybody needs an Earl working for them. You ever need anyone to put up a Web site for you, do up a few brochures, you call my man Earl."

"We already have a Web designer, thank you very much."

May made her way back to her SUV, cursing the slits in the boardwalk that kept grabbing for her cane. Once in her vehicle, she drove to Elise's neighborhood. Were there other witnesses? Was it too late? Would people even remember where they were five days ago? It was still worth a shot.

What about Earl? Could it have been Earl? Carl and Earl were both medium height and overweight, although Earl was heavier with thinner hair and a paler complexion. From his hours spent inside at his computer, she supposed.

She began with the house closest to Elise. She thought she knew everyone in Fog Point, but she didn't know the tiny bald man in a plaid shirt who met her in the driveway. Madras. When she was a teenager that kind of shirt fabric was called madras. He squinted at her through thick glasses.

"I'm May Williams and I'm investigating a disturbance in the neighborhood that occurred late in the afternoon last Wednesday."

"Oh?"

He aimed his remote and chirp-locked his car, one of those new VW Bugs.

"Did you happen to notice anything unusual then?" May asked.

"Unusual?"

If he was going to answer every question with a question it was going to irritate her. "Yes, unusual."

"You're serious?"

"Quite. Your next-door neighbor, Elise St. Dennis. Did you happen to notice anything unusual at her house last Wednesday?"

He scratched his head. "What do you mean by unusual?"

"There was a report of someone walking through the backyards at that time, possibly a Peeping Tom."

"Are you saying this isn't a safe neighborhood? I had so hoped this was a safe neighborhood. I just moved here."

May glanced into his car. On the backseat sat a camera with a ridiculously long lens. He followed her gaze. "I'm a nature photographer," he said.

"And so you didn't notice anything, Mr....?"

"Watts," he extended his hand. "I'm Neil Watts." His hand was small and pudgy, like a baby's. May felt like she was shaking hands with a very fat, cold child.

"And you never heard anything? saw anything?"

"I can't remember, actually."

"Would looking at a calendar help?" May got out a little wallet one.

He peered down at it, then said, "I think that was the day I was photographing the marshes. There was this mist, with the sun shining through. No, I wouldn't have been here. Not here." He kept glancing at Elise's house.

May handed him a business card. "Will you call us if you remember anything?"

"Okay." He took it, put it in the pocket of his shirt.

No one was home in the place on the other side of Elise's, although May knew it belonged to a family named Fryer. Reed Fryer worked in construction, and Clara Fryer worked somewhere in Ridley. They had two or three children who would be in school now. She jotted a quick note on the back of a card and thrust it behind the screen door.

The people directly across the street, retired schoolteachers Floyd and Betty Ryson, couldn't recall anything out of the ordinary, but they'd be more than happy to contact her if they remembered anything.

Next to them a woman in her eighties came to the door in a blue track suit and matching blue slippers and said she remembered exactly where she was last Wednesday. She was Isabelle Browngreen, considered by some the matriarch of the Browngreen family.

"You do?" May asked.

"Of course," she said. "That was the day the paper was a little late. Rachel, the girl, is always very punctuious. I was sitting on my couch waiting for the paper."

"Did you see anything across the street?"

"Nope. I was just waiting for the paper."

"Did Rachel say anything to you about why she was late?" May asked.

Isabelle shook her head.

May thanked her, left a card, and walked out wondering if there was such a word as *punctuious*.

She went to one of the houses across the backyard from Elise. The first one belonged to a young couple, Colin and Marnie Nation, who'd lived there for a year. Colin was somehow related to the huge Nation family who filled page after page in the Fog Point phone book.

Colin, a fisherman, was home and said he did remember something. If it was last Wednesday, he'd just gotten in off the boat and was in the kitchen making coffee. He'd looked through the window and had seen a person jogging.

"Where was this person jogging to?" May asked.

"Come on in. I'll show you."

She followed him through a toy-strewn hallway into a kitchen complete with highchair, a Jolly Jumper, and some sort of contraption supposedly for holding a baby. It had all manner of straps and bells, with whistles and bright things hanging overhead.

"Marnie's at work," he explained. "The baby is at her grandma's. I just got in from the boat." Then he pointed out the window. "It was here. I was standing here drinking a cup of coffee, and I saw this guy jogging, sort of slouched down like. Yes," he paused. "That was Wednesday. He jogged from over there." He pointed in the general direction of Elise's house. "To there," and he pointed in the general direction of the Featherjohns two doors down.

"You didn't think it was odd for a jogger to be running through people's backyards rather than on the street?"

He shrugged. "You see a lot of things in this town."

"Do you remember who it was?"

"He looked familiar."

"Was it by any chance Carl Featherjohn whom you saw?"

He cocked his head. "I'm not sure. I really didn't pay that much attention. It might've been. I guess it didn't register that it was him because he's not the sort of person who jogs, you know?"

"I know."

A few more houses. A few more places where no one was home; a few more places where no one could remember that far back. May stuck business cards into the mailboxes. "I'm getting tired of this, Paul," she said out loud. "No one knows anything. No one sees anything. No one pays any attention. If people paid more attention, this world would be a safer place."

Now on to Lenore Featherjohn's house. *The best for last,* May thought.

Lenore answered the door with wet hair and a towel around her shoulders.

"May Williams! What brings you here? Come in, come in. I'll fetch us some tea. I'm about to make cinnamon swirls. And I've just finished coloring my hair. New color. What do you think?" She turned around and around in a kind of a prance, showing off all sides of her head.

That impossible shade of tomato might look quite snazzy on a supermodel, May thought.

"It's really something," May said. But really, she should talk. She hadn't colored her hair since Paul died, because what was so important about a hair color if you wore a baseball cap all the time? At least Lenore made an effort.

"Is Earl in?"

"Well, I don't know. I think so. You come in and I'll go fetch him. You probably want Web-site design, right? Come on in."

May followed Lenore through the grand hallway. It was an impressive old house with muted burgundy floral carpets and a wide staircase that led up to rooms Lenore rented out. The house had belonged to the congregation of the old church that she and Jake now owned, and it had been in the Featherjohn family for many generations. A decade ago Lenore had turned it into a B&B.

On the main floor were two lounges and a large oblong dining room with tables already set for breakfast guests. An old dark-wood piano stood against one wall of the dining room, and on it perched framed pictures of her grandchildren, offspring of Carl and Earl's older brother who had left Fog Point some time ago. At least she had one son who was providing her with faces to put in picture frames.

May followed Lenore to the kitchen, where a radio happily played oldies, and flour, a mixing bowl, spoons, and sugar cluttered the counter.

"Like I said, I'm making cinnamon swirls for my guests. Tea? You'll have tea; sure you will." Lenore put the kettle on the stove and placed an assortment of tea bags in a small wicker basket on the table.

"I really came to talk to Earl."

"Just downstairs." She opened a door that led to the basement, stuck her head in the doorway, and yelled, "Earl!" Turning to May, she said, "Or do you want coffee? Tea or coffee, choice is yours." Then in a flash, she turned back toward the stairs. "Earl! You got company! Earl!"

"Whatever's easiest. Tea's fine."

May thought she heard a mumbled "yeah, yeah" coming from the basement.

"You can go on down." Lenore shooed her. "Go on, go on. Go on down. I always do. Afterward, come back up and we'll have tea and a nice chat."

May's cane clattered as she descended the steep steps, ensuring that she would be well announced.

The basement ran the entire length and width of the house, but all that had been done to this cavernous space was a bit of blue paint on the water pipes and furnace and some raggy carpets here and there on the uneven cement floor.

Earl and Carl were in their thirties, yet this basement looked like the dorm room of teenage brothers. Two single beds took up two corners. Sheets and dirty clothes lay in tangled messes on the beds and on the floor. All the drawers in one dresser were open, their contents spilling onto the floor.

Plus, it was still the cellar of an old house, meant for storing carrots and canned goods and potatoes, and nothing could eradicate that smell of earth and rust and old pipes and mildew and bones. Another smell drifted over the top of the cellar smells, that of unwashed sheets and feet.

Earl sat barefoot and pasty-faced in front of a large desktop computer. He grunted but didn't look at May. She wondered if what he was wearing qualified as clothes, or if he was still in his pajamas, these black, ripped track pants and a T-shirt. He was surrounded by a whole lot of high-tech equipment: fax machine, another computer, printer and scanner, and various other pieces of office equipment whose uses she could only guess at. A large camera on a tripod stood next to the tower of equipment. Their photocopier was huge and industrial, the kind you'd find in a Fortune 500 company.

"Hey, Earl."

"Yeah." He still didn't look up but remained leaning forward into the massive screen of his computer.

"I'm trying to figure out where your brother was at three o'clock last Wednesday."

"Why don't you ask him?" He still didn't look at her.

"I did. Now I'm asking you."

"How am I supposed to know what he does?" Earl finally turned toward her; his wide, oily face and blotchy eyes were a blank.

"Look at your PDA; see if anything twigs."

He turned back to the computer and said, "Down at the boat. He wasn't here. He hasn't been home in a week."

"A week?"

"He sleeps there, eats there. Summer's coming."

"How about you?"

His fingers paused on the keys. "Me? I was here working."

"So you weren't running around poking your face into people's windows and leaving your footprints under windows?"

He swiveled his chair toward her and planted his sausage feet on the floor. "What are you mumbling about, woman?"

"Someone spotted you or your brother peering into a window, making faces into it."

"I assure you, lady, neither my brother nor I are in the habit of peering into people's windows for fun. We both have too much to do." He turned back to the computer.

"And you never saw anything, either?" May looked around doubtfully. The few windows were set high on the wall and surrounded outside by window wells.

He shook his head.

"Well, here's my card if you remember anything. If anything turns up, give me a jingle."

He peered at the card. "You could do with a new card design, you know."

Upstairs the kettle was boiling, and May chose a little packet of green tea from the basket of tea bags. Green tea was supposed to be healthy. At the counter, Lenore's hands were covered in flour. She was making cinnamon swirls, which were like cinnamon buns, she explained, only smaller, much smaller. "You can eat them in one bite," she said. "So what did you need to see Earl about? He does a fine job with brochures if that's what you want. Oh, wait…" She wiped her hands on a dishtowel hanging from the stove and raced to the front hall, all that red hair bobbling around her head. She came back and placed a three-fold brochure down in front of May. "Earl did this for me. He does wonderful work. I'm so proud of him." She pressed a hand to her chest. "Oh my. So busy. Both my boys are. Between the three of us, me with the bed-and-breakfast and my boys with their ventures, there's just not a moment to spare around here in the summer."

"I'll bet," May said. The brochure wasn't half bad.

"And now that Carl has a new girlfriend, well, he's just as busy as ever," Lenore said.

May pushed the brochure across the table.

Lenore pushed it back. "Keep it," she said. "I'll give you a stack if you want to give them out at your store."

May pocketed it. "So," she asked, "Carl has a new girlfriend?"

"Oh yes. Some woman who cooks on boats. A chef on boats. She's going to be working for them. She seems like a nice enough young woman. It's about time Carl settled down."

May raised her eyebrows at that. "Let me ask you something, Lenore. Did you happen to see anyone running through the back-yards last Wednesday around three in the afternoon? Can you remember back that far?"

"Running through the backyards?" She rolled the pastry dough. "I think if I'd seen something like that, I would remember."

"Does Carl keep his boots here?" May asked.

Lenore slapped down a piece of dough. "His boots?"

"Yes. Does he keep his boots here?"

"He keeps his boots on the boat, May."

May thought about the rubber boots Carl was wearing. They were the kind worn by every fisherman in Fog Point. According to Jake, the boot print he had seen would not match that kind of boot. And Earl? She was inclined to believe Lenore that Earl seldom roused from his molelike existence in the basement.

After a few more sips of the green tea, May said, "I better be on my way." She started to rise.

"No, no, you sit." Lenore pointed with a floured finger. "Just because I have to work doesn't mean I don't want company. You finish your tea and tell me all about your life. I would love the company. Can you hand me that rolling pin over there?"

May did so and ended up helping Lenore make cinnamon swirls.

Talk about your nutty old ladies. I'm just as cracked as Lenore.

Lenore talked the entire time they worked, mostly about her oldest son who was a minister in Nebraska. "Carrying on the Featherjohn tradition," she said. And May realized that if they were two crazy old ladies, Lenore was the most fortunate. She at least had a family to talk about.

22

Moon held the weight bar above his head for a moment. He strained and strained until, with an exhausted *thunk,* he laid the bar on the rack above his head, all 125 pounds of it. After a few more reps, he'd move on to fifty push-ups followed by fifty chin-ups. Then he'd do the whole thing over again.

Moon had added a weight room to the basement of the apartment building. This rather large room originally was supposed to be some sort of meeting room, but Moon had turned it into his own weight room with a state-of-the-art treadmill, a stationary bicycle, a weight bench with all manner of free weights, and a couple of weight-training machines. He was supposed to make this room available to all of the tenants; that's what Davenborn, the building owner, agreed to. But what Davenborn didn't know didn't hurt him. It was Moon's private place. Moon never told any of his charges about it. If Davenborn ever questioned him, he'd say that he had put up a notice about it. It wasn't his fault if no one used it.

In the corner was a television he had rigged up to steal the satellite signal from next door. An old episode of *Survivor* lit up the screen.

He'd been working out now for five years, almost six. Long enough to completely reshape his body. No one from the old days would recognize him. Not with his reshaped nose and his shaved head. His own mother—if she was alive—wouldn't even recognize him. He wondered if she was.

Moon wiped his towel across his head and sat up. The first episode, and they were voting some poor schmuck off the island. How humiliating, being the first to go. That would never happen to Moon. Not if he got on *Survivor*, it wouldn't. He could see through their phony, half-baked alliances. Even though he was sure he would win, he would never go on *Survivor*. Not anonymous enough. *Fear Factor* was more his style, since there were new people each week. He'd applied three times to be on it, but so far no one had called. But if he ever did get on, he'd win the money. He was strong. Plus, he could stomach things most people couldn't. He also knew what happened to people when they were shot. He'd seen plenty of blood.

Chin-ups were next. Yes, he'd come quite a long way since he was a scrawny bucktoothed kid from the trailer park. A place where murders happened.

When Moon was sixteen he'd left for school one morning and had simply kept walking. He figured it would take his drunk father and blitzed mother about a week to even realize he was gone. By age twenty, Moon was on his way up, and now, at twenty-three, he was well on his way.

He became Moon. A year ago he'd had his name legally changed. The government told him they needed a first name—he couldn't just be Moon—so he'd chosen Steven, for Steven Seagal, his favorite movie star. He was now officially Steven Moon.

Just as soon as he finished here, he'd go upstairs and call that Jake whatzehoozitz, that person asking all the questions about Cain. For fun, when the time was right, he'd throw out the name Sarah McCarthy and see what got reeled in.

23

I t was *Carl Featherjohn?* Jake wondered. *All along it was* Carl? That's what Elise's daughter had told Carrie, who told May, who phoned Jake as he stood in the rain in Pop's boatyard.

"Carl? Carl was the Peeping Tom?" Jake asked. It was launch day for the *Constant,* and he and Ben were at Pop's, readying her in the Travelift, when May's call came. He found it difficult to believe that Carl had been the Peeping Tom, and so did May, apparently. First of all, Carl Featherjohn and Wesley Stoller looked nothing alike. And second, Carl seemed to have a pretty good alibi for the date in question. He was in Ridley at a business meeting. May was trying to find JoMarie Jardine to verify. So far she'd been unsuccessful.

Jake had seen Elise twice since the face-in-the-window episode last week. They had coffee briefly at Noonan's, and then he stopped by her studio on Saturday evening. At Noonan's she'd talked on and on about a new snake-brooch design she was working on. She even drew him a picture on a napkin.

But the second time he saw her, she seemed distracted. "I'm not myself," she told him. "When this whole Wesley thing is over, I'll be better."

In the past few days, nothing new about Stoller had surfaced, so

Jake's daily focus shifted from Elise and Stoller to the *Purple Whale* business.

"Plus," May was telling him on the phone now, "I've got some new information on the case. My Internet-connection friend, Sol, came through. When your boat's in the water, hop up to the office."

Sol found people. He was a shadowy person May met six years ago when she began researching the Allentown Gas Station sniper, Paul's killer.

It was during this time, Jake knew, that May had truly honed her computer research skills. She had signed on to listservs and loops and had gone to chat rooms about the murderer. May had even set up a Web site devoted to finding him, a place where the victims could talk. She had met Sol in the chat room. The sniper had also killed his brother. Sol seemed to have connections, and as a result of his brother's death, he developed his own Internet PI service with a specialty in finding people. He charged a lot, but he always came through.

The sniper shot and killed two more people after Paul—a little boy who was walking with his mother to the gas station rest room and a gas station attendant—before simply disappearing.

May thought he was still out there. Jake would often come upstairs to the office and find May on the victims' Web site, tracking down leads. It was the ultimate irony that the one person Sol wanted to find was the one person he couldn't find.

"When we're finished here, you can show me what you've got," Jake told her.

Twenty minutes later Ben and Jake directed the *Constant*'s placement on the Travelift and then launched her.

"She looks good out there," Ben said. "Back in the water where she should be."

Jake guided her to the wharf, locked her up, and told Ben he had to return to the office. "May's panicking. I've got to get back to work."

May was leaning into the computer when Jake arrived. "Okay, here it is." She handed him the short e-mail she'd printed. "What do you think of this?"

> May,
> Your subject, Elise St. Dennis, poses an interesting challenge.
> She doesn't seem to exist prior to nine years ago. Nine years
> ago, in May, she began filing income tax under that name. Prior
> to that I can find nothing. No driver's license, nothing. You must
> understand, May, that I could be wrong. I make no guarantees.
> I urge you to get a second opinion.
> Sol

"You called me back for this?" Jake said. "How much are we paying this guy?"

"He's expensive," May said, "but this one's free, he told me. You get one freebie from Sol, and then you have to pay."

"Just like drugs," Jake mumbled.

She said the words slowly. "Sol can't find anything about her prior to nine years ago. Don't you see what this means?"

"It means your friend Sol isn't as smart as he thinks he is."

"Here's what I think it means. Could she be in witness protection? Think about it."

Jake frowned and read the e-mail again.

"Do you think Wesley could've met Elise's father in prison? Think about that, Jake. The only point of commonality in this case is the prison. I also found out a bit more about Wesley Stoller. Take a look at these."

She had found three articles on the Web and a few more pictures archived in newspapers. She'd printed off everything she could find.

Jake picked up two additional photos of Stoller, plus one of his brother who was killed, plus a couple taken of the people who were there at the trial—witnesses, spectators, and family members. She'd done a lot of reading and was surprised, she told Jake, at the harshness of the sentence, since Stoller claimed to be drunk at the time and therefore didn't remember anything he'd done.

But the "I was too drunk to know what I was doing" plea did not go over particularly well with the judge who sentenced him to life in prison. Had they lived in a jurisdiction where murder was punishable by death, Stoller would've been given the death penalty.

Jake picked up one of the crowd photos. It showed the back of a young woman carrying a baby in one arm and holding on to the hand of a girl who appeared to be about twelve years old.

"Look at that, mothers bringing their babies to a trial," said May, looking over his shoulder. "I think that's awful. Everyone wants to see a public execution. If they set up a lethal-injection machine in the likes of Madison Square Garden or the Rogers Centre in Toronto, you'd have a sellout crowd to watch the final moments of a Jeffrey Dahmer or a Saddam Hussein. They'd have tailgate parties in the parking lot and sell T-shirts."

The other crowd photo showed a tall man in a suit leaning down to get into the backseat of a car. Another man, shorter and heavier, stood beside him, his hands up to ward off the cameras. At the back of the photo, a skinny boy leaned over the trunk of the car. He seemed to be trying hard to get a glimpse of the man getting into the car. More people stood behind him, also looking in the direction of the camera. The streets were lined with people as if it were a parade.

"More e-mails," said May, who was in front of the computer again. "They're coming in by the dozens these days. I hope we can handle them all. Oh, here's one from the daughter."

"The daughter?"

May read it aloud:

Dear Whale People,
I was wondering if I could borrow one of your whale posters for my room. Thanking you in advance.
Rachel St. Dennis

P.S. I think you know my mother.

Jake opened the office closet. It wasn't as if they didn't have any whale posters. He got out a couple and laid them aside.

"You could deliver the posters," May said, "and at the same time you could ask what the girl really saw."

"I don't know. She's only eleven. Elise is very protective of her. Let's go with what we've got for now."

Jake looked again at the pictures of Wesley Stoller. How could Elise have mixed up his face with Carl's, unless he had changed a lot in ten years?

"I think Elise is a very troubled woman," May said without looking up from the screen. "The more I think about it, the more sure I am."

"She had a difficult childhood. She told me that."

May swiveled in her chair. "Just be careful, huh? I still don't trust her."

$\sim$

Two things happened the following day, and if it hadn't been for the case Jake and May were working on, the events might not have been seen as related. The first was that Loren Hayes, star of the TV police drama *Next Stop Murder*, talked about one of Elise's dragon barrettes on a TV interview; the second was that Elise's next-door neighbor, Neil Watts, shot and killed himself.

Jake happened to be at Noonan's Café when Nootie came running out of the kitchen, her hands smothered in flour, yelling, "Turn on the TV! Turn on the TV!"

Buzz turned on the one in the café, the one they used for sporting events. "Hurry, hurry!" she said, jumping up and down.

Nootie explained that she had been making pies and watching *The View* because Loren Hayes was on, and she had a big mansion in Fog Point.

"Get a VCR tape in quick, Buzz. Hurry!"

Images came into focus on the TV screen, and there sat Loren Hayes, famous movie star, wearing one of Elise's dragon barrettes in her hair. It probably would have gone unnoticed had not one of the hosts on *The View*, the older one, the funny one, commented on her hair and the huge dragon with the green gemstone eyes.

"Do you like it?" Loren asked and unhooked it, letting all that blond hair tumble down onto her shoulders.

"It's this clip. It's a neat way to hold your hair up," she explained. "You clip it this way and twist it slightly. Now, the woman who designed it? Her hair is short, short. But she told me she used to have long hair, which is why she invented it."

And then Loren proceeded to show *The View* hosts the barrette and how it was made of cast gold, gold leaf, and emeralds.

"Let me see that again," the older woman said, taking the barrette. "This is nifty."

The camera zoomed in on it.

"I have a summer home in this great little community on the coast," Loren said. "Fog Point, it's called, and for those of you who've never heard of it, it's a wonderful little place, full of charm. I made the acquaintance of the designer herself, a fantastic artisan named Elise St. Dennis, who has a marvelous studio there."

Jake looked around. Suddenly it seemed that all of Fog Point had gathered at Noonan's to watch Loren Hayes cross and uncross her long legs and extol the virtues of Fog Point and Elise's Creations.

By that time Nootie was literally jumping up and down and calling people off the streets. "Our little Elise!" she was saying. "You just wait. She'll be on *Oprah* next! On Oprah's Favorite Things. And in the magazine, too! You just wait." Nootie watched a lot of television.

Jake moved to where he could get a better look and had Buzz pour him another cup of coffee.

"I'm going to go get her," Nootie said. "Buzz, you make sure the tape is running."

Jake was amazed at how quickly the place had filled up with people eager to hear Loren Hayes praise Elise St. Dennis and Fog

Point. Especially since they complained about Loren when she was here, referring to her and all the other summer people as stuck up and demanding divas.

Jake drank his coffee and watched. The segment ended, Buzz rewound the tape, and everyone watched it again and again and again.

He saw Elise enter the room. People clapped. He waved, but she didn't acknowledge him. Maybe she didn't see him.

At the same time the mail carrier came in with the morning mail and told everyone that somebody named Neil Watts, a stranger, had shot and killed himself in his house. He'd been living at Browngreen's rental place, the house next to Elise St. Dennis's. "The police are all over the place. I couldn't even deliver the mail."

Jake looked over in time to see Elise break away from Nootie's grip and flee. Jake wondered if she had run because of what she'd seen on television—or because of the death of her neighbor?

25

I t had been a letter this time. A real honest-to-goodness letter that had been delivered to Elise's studio, not her house, and delivered with a cheery smile by Jess, along with all the other mail.

It had her name and address on it, and when she saw it, she wanted to cry out. Instead, she shivered, feeling cold all over on this warmish morning.

It was happening. It had been set in motion, and it was happening. And there was nothing she could do to stop it. Not now. Not ever.

They say that every human being makes one crucial decision that changes the course of his or her life forever. Once made, this decision can never be revoked. Once it plays through, the tape can never be rewound.

Oh, Sarah! Sarah!

Elise was bent over the letter when Nootie came into her studio with a grin as wide as the pies she made.

"Elise!" she yelped. "Elise, do you have your TV on? Turn on your TV!"

"*My* TV?"

"Yes, your TV. You're on television." She was panting as if she'd run all the way from Noonan's, although she had in fact driven.

"I don't have one here."

"Oh, right, okay. That's okay. Come on. Buzz is taping it. Come with me." Nootie was breathless. "It's all about you."

"What...what are you talking about?"

But Nootie was beaming. "You're on *television!* You know that actress? The one in that police show? Loren Hayes? The one who has a house here? Well, she talked about you on television!"

Quietly, Elise shoved the letter into the pocket of her jeans. With Nootie literally grabbing her shirt, she had no choice but to go. They climbed into Nootie's old metal wreck of a car and chugged up to Noonan's. Nootie babbled the whole way.

"Buzz is taping it. Oh, I hope he got it to work. Sometimes that old VCR of ours has a mind of its own. But she was wearing your barrette, the dragon one."

Nootie helped Elise out of the car and into the restaurant.

As soon as Elise entered, the entire place burst into applause. Nootie held onto Elise tightly, leading her to the front while Buzz fiddled with the video player. And there she was, Loren Hayes. She was showing Elise's dragon barrette to the other women on *The View,* they were commenting on it. Then Loren lifted up her long hair again and secured it. Buzz rewound the tape. The clip came out, the hair tumbled down. Loren Hayes talked. The camera came in for a closeup. Then the hair went up again. They played the tape again and again and again. Then the mail carrier entered and told everyone about Neil Watts.

Elise felt dizzy. She had to leave. It wasn't Neil Watts. It wasn't Loren Hayes. None of them made her run. It was the letter that lay tight against her body in the pocket of her jeans.

26

M oon was quite proud of his Harley. It was a Softail, electric cherry, and he'd had it done up with a customized paint job. A kaleidoscope of diamonds scattering down the fuel tank.

It was the one shiny thing he loved just about more than anything in the world, because it represented what his future could be when he made a few more big hits. What his future *would* be. He took his Hog out as much as he could. If the roads were good, if it wasn't winter and snowing, he drove his Harley. He had a Ford F-150 that he drove in winter. But today? A fine day like today? It screamed for a Harley.

He was on his way to Aybeez Car Wash, but not to get his Hog washed. No, he did that himself. He wouldn't trust anyone else to wash it. He was on his way to Aybeez to find Cain. And as a secondary measure, to bug the place. A person like him, in business for himself, had to take advantage of every opportunity.

For example, by listening in on Barbie and Ken's bugged phone, Moon learned that the owner of the gym where the couple worked was carrying on quite a steamy affair with one of the young personal trainers. One of the trainers who was a guy. The homosexual angle was always worth a bit more, especially if the extortionee was firmly in the closet. Especially if the extortionee was married. And especially if the extortionee had children. The owner of the gym was all of these. So Moon demanded a one-time payment of forty grand, and he got it. No questions asked. Enough to order a brand-new Harley Softail Classic with all the bells and whistles.

But the first thing Moon did with his money was to get his teeth fixed. It changed his whole appearance. Of course, getting his nose broken in the one and only fight he'd ever been in also helped to alter his face. No, no one from the old days would recognize him: new teeth, new nose, new body, no hair. And with the mirrored sunglasses he bought on the Web, no one, not even his own family, would recognize him.

On that day, driving his Softail Classic to Aybeez Car Wash, he could feel his luck changing. Sarah McCarthy, the woman Cain was so eager to find, was the key to pirate treasure.

As he drove around Aybeez to get a feel for the place, he made a list. There were two things on his agenda: (1) Plant a bug in the owner/manager's phone, and (2) schmooze Cain and offer to do some PI work for him.

The car wash had six bays where customers with enough quarters could drive in and wash their own cars with high-pressure hoses. In five of the bays people were doing just that. Next to those bays, two large garage doors opened and closed over bays where employees washed the cars and did the detailing, which was a fancy word for vacuuming. A drive-through touchless car wash stood at the corner of the lot. Next to that was a small office. The owner's? A little dinky for an owner.

Big blue arrows on the cement guided drivers where to park if they were interested in detail work. Moon ignored them and drove around to the back; sure enough, he spotted a nice big office. He parked in front and walked inside. And darn it all, a meaty guy in a golf shirt and khakis sat there staring at a computer screen. He was big and hairless and pink, with jowls and a thick neck. His small eyes seemed too close together at the front of his head. He looked like an insect.

"Can I help you?" The guy looked irritated, probably because Moon had ignored the blue lines.

"Yeah, I'm looking for Wesley Stoller. He around?"

"Oh, you won't find him here, not in the office area. He'd be around front. Just follow the blue arrows, but in the opposite way."

"You the owner?" Moon asked. "Nice place you got here."

"Yeah."

"So you need any more employees?"

Without saying anything, Insect Face shoved his chair back, went to a filing cabinet, pulled out a drawer, fingered through some files, and then handed Moon a sheet of paper. "Go fill this out and give it to Ernie."

"Ernie?"

"He's the guy in the front office. Fill this out and give it to him. We're not hiring now, but guys quit all the time."

Moon took the application and left, but he'd be back. Insect Face probably had lots of secrets he'd be willing to pay to keep as secrets. He followed the blue arrows back around to the front, parked his Harley across two spaces, and went to find Cain. No one was in Ernie's office, so Moon went in and planted a quick bug in the phone.

Then he walked out to the bays, where a couple of guys were vacuuming the inside of a Ford Taurus. Moon grinned and headed toward them. A tall, skinny kid, who looked as if his bones were too big for his body, walked over with a geeky-looking, big-nosed, mustached guy, who looked as if he were wearing one of those glasses-nose-mustache combos. Moon resisted the urge to rip it off the guy's face.

"Something we can do for you?" Bones asked.

"I'm looking for Ernie."

"You're looking at him," Mustache Mask said.

"Nice to meet you. I'm looking to get my vehicle detailed."

Bones looked out at the Harley and frowned.

"Not this. I got a regular car at home."

"Nice. Is that a Harley?" Bones asked, shaking his big skeleton hands.

"Yep. That's a Hog all right. Stoller around?"

"At lunch," Ernie answered. "He'll be back soon."

"Great. He's a friend of mine. He recommended this place."

"He did?" Mustache Mask said.

"You mind if I have a look at your bike?" Bones asked.

"Knock yourself out."

While Bones and Mustache Mask went outside, Moon sidelined himself around the bay. One never knew where one could pick up things. Then Moon joined them outside and began giving them the grand tour of his Harley. When Moon looked up, he saw Cain walking toward them holding a bag from KFC.

"Hey," Moon said as Bones and Mustache Mask left.

"Well," Cain said, "that Softail yours?"

Moon nodded.

Cain walked around the bike the way people did when they saw it. The guy was practically salivating.

"I didn't know you had one of these."

"Yeah, well, I do. I do a lot of surveillance on it."

"You do what?"

"I'm a cop."

"You're a cop?" Cain's eyes went wide at this one.

"Private. I'm a private cop. I'm a licensed PI. Eventually I want to quit the apartment stuff and open my own detective agency. Got my license a year ago." A lie, but he didn't think Cain would check into that. "Just something I want you to know. If you ever need a PI, keep me in mind, okay?"

Cain stopped and stood there looking at Moon. They were exactly the same height and could look eye to eye. But Moon had a good forty pounds of pure muscle on the guy.

"You think I need the services of a PI?" Cain asked quietly.

"Oh, I don't know. My experience is that people in your position, people just out of prison, often need PIs to find people for them, stashes of money, drugs, you name it. I've worked with a lot of ex-cons. I could tell you stories."

Cain started toward the bay. "I got to get back to work."

"Yeah. No problem. Just keep me in mind, will ya? I'd even work your case pro bono."

Cain turned. "Pro bono?"

"That means for free. While I build up my client list. And I like you. You're a decent sort. I can always tell."

Cain looked at Moon for a long minute before he went inside.

27

To my mother, the television jewelry star,

Ashley's mother told me about the television program and how that actress on the program was wearing one of your dragon barrettes in her hair. Ashley's mother told me after school, and I was so excited that at supper I said to you, "Hey, Mom! I heard you were on TV!"

"Oh, you heard?"

"Ashley's mother told me."

And then instead of talking about the TV program, you said, "I don't like you spending so much time with Ashley."

But Ashley is my friend. Actually, she's my only friend, if you want to know.

The reason I don't have any friends besides Ashley is that every time I bring someone home from school, you start acting sort of sad, like I'm going to start liking them more than I like you. But you're my mother, and they're just friends. It's different, but you don't understand that.

I could tell this was happening when I first started having Ashley as my friend. When she first came over, you started asking her all about her parents and what her father does for a living and what her mother does, and you kept hanging around us. But when you started asking her all these questions, I just rolled my eyes at Ashley, and she burst out laughing.

You see, before she met you, I told Ashley that you were a famous actress. You'd been on television, and you were always practicing. Your best practice was asking strangers stupid questions and acting dumb around people.

I don't know if Ashley believed me or not, but now every time you start in on her, I give her the little look, and she bursts out laughing. The funny thing is that Ashley is now giving you phony answers. Did you know that? Did you know I was doing that?

A couple of months ago, I told Ashley that you weren't really practicing to be an actress, that sometimes you're just scared I'm going to like other people more than you. Ashley told me she knew all along.

The thing I like most about Ashley is that she never says things like "You have a weird mother." She understands, because she has an aunt who's like that, she says. So she knows about strange people. I think Ashley will be my friend forever.

One night at the beginning of my friendship with Ashley, you came into my bedroom and started telling me that I didn't need any friends, that we had each other. And then you hugged me tight.

"I want one friend," I said to you. "You have one friend; why can't I have one?"

"You mean Jess? She's not a friend; she's my employee. Or do you mean Norah? If you mean Norah, she's just an acquaintance."

"No," I said. "I'm not talking about Jess or Norah. I'm talking about Sarah!'"

You stared at me then and didn't say anything for a long, long time. That was the first time I'd ever mentioned the name Sarah to you, although I've known about Sarah for a long time. Then you turned and went into your bedroom and closed the door. You never said anything about Ashley again. You're even nice to Ashley now.

I don't know who Sarah is. I just know that every so often you talk on the telephone, always in your bedroom, always with the door closed. Sometimes I sit outside on the floor and try to listen, but I can't hear much. Just a lot of silence and low murmurs of conversation. Sometimes I even hear you cry. But I do hear you say, "Hello, Sarah" and "Good-bye, Sarah."

The day after you talk to Sarah, you don't work on your jewelry. You usually stay in bed all day and say you're sick. A few years ago I realized that the only time you ever get sick is after you talk to Sarah.

The reason I'm writing all this is that yesterday you talked to Sarah again. I sat down outside your room but couldn't hear what you were talking about. I heard you crying.

Later, when it was night, I stood at my window and looked at you smoking on the deck. Across the way, Carl Featherjohn was watching you. I could see him through the branches.

Your daughter,

Rachel St. Dennis

28

The suicide of the stranger seemed to be on everyone's mind. No one knew this man, but everyone had theories about him. Some said he was in Fog Point because he was a jilted lover and came here to kill himself. It had all been planned. That opinion came from Nootie, who watched a lot of soap operas.

"He came here to die," she said theatrically. "He knew what he was doing when he came to this little town. It was the perfect place to die."

The wife of the mail carrier who'd announced his death to the group at Noonan's was sure it was autoeroticism. She'd seen an episode just like it on *Law and Order*. She was sure it was life mimicking art. Those were her words. She shut up after someone explained to her what autoeroticism really was.

Someone else said it had to do with a business gone sour, and someone even suggested that it had something to do with Elise. This came from Marnie Nation, who told everyone that her husband, Colin, had been asked about a Peeping Tom at Elise's only a few days before Neil Watts killed himself.

But May was trying to figure things out, and when May was trying to figure things out, she needed her solitude. This would be the perfect day to launch her own boat. She still had a few hours of daylight.

About a year after she moved here, May bought herself a seventeen-foot Boston Whaler with a ninety horsepower Merc. The boat had a center console with a steering wheel she could sit or stand behind, depending on her mood. It also had three bench seats—one in front, one in the stern, and one in the center. The one in the front doubled as the top of an Igloo cooler.

The guy she bought the boat from had added a custom-made, zip-in full enclosure for it. If May had liked camping, she could conceivably have taken the thing out and slept on it overnight. But this was something May never intended to do.

Launching her boat wasn't a major undertaking, and she had perfected a way to do it herself. Hook her boat trailer to her SUV. Little by little, back her SUV down the launch ramp, put on the brake, then step out to check the boat, make sure things were going into the water the way they were supposed to, then get back in the SUV and back the boat down another five inches, then put the brake on, get out, and check the boat again.

"You'd be proud of me, Paul. Doing all this by myself."

But you were always independent, babe, she could imagine him saying.

"Hey! Hey, May!"

She looked up. Not Paul. It was Johnny Browngreen in his rubber boots, still wearing his purple rubber bolstering gloves. "Hey, I can get some guys. We'll help."

May could launch her boat by herself, but she seldom had to. Even though she hadn't grown up here, she was almost accepted. Almost. She never would be, not really. True Fog Pointers had grand-

parents buried out behind the Stone Church. But having Carrie Maynard as a close friend certainly helped. The Maynards had been part of
the Fog Point roster for hundreds of years. There were certain names
that resounded through the landscape: Maynard, Noonan, Browngreen, Nation, and Featherjohn. And even though Carrie had left Fog
Point when she was a young teenager, because she was a Maynard,
when she came back she was accepted as if she'd never been away.

Fog Pointers were a tolerant bunch. They had to be. Even in the
early days, Fog Point had attracted its share of artists and authors and
other eccentrics. In the 1920s this whole neck of land was a party spot
for writers and film stars. Some of the mansions on the point were
built back then and had now been refurbished for a whole new crop
of rich, young movie stars.

Fog Point had also had aging hippies, people who came here
protesting the war in Vietnam in the 1960s, built log houses, hid out
in the woods, and stayed there. Some still lived there.

And now there were the contemporary artisans, a younger,
vibrant group of political liberals who drank chai tea, had business
savvy, and made five-year plans. Elise St. Dennis was one of them.

Elise who came from nowhere.

Once May backed the boat far enough, Johnny unhooked the
line, pushed the boat into the water, and let it float. Then, with the
long line in one hand, he guided the boat to the wharf. May drove
back up the ramp and parked her vehicle.

"You have a theory about that guy who died?" he asked, handing
her the line.

"Nope."

"You know what Larry heard today? That it was really a murder.
Everybody's saying it was murder now."

Murder? People love this sort of thing, especially in a town like Fog Point where the biggest crime the police usually dealt with was people stealing firewood from each other's stacks.

"Where'd Larry hear that?" she asked.

He shrugged. "Just around. But if you ask me, the killer had to be someone from away."

May climbed aboard her boat, intending to take it all the way to Thunder Island, maybe around the island and back again. Get the kinks out. Get some fresh air; try to figure out what was going on. She started the engine. It turned over first crank. "Thank you, Pop," she breathed. He tuned up her outboard each year, and everyone knew that he was the best mechanic around. Well, actually, he was the *only* mechanic around.

Had to be someone from away? Well, of course. Things like this didn't happen in this town. But that was the attitude. Something bad happens, blame the outsiders. This death of a plaid-shirted stranger didn't concern them, except in the most speculative way.

She put her VHF radio on channel 16 and motored slowly out past the markers. Ahead of her on the bay, a flock of seagulls cawed as they dipped into the water. The tide was out, and up by the point where the boardwalk ended, a group of clammers in black boots were digging with rakes.

"Paul, you would like this," she said loudly to the wind. "You'd really like this today."

Out past the moorings, she felt truly alone. Thunder Island lay five miles ahead of her; the wharf and all its problems behind her. She aimed for the island, black water speeding underneath her boat like a solid sheet. She liked speed. Everyone in this town liked speed. This was a place where kids got fast boats before they got cars.

Ten minutes later she reached Thunder Island. The island was a favorite picnic spot for Fog Pointers. The two-mile-by-one-mile island used to be home to about six fishing families, but twenty years ago a fire destroyed most of the island. The one casualty, a child, was said to haunt the island. Shortly after the fire, most of the families moved to Fog Point. Only one person, an irascible black sheep and distant cousin of the Maynards, lived there now.

Five minutes later May was on the outer edge of the island, the sea side. The water was surprisingly calm, not even any swells. She circled the island slowly. A few seals raised their heads and looked in her direction. Dolphins arced over the waves in the distance. She thought about Elise and Neil Watts and wondered if they possibly could be related.

It wasn't the Witness Protection Program. Jake pointed out that if it were, Elise and her daughter would have been given a past. That's what they do in witness protection. So what kind of woman comes here without a past? A woman who's running from something.

Around the island to the north she came upon a kelp bed with pieces so huge they looked like mermaids swimming behind her.

She heard the cry of gulls, saw the way they clustered around a distant lobster boat, seeking leftovers. Ahead of her a group of gulls swooped, then hovered over a piece of floating carrion. Without sea gulls, dead fish would litter the waterways. Proof of God's creative plan, Carrie always told her.

"Yeah, you'd think with all God's creative powers he could keep them away from my boat," May would grumble, as she sponged away bird droppings from the seats of her Boston Whaler.

As she moved closer to the gulls, she could see what they were feasting on. A dead sea gull, one of their own, floating on its back, stomach exposed, while the others picked and picked, squawked, and called others to the feast. She didn't know why, but the sight of this strange cannibal feast unnerved her, made her want to leave.

She avoided the dead bird and set her sights for home, to Pop Maynard's floating dock where she kept her boat.

When she arrived, Carrie was pacing the dock, waiting for her.

"They're looking for Stuart," Carrie said. "They think he had something to do with the murder of that man."

"Who's looking for Stuart?" May threw Carrie a line and climbed out of her boat.

"The police. They want to talk with him. They want to arrest him."

"Let's go find him," May said.

29

Early the next morning Jake and Ben jogged up the cliff path toward the gazebo while Ben reviewed the points of his upcoming Sunday sermon. This was Ben's habit, with Jake offering input from what he called the "backslider's point of view." Jake often told him that since he heard the morning sermon prior to Sunday, he really didn't need to go to church.

"It would be like watching a rerun," he'd say.

The steep cliff path was proving to be a workout, but neither one suggested stopping, even for a breather. But as the path wound steeper, Ben's sermon recitations lessened until they quit altogether during the last fifty feet. In the silence Jake thought about Elise. He was worried about her. He hadn't seen or spoken to her since she'd fled Noonan's Café yesterday morning. He'd tried calling her. He'd tried every half hour for the rest of the day, but she hadn't answered. He'd tried all evening. Still no answer.

They were at the top of the path now, and ahead of them, the gazebo. This early in the morning, they were the only ones up here. In the summer this place would never be empty, even at this hour. Hikers who climbed to this spot could see well past Thunder Island, and on clear days, whales had been spotted. To the right, summer mansions were perched on the edges of cliffs or set back in patches of woods. If it had been a clear morning, Jake and Ben would have been able to see some of the roofs, a few attached swimming pools, and tennis courts. Ben stood very still, looking through the patches of fog out to the sea, while Jake stretched and gazed back toward the town, still asleep in the predawn.

"'All who wander are not lost.'"

In the middle of a calf stretch, Jake looked over at his friend. "What?"

Ben just stood very still, his eyes to the sea.

"'All that glitters is not gold. All who wander are not lost.' Shakespeare. Well, it's attributed to Shakespeare but quoted later by Tolkien. It's in the book I left for Jana."

"I'll be sure to give it to her." Jake was running in place now.

The fog had cleared slightly, and Ben stood very still. "Whenever I stand here at the edge of the ocean, I cannot help but be reminded of my own mortality, my own vulnerability. It always makes me think of God. 'All who wander are not lost.'"

"Is this for your sermon? That quote?"

"No. It's for you, my wandering friend."

They started down the path to the other side. Eventually the trail led to a cliff near the summer homes. It became extremely treacherous after about half a mile, and signs warned away would-be hikers. Jake and Ben would go as far as it was safe and then turn back.

"Wandering friend?" Jake asked.

"It's okay, Jake, not to have all the answers. It's okay to wonder and be confused and to run. I know you're troubled about your daughters, confused about your feelings for Elise."

Jake didn't say anything.

Ben continued. "Sometimes I think of the entire church as a loose association of wanderers. No one quite knowing for sure, no one having quite enough faith, but believing anyway. All of us wanderers."

"Wandering," Jake said. "I had enough years of wandering in my boat. I like to think I'm through with the gypsy life."

Ben spoke quietly. "Wandering. Mystery. All of us writing the stories of our lives. The mystery of God. Represented by a part of God's creation. The sea. The wandering, restless sea."

They turned around and headed back.

"That's what I like about you, Ben," Jake said with a laugh. "You speak in such clear English."

"I said this was for you, my wandering friend. You may think you're lost, Jake, but you're not. You once loved God, didn't you? You even went to Bible school for a year; you were baptized; you dedicated your life for service. I know you, Jake. You've taken a few wrong turns, made a few wrong choices, but God is still there, waiting.

"Sometimes it's in this very wandering that God meets us. Look at the children of Israel. They wandered for forty years in the wilderness, but were they lost? No. God knew exactly where they were. Look at Hagar, banished to the wilderness, but had God forgotten her? No. The exact place where we thought we lost God is often the very place we find him again."

"My mystical friend," Jake said. "You should be living in a cave somewhere with all the other mystics."

"Nah. Not me," he said. "I'd miss the sex too much."

They were back at the gazebo now, where about a half-dozen members of the local art club were setting up easels.

"You're confused. You're still struggling. But you're not lost; I know you're not," Ben said as they parted.

Back at the Purple Church, Jake grabbed a quick shower and then headed down to Elise's Creations. It was still too early and the Closed sign was firmly in place, but he went around back and knocked. No answer there, either. Where was she? Did this have to do with the TV program? with her neighbor? He drove to her house. By now Rachel would be in school. Elise wasn't there.

He drove back to the boardwalk, parked, and walked to Norah's. Maybe she knew where Elise was. Norah's Inner Healing Books and Gifts smelled of incense and camphor and sounded like pan flutes and waterfalls. Norah sat on a chair in the back behind her cash register, her curly, brown head bent over a book.

"Hello there, Jake," she said, taking off her glasses.

"You're open early."

"I'm not officially open. I'm just here." She smiled at him.

"I'm looking for Elise. Have you seen her?"

"Not today. Last night I did."

"You saw her last night?"

"She came to me. She's in such distress now."

"I thought her spirits would be pretty high now, what with being on TV yesterday."

"Such good things like that can be overwhelmed by the bad energy of someone next door killing himself. It's not good to be that close to such negative energy. She's been close to negativity all her life. Sometimes it all piles up. She came to me. We did a meditation. With candles. Rachel joined us. She's an indigo child, you know."

That word again. Jake blinked.

Norah got up, came around the counter, and sat on it. Wherever Norah walked, she left behind a trail of incense, and sometimes talking to her was like talking to someone who spoke another language.

About a year ago he and Ben had seen her in Mags and Hermans cuddling a teddy bear while she drank a cup of hot chai tea. When she saw the two men eyeing her bear, she said happily, "I'm going to be selling these good-feeling bears in my shop, and I'm just carrying this little fellow around so I can imbue him with good and happy energy. I want him to get a feeling for this place."

Jake laughed. She was joking, of course. Or maybe not. He said, "Norah, it's a stuffed bear. A toy."

To which she'd replied, "I firmly believe that inanimate objects carry the life of their creator. Just like we carry the life and energy of our Creator. And," she added, "*toy* is a derogatory term. It implies use. We prefer *stuffed companion*."

Jake couldn't help it. He guffawed, nearly sputtering out his coffee. But Ben, who always enjoyed a good discussion about God, had taken his coffee cup over to where Norah was sitting. By the time Jake had left, the two of them were deep in conversation.

This morning Norah wore some kind of Indian shawl with tassels on it, the kind he'd seen on shade pulls. "Elise and I have been friends for a long time. She's had so much pain in her life. I know, too, that she thinks highly of you, Jake. Don't let her down."

"I'll try not to."

"She needs you now more than ever."

"I haven't spoken to her since this thing with her neighbor and the TV program. I've been looking for her…"

Norah stood very still and cocked her head. "This is very interesting. The yin and yang. You have the overpowering negative energy of a person next door ending his life, and you have the overpowering positive energy of being recognized for your achievement. I believe she is in a state where she cannot cope. You need to find her, Jake.

I know she's looking for you. Even if she's hiding, she's looking for you."

"Do you know where she is?"

"She's been through so much in her life."

"But do you know where she *is?*"

"Her husband was so abusive. So was her childhood. Terrible. She's had such tragedy. A long time ago, when Rachel was just a baby, he was drunk and drove off a bridge. She came here to start over."

Jake waited.

"Elise comes from very negative energy. But she's come through it all. We even did a rebirthing for her once."

"A what?"

"A rebirthing. You've heard the expression *born again?* You have to go back to the womb and become born again. I don't do it, but there is a practitioner in Ridley who does. I facilitated the rebirth. I'm hoping to become certified in it. It involves being bound, like you're in the womb, then being reborn in stages. We did that with Elise. She's such a gifted artist, and most of her giftedness comes from what she's been through."

Jake said, "Did you know she was writing to prisoners?"

Norah looked up, frowned, shook her head. "I wonder why she would purposely go back to that space. I'm sure she had her reasons. We have to trust that inner part of us." She put her hand to her heart. "The inner part of us that carries its reasons. We need to listen to that."

The Indian bells jangled, and Norah waved to the customer entering the shop, inviting her to look and feel free to ask questions if she had any.

Then she turned back to Jake. "Elise is fortunate to have Rachel, though. Rachel is an old soul."

"A what?"

"Indigo children are different from other children. I call Rachel an old soul. She's been around the block a few more times than the rest of us."

Jake looked at Norah. The child was eleven.

"I'm just glad that Elise has Rachel at this point in her life as her guiding light. Rachel is very gifted—not as her mother is gifted in the arts, but in her mind, her intuitive spirit."

The customer came to the counter with a few aromatherapy candles and a package of tarot cards.

"So you're saying you don't know where she is, then?"

"Not at present, no."

By the time Jake left Norah's, Elise's Creations was open. Jess told him that Elise wouldn't be in. She was in Ridley teaching a seminar at a jewelry show.

"Really? She's in Ridley?"

Jess nodded. "Well, it's really more like a conference than a jewelry show. She left early this morning, just after Rachel went to school."

"I wanted to call to congratulate her about the TV program, but I wasn't able to get ahold of her all day yesterday."

"Yes! Isn't it marvelous? I'm so pleased for Elise."

"She didn't seem all that pleased, though," he said. "She ran out of Noonan's."

Jess frowned. "Well, maybe that explains it then."

Jake gave her a questioning look.

"When she got back here, she was sort of subdued. I kept asking her about it, but she wouldn't talk to me."

"Is this common? Her not talking to you?"

"We're business associates. I do a lot for her, but she has this outer shell that's impossible to break through. She's one of those people who's hard to get to know, ya know? You think you know her. You have this real heart-to-heart one day, and then the next day she barely speaks to you. I call it her artistic temperament and just try to ignore it."

Jake nodded. He understood that. Maybe Elise just needed more understanding. Maybe he just needed to be patient with her.

"How long will she be in Ridley?"

"I'm not sure. I think she'll be home in the afternoon." She bit her lip. "But if you wanted to go to the conference to see her, you could."

"How much would it cost to get in?"

Jess laughed. "No need. I've got a name badge." Her eyes flickered, and her expressive mouth curled into a grin. "It has my name on it, so if you want to be me for the day, you're welcome to it. Elise got two registrations, but I'm not going to be able to make it today. Maybe tomorrow." She reached for the badge under the counter. "Here you go, Jake."

He looked at it. "I'm sure they're going to notice that I'm not Jessica Gurney-Forrest."

She waved her hand. "You know what? They never even pay attention. You go in with the badge turned around the other way, like the wind blew it or something, and you'll have full access. I'm sure you'll find Elise there. Here,"—she handed him the brochures for the show—"go. Have fun."

He pocketed the stuff. A quick trip to the Purple Church to tell May where he was off to, and he'd be on his way.

But when he arrived, Bill from the Fog Point police department was there talking with May. Neither one looked very happy.

30

To my mother, who shoots guns,

You have a gun. I know you do because this afternoon that sleaze machine Carl Featherjohn came over and gave it to you. Or maybe you bought it from him, because I did see you give him some money.

Here's how it happened: I was supposed to be spending the afternoon at Ashley's. School's almost out, so we were going to make our plans for the summer, beginning, I might add, with a week at church camp. How cool is that?

But I ended up coming home from Ashley's because her brother was throwing up sick, and Ashley's mother didn't want me to catch it. I walked home and came in the back door and went right to my room so I could write in this book all about summer camp. You didn't see me come in. You were too busy staring at a candle on the kitchen table.

So I went upstairs and was about to plug in my MP3 earphones, when I heard the front doorbell ring. I thought maybe it was Ashley, like maybe I'd left something there by mistake. So I opened my bedroom door and was ready to go

downstairs, and who did I see in the doorway but loser Carl
Featherjohn. He looked as lame as ever with a toothpick sticking out of his mouth and his greasy hair all over his head. I was
wishing Ashley was with me so we could point our fingers
down our throats and make gagging noises. He was carrying a
black suitcase, and I thought that finally his mother had kicked
him out of the house and he was coming to see if we'd take
him in. Yeah, good luck, Carl. My mother hates you too.

"I didn't expect you today," you said to him.

"Well, I was in the area, darlin'." He was chuckling. In the
area. Like he'd just made the joke of the century. And what's
with the darlin'?

"Come in, then. I don't want this to take long. My daughter
will be home soon."

So you went into the kitchen, and I thought this was too
good to miss, so I came downstairs as quietly as I could and
sat on the floor next to the couch in the living room, my journal on my lap.

Carl grunted and plunked the suitcase on the table, and
you blew out the candle and put it by the sink. There's this
smell that follows Carl Featherjohn around, like oily hair and
oily cars mixed with some sort of bad food. I could smell it all
over the house.

I didn't hear anything for a while, but I could hear the click
of the suitcase opening. And what I saw made my eyes go
wide. Guns. He put like five or six guns on the kitchen table. I
couldn't believe it. And there you were, picking them up and
looking at them and asking questions like you knew what
you're talking about.

And then I heard you say something like "I'd like this one, Carl. But I need to learn to shoot it."

Then he was packing the other guns away, and next thing I know, you were making plans to meet in a couple days for shooting lessons.

When I saw he was going to leave, I climbed behind the couch. I can fit there if I squeeze in tightly. After you went upstairs with your new gun, I got out and went upstairs and sat in my closet.

Your daughter,

Rachel St. Dennis

~~~

The Teeny Tiny Minke Whale
By Rachel St. Dennis

Minke whales are one of the smallest species of whales on the East Coast. They get to be twenty-eight feet long, which seems big to me, but in the whale world, that's pretty small. But don't let their small size fool you. They are active and very smart and know exactly what they are doing.

The big whales don't scare them at all. They just go right out and swim where they want, making very loud sounds.

Minke whales make very loud sounds. I read this one place where they said they can scream as loud as a plane taking off. They are also very powerful, so it doesn't matter that they are small.

I plan to see them when I'm older. I think I'd like to have my own boat so I can go see the whales whenever I want to.

31

May sat at her desk frowning as she capped and uncapped her pen. Bill leaned forward with his glasses up on his forehead as if he had a second pair of eyes.

"What's up?" Jake asked.

"I'm glad you're here," Bill said. "Sit down."

May sighed, shifted in her chair, and pulled her cap down over her eyes. Jake knew this body language. May was not a happy camper.

May said, "Bill's got his knickers in a knot because Neil Watts, the guy who died, apparently had one of our business cards in his shirt pocket. I told him it was nothing. Just a routine investigation carried on for a client." She put the pen on the desk. "But Bill here says he thinks the whole thing has something to do with terrorism. If you can imagine such a thing in Fog Point. And he thinks Elise is involved."

Terrorism? Elise? Jake pulled his chair closer to them.

"I told Bill that our client, for whatever reason, has chosen not to go to the police, and we have to honor that. We can't violate that trust."

Jake looked at her as she continued. "And Bill here is trying to persuade me that I need to tell him about our case. He doesn't understand that this case has nothing to do with Neil Watts or terrorism. We have no idea who Neil Watts was or where he came from. I spent less than fifteen seconds with him, Bill. Fifteen seconds. Possibly less. I never saw him before. He's not a part of the case we're working on. He was just a possible witness. He had nothing to do with our client."

"What's this about terrorism?" Jake asked.

Bill dropped his glasses to the proper place on his forehead and looked down at some notes in his lap. "I've got a murdered guy, a member of the so-called paparazzi…"

"A murdered guy? So it was murder?" Jake asked. "We heard rumors."

Bill looked up, nodded. "It's no secret, I guess. Press already knows. It was a pretty amateurish attempt to make it look like a suicide."

"Did you say paparazzi?" Jake asked.

"Again. That's no secret. This Neil Watts; he'd been here before," Bill said. "And he didn't endear himself to the summer people. The complaints against him are a matter of public record. Although we aren't sure why he was here now, since Hollywood hasn't descended yet for the summer."

Jake remembered his argument with Elise. "You get his camera?"

Bill nodded.

"What was on it?" Jake asked.

Bill eyed him and said, "First, I'd like a bit of information from you."

Jake sighed, put his hands on his knees. "You know we can't tell you anything, Bill. We would if we could."

"Well…okay. I guess I can be straight with you even if you're not straight with me. First of all, there were pictures of his neighbor, Elise

St. Dennis. Lots of pictures of her. He had a camera rigged right from one of the windows in his house into her house. It was the perfect setup."

"He was a Peeping Tom." And as Jake said this he wondered. Had Watts been the one at her window that afternoon? He looked at May. She inclined her head slightly. She was thinking the same thing.

"But that's not all we found," Bill said. "On that same roll of film we found lots of pictures of known terrorists. People on the FBI list. And that's why I need you to tell me what you know. Watts shows up murdered, and he had your business card in his pocket. He took pictures of Elise, and you, Jake, have been seen around town with her. That's why we're interested. Especially with Elise and what she does for a living."

"She makes jewelry," Jake said.

"And terrorists make jewelry," May mumbled. "Everyone knows that. It's a real cottage industry with them."

Bill ignored her and went on. "Both her home and her studio on the boardwalk have state-of-the-art security and alarm systems that are connected right to the police department. The only other homes that well secured are the summer mansions."

"Because of the gold," Jake said. "And the gemstones."

"But more important, the chemicals," Bill said.

"What chemicals?"

"Jewelers keep enough chemicals on-site to blow up a small country. Acids and stuff." Bill shuffled his papers. "They need that and other stuff to clean gold and things."

"But what about everyone else who has chemicals around?" May asked. "Pop has chemicals. So does the hospital. Dentists, too, for that matter."

"But they aren't being photographed by someone with known terrorist connections."

"Aren't you being a bit overdramatic, Bill?" May said. "Terrorist *connections?*"

"Watts had pictures of people wanted by the FBI. We have proof that he not only took their pictures but met with them."

"What proof?" May asked.

"I'm not at liberty to say," Bill replied as he put his glasses back up on his forehead.

"Then why arrest Stuart Maynard?" May asked. "Carrie was beside herself. What did he have to do with anything?"

Stuart? Arrested? Jake looked at her, looked at them both. "Are we talking Stuart Maynard? Someone please tell me what's going on, from the beginning."

"Stuart wasn't arrested. He was merely a person of interest. A witness said he saw Stuart behind Watts's home yesterday morning, and we were just questioning him. That's all. He hasn't been arrested, May."

"But you *do* believe that Stuart is mixed up in all this," May said.

"We do not, May," Bill said. "He was only brought in for questioning, to ask him if *he* saw something. Someone saw him. We have to follow up on that."

May drummed her fingers on the table. "But you know Stuart doesn't understand these things."

"That's not our problem."

"Bill, the kid is mentally ill!"

"I didn't mean it to sound harsh. Our problem is finding out who killed Watts."

"We don't know anything, Bill. Really, we don't. We're doing a job for a client. That's all. And the job has nothing to do with Neil

Watts or Stuart or terrorism. It's just an embarrassing personal matter our client wants cleared up."

But Jake was already wondering. *Why had Watts been filming Elise? Was he merely a stalker who happened to become taken with the pretty girl next door?*

After Bill left, Jake said, "We need to persuade Elise to see the police."

"I've been saying that all along, Jake," May replied.

32

J ake and May's first whale-watching tour was only a week away, and while Jake got ready to leave for Elise's jewelry show in Ridley, May was to supervise the launch of the *Purple Whale*. Client confidentiality was important to May. Up to a point. But the law wouldn't be on their side. Client privilege, client confidentiality, and the seal of the confessional pertained only to lawyers, doctors, and people of the cloth. Not to mere PIs. Even though May was sure that Elise and her problem with Wesley Stoller had nothing to do with national security, she wondered how long it would be before the police would come knocking at their door again.

As May walked down the path to Pop's, she tried to put the pieces together. They refused to fit. Neil Watts, a paparazzi, had moved in next to Elise and had taken pictures of her. Watts had also taken pictures of terrorists. Then he's murdered. Stuart Maynard just happens to be in the neighborhood, and someone happens to see him running from Watts's house after the murder. And what about these chemicals in Elise's house? Is there anything there? And the million-dollar question: Does Stoller fit into the mix at all?

"You talking to yourself again, May?"

She hadn't even seen Pop at the end of the path.

Had she been saying these things aloud? *This case must be getting to me.*

She said, "Call me the crazy lady."

Down at the boatyard, the *Purple Whale* was already in position on the Travelift.

"Everything is already ready," she said, surprised.

"Matt's been down here all morning. You got a good worker in that one," Pop said.

"Well, great, then." She was not in the mood to have to supervise the moving of the huge whaleboat. Someone as independent as May would be the last to tell anyone that it was a job for a man, but in this case it really was. The straps were already in place underneath, and the Travelift straddled the special launch ramp designed to accommodate the rig. She looked at the boat, gleaming with fresh purple paint. Lead weights hung from the straps so they wouldn't foul the boat when it was placed in the water.

May watched the massive boat being lowered into the water. Matt was aboard, and when the boat was afloat, he started the engine.

Carrie stood beside her. May hadn't seen her come over. "Well," Carrie said. "That was easy enough."

"Thanks to Matt."

"I heard you had a visit from the police too?" Carrie said.

News travels. May nodded. They began to walk.

"So it's not just Stuart."

"No, it's not just Stuart. How is he, by the way?"

"He's in his room and won't come out. He says he won't come out because he's embarrassed and deeply ashamed that he was arrested."

"He wasn't arrested," May said. "It was just for questioning. They talked to us, too. They talk to everybody when someone's murdered, especially when people are talking terrorism."

Carrie opened her eyes wide. "Terrorism? You mean like bombs? You're saying Stuart knows something about terrorism? What's going on?"

May looked at Carrie's stricken face and said, "I don't know. It was just an idea they threw out."

"Well, I don't understand *that*. That's just plain weird. Especially when it has to do with Stuart."

"Agreed."

May and Carrie were on the wharf now. May watched Matt throw a line to Carrie that she secured to a cleat on the dock. Carrie was young and strong. They didn't need gimp lady helping.

Later, in the Purple Church office, May checked e-mail and voice messages. One was from Clara Fryer, Elise's neighbor. The Fryers' house was one of the many places May had left business cards. She returned Clara's call.

"I got your card," the woman said. "You said you wanted to know if we'd seen anyone in the backyard."

"Yeah."

"We saw Stuart Maynard. You know him? He's not quite right in the head."

"You saw Stuart? You're sure it was him?"

"Of course. We know that boy. Everyone does."

"And you told the police this, too?"

"We were home when they came around, so yes, we told them. Is this what you wanted to know?"

May took careful notes as Clara Fryer relayed that she and her husband were out on the deck just as it was getting dark. They thought they saw a person walking through the backyards. "And that's not an easy feat because there are so many fences. We didn't stay outside too long because of the bugs. And we didn't think anything of it, because, you know, Stuart has been found in various places and all. My husband just commented, 'Oh, there's Stuart.' And that was about it. We didn't think anything of it until we heard that poor man, Neil Watts, killed himself. But I guess now they're saying murder."

"Yes, now they're saying murder."

When May asked Clara if they knew Neil Watts, she said no. "He was kind of quiet. Kept to himself. One of those people."

May rubbed her forehead. "Kind of quiet, kept to himself" was how people described serial killers and sociopaths who build bombs in their basements and shoot up schools. *Don't even go there, May, you're barking up the wrong fire hydrant.*

"How about a week ago," May asked instead. "Did you see anyone in the backyards? That would've been last Wednesday around three?"

"We weren't home then."

May hung up the phone, but questions persisted. Her head ached. *Stuart?*

"May?" Lyndsey stood in the office doorway next to a woman, a man, and two boys who looked like twins about ten years old. Huge expectant smiles lit all four faces.

"Yes?" May took off her computer glasses.

"This is Mr. and Mrs. Blazovik and their two sons. They just flew in from Wyoming. They've signed up for a kayak tour next week. They're staying over at the Dew Drop Inn on the highway, and they just wanted to meet you."

Mr. Blazovik said, "We're delighted to meet you. All of us are so excited to try ocean kayaking. We love your Web site. We've never been out here before, and we're expecting the vacation of a lifetime."

She shook their hands, smiled, walked them down to see the kayaks and the water, told them what to expect, and introduced them to Matt, who was taking out the first crew. He'd get them set up. May was used to this switching of gears. Run of the mill in a business that combined PI work with whale watching and kayak weekends.

Still, May's mind flitted back to Clara Fryer's troubling report about Stuart. A second person seen in the backyards behind Elise's within a week?

33

There was a trick to it, and Moon knew what it was. Don't get greedy. He crouched behind the closet door in the tiny bathroom off the staff coffee room down at the Shop 'N Save. Employees escaped there for a quick coffee, lunch, and fifteen minutes of gab.

He always came in at a time when no one would be there. He'd memorized the break times. He knew how to sneak into the coatroom where they kept their bags and coats. Tweedledee kept her ATM card in her wallet, which she kept in the pocket of her coat, which she hung on a hanger. Stupid lady! Most of them kept their purses in the locked cupboard in the back, but not her.

He was here, like he was every week, in the scummy little bathroom, waiting until everyone left. Finally, that last stupid cashier, the fat one, Miss Wiggle Arms, rinsed out her coffee mug, placed it on the shelf, and was gone. This wouldn't take long. Moon was good at this. He sidled out, grabbed the wallet, and removed the card before anyone had a chance to say, "Hello, how's your day?" Then he was out the back door. The rest was easy. He went around the building, walked back in the front door, waved to Tweedledee, and then proceeded to the ATM in the corner of the store and withdrew forty dollars with her card. Then he picked up a couple of cases of beer and got in her line.

"Hey, how's it going?" Tweedledee asked as she rang his beer through and made change.

"Nice to be here buying beer from one of my favorite tenants."

Then he headed back around the rear of the store, punched in the number code to unlock the back door, and carefully put her card back in her wallet.

He'd been stealing forty dollars a week from her since she'd started working there. That was the trick of it. Use ATMs close to where his marks lived or worked. And above all, *don't get greedy*. This principle applied to all his schemes, from stealing ATM cash to stealing credit-card numbers to extortion.

It was all based on a person's annual salary. When extorting money he could reasonably demand ten percent of a person's annual salary and get it. If he demanded more, people got nervous and called the police. So, based on his theory, a person who made a million dollars a year warranted a demand of one hundred thousand dollars. No more, no less. A person who made fifty thousand dollars, a demand of five thousand dollars. No more, no less.

Moon made it his business to unearth people's skeletons and then blackmail them for just enough so they didn't get nervous and go to the police. It was lucrative when he did it right. And Moon did. Like today. Blake Arnold of Arnold's Bakery on the south side was going to pay him a one-time payment of four thousand dollars. He'd arranged that just before walking down to the Shop 'N Save.

"One-time payment? How do I know you won't keep coming after me?" Blake had asked.

"You don't. But I won't. You pay me this money, and you won't see me again. I'll give you the photos and the negs. They're yours, all yours for four thousand dollars."

Moon meant it. He always kept his word. It was important to him to be honorable. The trick was coming up with enough situations. That's what Moon called them—"situations." And he scavenged through the newspapers and through his peepholes for these situations.

He also had a theory about disposable cash. He figured that about five percent of everyone's salary was disposable. That is, they could lose it and not miss it. He'd heard one budgeting guru refer to this money as the "latte fund." When Moon heard that, he decided that's what he'd go for, people's disposable cash.

When he got home, he put on his tool belt, his Glock, his cell phone, and his sunglasses, just in case he bumped into Cain. There could be no more mistakes when it came to Cain. Then he let himself into Barbie and Ken's place. They'd complained about a leaky kitchen sink, but before he climbed under their sink, he logged on to their computer and ordered himself a DVD from Amazon, using their account, of course. The two of them had about a gazillion CDs they'd ordered from Amazon; they wouldn't blink over a few more. He'd been doing this for as long as Ken and Barbie had been living here.

He logged out of their computer and found his way underneath the kitchen sink. He knew how to fix pipes. Yes, he did know how to do some stuff that was legit.

His cell phone buzzed. He answered it underneath the sink. It was Troy Davenborn, the owner of the apartments.

"Hello, Mr. Davenborn." All friendly-like, he was. Little did Davenborn know that he was going to be Moon's big hit. He currently had digital photos on a CD, which he had meticulously burned three months ago, of Davenborn with a hooker down on Beaumont Street. But he wouldn't demand payment yet. It would be just before he was ready to move on up from this place. And he was going to demand nine hundred thousand dollars. Not a penny less. Not a penny more. That's how rich the guy was.

"I'm wondering how things are going with your new resident," Davenborn was asking.

The idiot called them *residents* instead of *tenants*.

"I assume you mean Mr. Wesley Stoller? He's getting along just fine."

"Because you know I don't usually like having former prisoners living in my residences."

"I know that, sir." This was something Moon worked on for years, making sure that when Cain got out of prison, he came here. It hadn't been easy. He had to convince the parole board and several guards, all without Cain's knowledge, but money both talks and ensures silence.

"But since you specifically asked for him, I thought I would make an exception. I trust your judgment, son. You're one of my finest managers, Mr. Moon."

"Thank you, Mr. Davenborn. It's a pleasure to work for you, sir."

"And how is school?" This guy, always with the small talk.

"School is fine, sir. I'm so thankful I have a job that allows me to attend accounting classes part time."

"You'll be a fine accountant. And student loans, you're managing with them?"

"Got no student loans, sir. I'm paying as I go, sir."

"That's wonderful, son. I just want you to know that if at any time you wish to evict Mr. Stoller, you contact me. If he ever gets unruly or causes any problems."

"I will, sir. You've got nothing to worry about."

"Good, son, because I see you moving up in this business."

"Thank you, sir. I won't disappoint you."

34

B efore Jake left for Ridley, he changed out of his stained boatyard jeans. *What does one wear to a jewelry show,* he wondered. He settled on a pair of just-washed khaki pants, a blue golf shirt, and loafers. Placing the name tag on the seat beside him, he set off in his pickup toward Ridley Harbor.

The Jewelry and Antique Faire was held at the Marine Exhibition Center in Ridley Harbor, a place he'd been before. It was right on the water and had its own launch ramp, so it was a favorite place for boat shows, recreational or commercial. He had gone to both. When they renovated the church basement, Jake and May even took in a home show or two here. It was here they'd also found several buyers for their stained glass.

Interesting, having your windows be your bank, he thought.

It was past noon by the time he arrived in Ridley. The parking lot down by the exhibition center was full, so he had to parallel park his truck between a red minivan and a Jeep a dozen blocks up the hill. He grabbed the name badge and started down the sidewalk toward the exhibition center. The parking lot was crowded with jewelry-minded people emerging from the exhibition center with plastic bags proclaiming Gold World. Whether that was a seller of gold or of life on a new planet, Jake didn't know. He threw his Gurney-Forrest name tag around his neck, making sure to reverse it, and walked through the entrance. He ignored the oversized woman at the entryway, the seller of badges and passes and giver of Gold World bags and programs.

"Sir? Excuse me, sir?"

Uh-oh. Busted. "Yes?" he leaned back quite innocently.

"Did you want your program for the day, sir?"

"Oh yes. Thank you."

She handed him a trade-show bag filled with all manner of leaflets and brochures. "There's an invitation to the wine-and-cheese reception sponsored by Beads 'R Us. It's at the bottom. Are you registered for the conference or just the trade show?"

He had no idea, so he mumbled something indecipherable and walked away. A few yards away he stood in an alcove and studied the booklet. He discovered that Elise had given a two-hour seminar called "Fundamentals of Gems Work" at ten o'clock for conference participants. Upstairs. He knew where that was. He'd been in those same conference rooms for demonstrations of fire extinguishers and VHF radios. Attendance at those workshops required a special conference badge. He looked at what he wore around his neck. It was just the trade-show color, not the yellow badge for conference attendance. Oh well, he'd keep his badge turned over and feign innocence. After all, it was always easier to ask forgiveness than permission.

It was now twelve thirty. He headed down the aisle. Instead of the PFDs, bottom paints, radars, and GPS's that had lined this hall last time he was here, there were booths with, well, jewelry. He walked down the first aisle past displays of gemstones, beads, silver, rings, hair ornaments, and diamonds under glass. He passed a booth where a guy in an apron stood behind a counter hammering a piece of silver over a piece of wood shaped like a log.

At the next booth gemstones were being sold at wholesale prices. There were, of course, the ubiquitous free draws. Jake walked past booths laden with rolls of gold chain in various widths and styles. It seemed jewelers bought chain like marine rope, by the yard. There was even a booth displaying kilns. Clearly this was a world he knew nothing about.

He headed through the doors to the conference center and took the stairs two at a time. The room Elise had been in was empty except for two men and an older gray-haired woman who was holding a book and a folder. Predictably, all three wore a lot of jewelry. Big showy pieces hung from the woman's ears and around her neck. The younger of the men wore an earring and a rather gaudy pendant that looked like the inside of a conch shell and hung on a gold chain nearly to his waist.

Jake figured the other fellow to be somewhere near his own age. He wore a button-down shirt with the sleeves rolled up and a fancy silver monogrammed tie tack attached to his shirt, although he wasn't wearing a tie.

"Hi…uh…I'm looking for Elise St. Dennis," Jake said.

"You just missed her," said the woman.

"She was just here," said the young man with the earring.

"Do you know where she went?"

"You might check the college booth," the tie-tack guy said.

"The college booth?"

"College of Craft and Design. She's been known to hang out there."

"I'm sorry to have missed her seminar," Jake said. "Was she any good?"

"She was excellent," the guy with the earring said.

"I don't know, though," the woman said. "Didn't she seem a little distracted to you, Peter? I've heard her before."

The older man cocked his head sideways and kept it that way. Jake wondered if the guy had a crick in his neck. "Could be she's just tired," he said.

"We're *all* tired," the woman groaned. "It's been a long few days for all of us."

"I'm Peter, by the way," said the tie-tack man, extending his hand.

"Jake."

"And I'm Morgan," said the woman.

"She's the antique part of the jewelry conference," the young man, whose name tag said Bluey, offered. The three of them laughed loudly at that. Jake figured he must be missing something. He grinned anyway.

"They call me that because I collect antique jewelry and copy the techniques for my own work," Morgan explained. "But try the college booth. Also try outside. Picnic tables are set up outside by the water. Elise could be anywhere."

"She could even be on her way home by now," Bluey said.

"Thank you." Jake turned to go.

The booth housing the Ridley Harbor College of Craft and Design was near the food court, bustling now with the noon crowd. He scanned the booth and the tables, but Elise wasn't there. The young woman behind the booth said she hadn't seen her all day. "She's usually easy to locate. She teaches tons of classes for us and always comes by to say hello."

"You don't know where she might've gone?" Jake asked.

"My guess is that she's heading home already. She seemed anxious about something."

"Anxious?"

She paused. "Maybe just busy. With her studio and all. And then, of course, all of us heard about her dragon barrettes being featured on *The View*, so I imagine a lot of people want to talk with her. But try out back. Lots of people go out there for a smoke. She might've."

He thanked the woman and raced toward the exit. He'd head outside, and if Elise wasn't there, he'd make a quick sweep through and then drive home. Clusters of jewelry designers and aficionados mingled in groups. Conference attendees filled picnic tables, drinking out of cans with straws and looking through brochures. The one common denominator was that every one of them wore some sort of jewelry—necklaces, bracelets, things in their hair.

Jake walked past the milling crowd at the picnic tables, away from the conference grounds, and around the back of the exhibition center.

Then he saw her. Ahead of him, staring out into the water from her perch on a nearby rock, sat Elise. With her left hand she flicked ash from her cigarette onto the rocks at her feet, and with the other hand she massaged her forehead. She held something in that hand, a piece of paper, scrunched in her fingers. He made his way toward her. She didn't look up.

When he got close enough, he said, "Elise?"

She still didn't look up, although she must've heard him.

"Elise?" He sat down beside her.

She turned, and her eyes widened with recognition.

"Jess told me you were here." He kept his voice soft, as if speaking to a child. She shoved the piece of paper into her pocket, picked up a small stick, and swirled it in the sand. The sun was so bright, so glaring, he could see the small flaws in her skin, the tiny lines around her eyes.

She stubbed out her cigarette on a rock. "I don't usually smoke. I shouldn't smoke. It's a bad example to Rachel. She's all I've got. She and I…" She swiped at the edges of her eyes and sniffled a bit. Her skin looked so pale, transparent, as if it were too thin to cover her soul.

She looked out toward the sea. A black freighter inched across the horizon. "I have bad karma," she said.

"Don't say that," Jake said.

"People die when they're around me."

"You're talking about your neighbor."

She nodded.

"Did you know him, Elise?"

She threw the stick down. "I didn't know him at all. I never even spoke to him. Not once. He was a stranger to me."

"He was taking pictures of you."

She looked up suddenly.

"The police came by," Jake said. "They told us."

"I can't help that. That was him; it wasn't me."

"But you knew about it?"

"I saw the cameras. I saw him do it."

"But you never spoke to him?"

She shook her head, retrieved the piece of paper from her pocket, flattened it on her knee.

"Elise, I saw you with him. I saw you talking to him. You were arguing."

"I wanted him to stop."

Jake studied her quietly, not saying anything. She rested her head on her knees, didn't look at him.

He looked at a place on the back of her neck. "Elise."

She didn't look up.

"I know you're afraid. First, there's Stoller, and now a neighbor…"

"You said to tell you if I heard from him?" She handed Jake a piece of paper. "I heard from him."

He looked at it. "Wesley Stoller sent you a letter?"

"Read it. And then you'll know why sometimes I say things wrong or get things mixed up," she said. "I haven't been able to breathe since it came. I haven't eaten. Nothing."

He opened the letter and read.

Dear Elise,
I want you to know that I'm coming for you and Rachel. We all belong together. I know that in the deepest part of your heart you know that too.
        Wesley

She shivered and moved closer to Jake. He put his arm tentatively on her shoulder. She came into his arms then. For a long time he held her like that, his hands on her hair. "I wish everyone would just leave me alone," she said, shaking.

"When did you get this?"

"It came the same day as *The View*. Now I know he knows where I live." She moved away from him slightly. "I can't stay here. I have an appointment with Rachel's teacher later today. I have to go. Rachel, she has problems sometimes…"

"She seems like a nice kid."

Elise rose, brushed herself off, kept ahold of Jake's hand. "She has problems. Like her mother. Social problems."

"We should really go to the police with this, Elise." He was still holding the letter.

To his surprise, she nodded. "I'm thinking of that now. I really am."

"As soon as you get back."

"I'm afraid."

"I know. I'll go with you," Jake assured her.

"Would you?"

"Certainly. How about we have a nice lunch first and then go see Bill?"

She smiled. It lit up her face.

They held hands as they walked to her car and arranged to meet at a restaurant in Ridley.

At lunch she said, "I have to tell you something. I know what you're going to say, but I have to tell you anyway. I have a gun. I'm taking shooting lessons. I have a gun, Jake."

35

A ll Elise meant to do with her life was to keep her daughter safe. And for ten years she had succeeded. Now, with Wesley free, there were no more guarantees.

"God," she said on the way to Rachel's school. "God, God, God." Whether this was a prayer, or an oath, she couldn't tell. She hadn't prayed in a very long time.

When Elise was a child she believed in God. It was a desperate belief, something she clung to frantically, like she clung to her sister at night, the two of them holding on to each other underneath the blankets, while downstairs their father harassed their mother—loud, insistent, cruel. And their mother, cowering, took it like she always did, as a "good soldier of the cross."

If Sarah couldn't take care of their mother, Sarah would take care of Elise. Sarah always took care of her, the way Elise now took care of Rachel, with a kind of desperate care, a frenzied love. When something bad would happen, Sarah would put her hands over Elise's ears and sing, "Yes, Jesus loves me. YES, JESUS LOVES ME. YES, JESUS LOVES ME, THE BIBLE TELLS ME SO!"

Elise had done the same for Rachel, covering her daughter's ears with her own hands, because in those early days with Rachel, Elise still clung to a belief in God. Still, after all she'd been through. *Yes, Jesus loves me, the Bible tells me so.* Loudly, loudly Elise sang to Rachel.

Elise and Sarah played a lot of games back then. Everything was a game to Sarah. Their favorite was one Sarah made up called "At Least It's Not..." where they tried to convince themselves that things weren't so bad by listing all the things that could make their situation worse.

Sarah would begin, "Well, at least it's not raining and there's a hole in our roof and we're getting wet."

"At least we're not getting trampled by elephants," Elise would answer.

"At least we're not sitting in a cold puddle of water and it's nighttime."

"At least we don't have cockroaches in our refrigerator."

"At least all the windows in the house aren't broken."

"At least the milk in our fridge isn't poison."

"At least we don't sleep in a cage and have only bread and water."

"At least we're not fat and have pimply faces and gross hair."

"At least I'm not a famous music person and I went to my concert and didn't bring my music."

"Or my mother packed the wrong music!"

"At least I'm not an Olympic gymnast and I got to my first Olympic game and when I got up, all I had to wear was a plaid leotard and tights with a big hole in the knee."

"Because I left my good ones at home!"

And they would keep on going until they collapsed in quiet giggles.

All the while, downstairs their mother would say nothing, meek as a lamb to the slaughter, as a lamb before her shearers is dumb, so she openeth not her mouth. "That passage from Isaiah is about our Lord. He chose the way of suffering. Demanding one's own way is not the way of humility, the way of the cross." That's what their mother told them.

Elise hadn't cried at her father's funeral. None of them had. Not even her mother, who had stood to the side, her mouth in a thin, grim line. Elise and her sister had both been there. Everyone had been there, and no one had cried. She'd held baby Rachel, who'd played with Elise's earrings the whole time. Elise had worn earrings that she'd made herself out of thin wires and sparkly beads, and by that act she had spit in the face of the man who'd forbidden jewelry in his home.

At least Neil Watts is dead, Elise mused, her thoughts shifting back to the present.

At least the police had believed her when she told them she didn't know Watts.

"I don't know why people stalk me," she had told the police officer while Jake held her hand. First Neil Watts and now Wesley Stoller. "I don't know why!"

At least Jake believed her.

It could always be worse.

At three thirty Elise parked in front of Rachel's school. She'd been here before. Lots of times before. *Rachel's smart and artistic, but we're worried about her social skills. Does she like playing sports? Being on a team might help.*

No, she doesn't like sports. She just likes whales.

As Elise walked down the hallway, no memories from her own childhood came back to her. Sometimes she wondered how different her life would have been if she and Sarah had been allowed to go to school. The children in her church had all been homeschooled in the church basement, a big group of them, all ages. The quintessential one-room schoolhouse of the 1980s. So as Elise walked down the hall, the smell of wood, books, and running shoes evoked no memories, only a vague longing.

The first time Elise had been to school was eight years ago when she enrolled in the Ridley Harbor College of Craft and Design and began indulging a lifelong love of jewelry. Since then she'd taken many courses and now was called upon more and more often to teach them. Her designs had even garnered a few awards of late.

Amy McLaren's door was open, and she was sitting behind a big metal teacher's desk. She looked up from her writing and smiled at Elise.

A smile's good.

"Come in, come in," Amy called. "Have a seat." She pointed her pen toward a child's desk.

Elise sat. The small desk fit her perfectly.

Amy was a matronly woman in her forties who looked forever tired. She was wearing a pink cotton blouse, quite wrinkled after a day of looking after fifth graders, and an elastic-waist skirt in a flowered print. The blouse strained across her ample bosom.

Amy folded her hands on the desk and smiled. "I've got some good news," she said.

Elise, who didn't believe in good news, merely looked at her.

"As you know,"—Amy shuffled a stack of papers—"Rachel is an extremely bright girl. After talking with the vice principal and others and looking at her test scores, we've decided to place her in a special gifted program. That is, with your approval."

Elise waited.

"It's a program where she will travel to other schools and have a chance to practice her skills, especially her science skills. She really excels at science fairs and loves them, as you know. Well, the vice principal and I have found this special program for girls who excel in science." She went on to explain that some of the travel would be outside the country. England looked like a good possibility for the fall.

"England?"

"Yes!" The teacher's eyes were bright. "Would you give Rachel permission to go to England?"

"Of course." Elise folded her hands on her lap and held them very tightly against her.

"We have one other girl going from this school. We'll be raising money, and we would expect the girls to raise money too."

"Rachel already has a paper route. I'm sure she'll be thrilled about this."

"That's great. We have only one week of school left, but we want to get this thing in motion for the fall. Now, we'll need her birth certificate because we have to get the passport thing rolling. She doesn't already have a passport, does she?"

"No." Elise looked down at her hands. She was quiet for a while before she said, "I don't think Rachel will be able to be a part of this after all."

"What?"

"You need a birth certificate to get a passport, right? I don't have a birth certificate for Rachel. It was destroyed in a house fire some years ago. All of our papers were. There's a mention of that in the school records."

Amy grinned. "Is that all? You can get a replacement birth certificate quite easily. Just write to the government office where she was born. It's very simple. It's nothing to worry about." Amy studied

Elise's face for a moment, then suddenly said, "I'm so sorry. I didn't know there was a house fire."

"There was."

"I'm so sorry, Elise. I didn't mean to make light of it."

But Elise got up and backed out of the doorway. Once out, she ran, the same way she had run out of Nootie's the day before. The same way she would be running for the rest of her life. And as she ran, she thought about birth certificates, two of them, safely stored in a bank safe-deposit box many, many miles from Fog Point.

36

A t the end of the boardwalk, beyond Pop Maynard's Boatyard, the whole texture of the land changed from rocks and beach and tide pools to mud flats and grass. Known as The Shallows, this place was the least desirable on the Fog Point waterfront. May's cottage was one of only two dwellings along this part of the bay. The other one was about a quarter mile up and had been in the Browngreen family for generations. No one lived there now.

It was low tide when Jake drove along the narrow winding road toward May's cottage. She'd been working at home all afternoon. She had a theory, she told him, and needed time and quiet to work on it. Now she wanted his input.

Jake had finally persuaded Elise to go to the police, and after lunch they had spent an hour talking with Bill. Elise said that she had never met Neil Watts until a few months ago when she noticed him in his backyard taking pictures of her house.

"Why would he do that?" Bill had asked.

"I have no idea."

"Did you confront him about it?"

"Of course."

When she'd given Bill the letter from Stoller, he'd read it, then put it into the envelope. He'd have it analyzed, he'd said. The police had promised to look into Wesley Stoller. A restraining order was not out of the question.

Bill had quizzed her extensively about the face in the window. "Could it have been Neil Watts?"

Elise had shrugged. "I was so certain it was Wesley Stoller," she'd said quietly.

She'd gasped when Jake had given Bill a copy of the photograph he'd taken of the partial boot print. "Where did you get that? I thought the film was ruined."

"I came back and took another photo."

For a moment, a brief moment, he'd felt her move imperceptibly away from him. Then Bill had asked her about her shop. Had anything gone missing lately? Gemstones? Chemicals?

At the mention of chemicals, Elise's eyes had widened. "No," she had said. "Nothing. Not that I know of, and I keep good records."

Jake continued along the lane that led to May's. At high tide this place gave the illusion that it was a waterfront like any other waterfront, but low tide turned it into mud flats and marshes. Local myth had grown up around The Shallows. It was said that at low tide, fishermen who had died at sea came to shore and walked around. If they didn't make it back before the tide came in, they haunted Fog Point for six hours until the next low tide, when they could leave. You could tell this was true, the locals said, by the pungent, murky low-tide smell. No one really knew where the stench originated from, and marine biologists had made many expeditions out to the end of the mud flats but came back with no definitive answers. To locals this was more proof that the dead came to shore from The Shallows.

It was a full moon tonight, an actual blue moon, which meant that it was the second full moon in a month, so the tide would be extra low, a low-low it was called.

Jake knew May liked it here. She told everyone she didn't mind the low-tide smell. It was the smell of life and the sea, she said. As part owner she could have lived in one of the apartments at the Purple Church. "No, thank you," she said. "I'm too old for dormitory life. Nor would I relish having to walk clear down the hall in the middle of the night to the bathroom. I'll live out on The Shallows with my screened-in porch and my own bathroom, thank you very much."

She had had a dock constructed out front, where at high tide she could tie up her boat. At low tide her boat settled into the mud until the tide rose again. She had also built a large screened-in front porch that ran the entire length of the cottage. One of the by-products of this part of Fog Point were insects, and lots of them. Jake could hear them as soon as he drove into the lane leading down to May's. He rolled up his truck window wondering how she could live like this.

May was sitting on a flounced rocking chair on her screened-in porch and talking loudly on the phone. She waved when she saw him, but her face was unsmiling. She motioned for him to come in quickly and close the door behind him, which he did.

"Yes, yes. I can be there at a moment's notice," May said. "If you need me. Fine, then. We'll wait and see what happens. What he does. Yeah. Keep me posted. I'm home all evening with lots of gas in the SUV."

A citronella candle burned on a wicker coffee table, and next to it sat a cake box from Noonan's. Rum cake, the same box Carrie had brought to his boat earlier that week. May's laptop was on the table. He sat down on a wicker rocker and listened to the bugs outside.

Finally May clicked off the phone. "Stuart's missing," she told him.

"Again?"

"Carrie doesn't know whether to just ignore the fact that he's gone or send out a search party. She checked his room earlier this evening, and he wasn't there. I think she's going to wait awhile before she gets nervous."

"Probably a good idea."

May took off her red baseball cap and laid it on the table next to the cake box, then ran a hand through her hair. She was so rarely without her cap that her head looked funny without it. "You want some iced tea, Jake? I've got fresh brewed. I have a theory about Elise. And this Neil Watts thing fits. I need to talk with you about this. I think I've got it all fitting together. I'm dying of thirst; don't know what's the matter with me lately."

She got up, went inside, came back with two teas, and set them on the table before saying, "Okay, you know me and my theories. Well, I'm working on another one. Here's what I've got: Elise suddenly appears ten years ago, no record of her existence prior to that, and all of a sudden she's here with a new identity. She didn't even have a driver's license prior to ten years ago. And she and Rachel are here alone. No family. Nobody but the two of them."

Somewhere out on the marsh, an animal's cry echoed mournfully.

"You were a cop once," May said, "and I was married to one for more than thirty years. You learn what people do. Nothing surprises you. Okay, here's my theory. Elise St. Dennis does not exist."

"Come again?"

"There is no Elise St. Dennis prior to ten years ago. There isn't even an Elise St. Dennis who conveniently died when she was a child, giving Elise, or whoever she is, a birth certificate. I checked that, too. And no Rachel St. Dennis, either."

"That's what your friend Sol says…"

"I believe him, and you should too. Mother and daughter just show up here. No history. Nothing. Okay, here's part two of my theory, maybe the reason why." She hefted her laptop onto her lap and opened it up. "So, okay, prior to ten years ago, Elise gets herself somehow, maybe unwittingly, involved in terrorist activities."

Jake opened his eyes wide and muttered under his breath.

May put her hand up. "I know. I know what you're going to say, but stay with me on this one for a bit. She's selling her stuff, the stuff she uses in jewelry making. I checked into that, Jake. Here, listen to this; I looked it up. She's got hydrochloric acid in that shop and tons of other chemicals she uses to refine gold or melt it or shape it. Or whatever else she does in there. She's selling the stuff, and someone's paying her and paying her big time. How else could she afford to advertise in the *New Yorker* for land's sake?"

Jake shook his head. This was outlandish. The Elise who'd shivered next to him on a rock and held onto him as if she were drowning was genuinely afraid. There was no other word for it. "I know fear, May," he said. "And this woman is afraid."

"Of course she's afraid. She wants to quit; they want to escalate operations."

"Your theory is a bit out there, May. You realize that."

"I know it is, but think Patty Hearst with me for a minute, okay? The police seem to think there's a connection between Elise and terrorists. And they sometimes have information we don't. Plus, it may not be anything she willingly got into," May said. "Perhaps she's being threatened. I'm quite sure she's being threatened now. She wants out. Trouble is, they aren't taking no for an answer."

Jake chewed on this for a while. He remembered lunch with

Elise. They'd sat at a table by the window, and she'd told him about her sister and her father. Her father had started his own religion, an oppressive patriarchal religion that forbade women to cut their hair and wear jewelry. He'd kept his hand firmly on them and their mother, regretting that he had no sons. Sons proved that a man was blessed by God. His lack of sons was his wife's fault, which he took out on her. And Elise had explained how he'd finally ended up dying in prison after one too many assaults on her mother.

She had told him all of that in an expressionless voice.

No wonder she was running. No wonder she had come here to try and reinvent herself.

May continued, "Perhaps selling off some of these chemicals was something she began years ago as a way to earn a bit of cash. Single mother supporting a child. So maybe she's been threatened by Wesley Stoller, who quite possibly is a terrorist. And then there's Neil Watts, which brings me to part two of my theory."

Jake nodded.

"He's a photographer, right?" May said. "Well, you'll never guess who took pictures at Stoller's trial. Voilà!" She handed him her laptop.

He looked down at the pictures of the trial, the two of Stoller and the two crowd scenes, the ones they'd already seen.

"Look along the bottom," she said.

Photos by Neil Watts. Jake looked up at May. "So Neil Watts was at Stoller's trial."

"He was there. And here's a picture of him." She reached over and clicked a few keys, and a staff picture from the *Boston Globe* filled the screen. "He used to work there," she said, "until he got canned."

"Why'd he get canned?"

"So far all I can find is insubordination, which is a catchall phrase that covers just about anything. But he was fired, incidentally, right after this trial." She tapped the screen.

While Jake studied the photos, May opened up the cake box. "Have some cake," she said. "Carrie brought it over. Okay, let's think about this." She cut two slices. "Watts takes pictures at Stoller's trial ten years ago. Stoller goes to jail. Watts gets fired. Elise writes to Stoller. He threatens Elise. Watts moves in next to Elise. He takes pictures of Elise. He also takes pictures of known terrorists. Elise has gold and chemicals. Watts is murdered. Do we see a pattern here, Jake? Would you say that Watts and Stoller are somehow in cahoots? And that maybe Elise unwittingly got herself mixed up in something bigger than herself?"

Jake shook his head. "I don't know. It sounds so far-fetched."

"The whole world is far-fetched now, Jake." May ate a forkful of cake.

"So according to your theory, the grand pooh-bahs of the terrorist world killed Watts and are now after Elise?"

"Yes, it's what I think." May nodded.

"So what about Stuart?"

"Nothing about Stuart. He just happened to be in the wrong place at the wrong time. Poor guy. According to Carrie, he was off his meds when it happened. Carrie says he writes poetry. He says he gets better ideas for writing when he's not taking his meds."

"I'll bet he does."

Jake ate a forkful of cake.

"Some birthday," May said.

"Pardon me?"

"This was Carrie's birthday cake. Nootie made it for her."

37

It was a gray afternoon when Elise got ready for her first shooting lesson. She kept her gun wrapped up in a cotton rag in a shoe box up in her closet, behind her shoes and next to the box that held the magazine articles and Internet clippings her sister, Sarah, had been sending to her through the years.

She'd received another news clipping yesterday, the same as always, in a plain envelope. This one was about a woman in Oregon who'd killed her wife-beating husband by systematically adding weed poison to his morning coffee.

It was a little after one o'clock when Carl Featherjohn pulled into her driveway in his gaudy red pickup with Schooner Cruises, a phone number, and a Web site freshly painted on the side.

Elise picked up her duffle bag with the gun in it and climbed into his truck. She didn't want to ride with him or go anywhere with him, really, and suggested that they meet at the shooting range. But he said no way. He'd drive. An ordinary car like hers wouldn't be able to take the ruts. Filled with water from the spring rains, they'd be impassable except in a truck or SUV. Reluctantly, she'd agreed.

She got in and sat as close as she could to the door. He grinned over at her, a toothpick in his mouth.

"You might want to rethink your footwear, darlin'."

She looked down at her high-heeled platform boots. "These are fine."

He shrugged. "Suit yourself." He pulled out of her driveway and went north on Main Street. They passed Jake's Purple Church on the right and Stone Church on the left. Then they passed the graveyard and the gravel road to the right that led down to The Shallows.

When they reached the outskirts of town, the paved road turned into a gravel road, which changed into a dirt road, which eventually became nothing more than a very narrow, rutted dirt path with deep puddles.

"Where are we going?" she asked.

He looked over, shifted the toothpick from one side of his mouth to the other. "To the shooting range."

She nodded and looked out the window. She should have taken a course from the gun-store people. One of those registered courses where people who weren't criminals taught you how to shoot. But then they'd have her name. She probably needed a background check even to join a legitimate gun club.

Some of the ruts looked knee deep, and Carl drove up one side and down the other, much too fast in her opinion.

About twenty minutes after they left town, the muddy path widened into a clearing of sand and gravel. He stopped the truck, jarringly so, and said, grinning, "Well, darlin', we're here."

"What is this place?" she asked.

"The shooting range. Used to be a gravel quarry until they decided the gravel was of too poor a quality. Now it's just a shooting range. Unofficial."

He opened his door and got out. Elise grabbed the door handle.

She had her doubts that the rusted handle would even work. She clenched it, pulled. It gave with a screech, but at least she could get out. She jumped down. Her boots crunched on broken glass as she walked over to Carl. There seemed to be broken glass everywhere.

From the back of the truck, Carl hefted a couple of cases of beer.

Elise put up her hand. "No, I did not come here to drink beer with you. I draw the line there."

He guffawed and set them down, shifting his toothpick. She could see now that they were empties. "You get real good, I'll even let you shoot one of these."

To the right of the sand piles were logs with rows of bottles set up on them. To his credit, he also had a bag of paper targets. "These we fasten to the wood frames up there," he told her.

"No one knows about this place?"

"Everybody knows about this place. The police don't care. There's never been a murder out here. First time a dead body shows up, well, then they'll have to patrol it."

"Kind of hard to do that, having to come all the way out here."

"Precisely, darlin', precisely. Okay. Now before we get down to business, let's take care of business."

She opened her duffle bag and handed him a brown manila envelope full of money.

"It's all here?"

"Of course."

"And this takes care of everything?" Carl pressed.

"Everything."

He stuffed the envelope inside his jacket. When she took out her gun, she thought of another gun and another time, and about the way the ends of that man's hair flopped forward as he fell, the way he grabbed and clawed at his chest, the look of surprise in his eyes. And he hadn't died right away. He cursed and swore as she picked up the baby and ran. At the end of the street, she could still hear him dying.

Carl brought out two sets of bright orange earmuffs and told her to put on a pair.

"Okay," he said as he laid the gun on its side on the makeshift wooden table. "This here's the barrel. The bullet goes in here. You've got a nice Smith and Wesson .38 five-shot revolver, a nice ladies' gun. Since it's a five-shot, you get to shoot five bullets before reloading." He picked it up and loaded it. She watched him carefully. She had to know how to do this. "Now the gun's loaded. Just one shot this time."

She nodded.

He held it out and aimed it into the quarry. Although Elise had braced herself, the blast was louder than she had expected.

Carl placed the gun in his belt and walked down to the sand pile and hooked up a paper target to one of the frames. He came back, reloaded, and shot some more rounds into the target. He opened the cylinder, emptied the shells, and said, "Okay, she's fine. Now it's your turn."

He handed her the gun. Once she had loaded one bullet, she turned the cylinder like he showed her. He then stood behind her, put his arms around her to show her how to position her arms. She hated the feel of him so close.

"And see, you look down through those two little ridges at the end of the gun. You sight them up with the target. Let's see what you can do."

He backed away. Her arm was shaking so much that her bullet went way wide of the target. She had to learn.

An hour later, after going through many rounds, she began to feel more comfortable. She was even able to shoot a beer bottle, her ultimate triumph, even though it was from fairly close range.

Close range was all she would need.

A few more shots, and he taught her how to clean the gun. "Very important," he said. She nodded again. As they packed up, another truck made its way into the quarry.

"We've got company," Carl said.

"Good thing we're leaving," she said. Two fishermen she recognized waved at her. She didn't wave back but bent low in the truck.

38

To my mother, who never lets me do anything,

I found out something today that is making me so mad. It's
making me mad all over, like I'm feeling hot and cold at the
same time. Ashley's mom told me. Not even you. I went there
after school because you're so busy with the store.

Ashley and I went downstairs for something to eat, and
her mom said to me, "Well, Rachel, I guess you're pretty
excited right about now."

And I said, "Excited about what?"

"About that trip to England."

I'm standing there holding my glass of milk and wondering
what she's talking about. What trip to England?

And then she smiles and says, "I guess I shouldn't have
let the cat out of the bag."

And I'm still standing there like an idiot because I don't
have any idea what she's talking about. And then, I don't know,
something told me I should play along. So I shrug and say,
"Oh, that."

And now Ashley's all, "What? What?"

"Honey, it's a real honor," said Ashley's mom. "You'll be representing Fog Point."

Meanwhile Ashley's just staring at me, her Popsicle half in and half out of her mouth. I'm there trying to give her the eye, like, "Be cool; I'll tell you later." But she can't stop jumping up and down.

To Ashley's mom I'm saying, "Yeah...well."

"To be chosen for that special program is quite an honor, Rachel. The whole town will be proud of you. I'm sure your mother is proud."

You never said anything. Why?

I can't wait to talk to you about this trip. I leave Ashley's, telling her that I have to go home and work on my whales report. I promise to call her later and tell her all about it. When I arrive at the shop, you're in the middle of one of your consultations, but I barge right in anyway because I'm so mad. Jess trails after me, "Rachel! Rachel!" and grabs my jacket. But I don't care. You should have told me this. I don't care about the old white-haired lady holding a poodle.

"Leave me alone. I need to talk to her!" I yell at Jess.

"It's almost over," Jess is saying. "Five minutes. Ten at most. Here, come sit in the back. Do you want some lemonade, Rache?"

"No!" But I'm back out of the consultation room now. You got up and locked it. Like you need to keep me out, your own daughter. Now I'm worse mad.

"What is it Rache, girl?" Jess puts her hand on my head. I have to admit, Jess is pretty cool. There are no customers, except for the frumpy poodle lady with you, and so I go to the

back with Jess, and she gets me a can of lemonade from the
fridge, and I tell her that I'm supposed to go on a trip to
England, and my mother conveniently forgot to tell me.

And Jess, she smiles at me and opens her eyes wide. "Oh,
Rache! I'm sure she means it as a surprise. And now you've
gone and spoiled it."

I know she's trying to make me feel better, but I also know
you. You've never planned a surprise party for anyone in your
life. No, this is something else. You just forgot. You're so
strange and tired and weird and cranky and quiet lately, no
wonder you forgot.

I drink my lemonade and nod at Jess, but then as soon as I
hear the poodle lady leaving, I yell, "MOM! WHY DIDN'T YOU
TELL ME ABOUT ENGLAND?"

"What?" Your eyes are very wide and then you look at your
pointy shoes.

"England. Ashley's mom told me I was going to England.
Why didn't you tell me?"

"Because you're not going to England."

"Mom!"

"I can't let you go. You're too young to be off all by yourself. You're not going."

I just stood there. I know you mean it. You turned and
walked back to the little room and closed the door, but I could
see that you were shaking. Maybe crying. Well, I'm crying too.
Plus, I'm still mad. It's just not fair!

Your daughter,

Rachel

~

The Wolves of the Sea
By Rachel St. Dennis

Killer whales or orcas are sometimes called the wolves of the sea. They are the worst predators. They kill and eat seals and small animals and anything that swims by them; for example, big fish and even small whales. They don't care. They just destroy everything in their paths. They think they are the kings of the sea. They kill and kill and kill and kill, and they just don't care. Nothing matters to them. All they want is for everyone to think they are so great. Like the king of the jungle, except with them it's the ocean. If I get to be a marine biologist, I'm going to kill all the killer whales. They should make friends with the sharks. That's what I think.

39

May was too old for this, all this running around after murderers and miscreants and making sure people got to their kayaks on time. There was a full moon; maybe that accounted for people's craziness and the worse-than-usual mass of saltwater mosquitoes that sought entrance at her screen in the morning. So great was their buzz that she actually thought it was her alarm clock. She leaned over, reached for her alarm, saw that she was an hour early, but decided to get up anyway.

She reached for her cane, pushed her body to a sitting position, and grimaced as she forced her legs over the bed. She moved her knee gingerly back and forth. There was a whole regimen of physical therapy exercises she was supposed to do daily. Sometimes she actually did them.

With one hand pressing down on the top of her cane and another on the wall, she groaned, pulled herself up to a standing position, and made her way to the bathroom. It was early, but this would give her a good start for the day. They were getting more and more requests for tours and information. There were a gazillion e-mails to answer, and the whole thing promised to turn into a scheduling nightmare. But that was a good thing. Maybe they'd actually be able to pay some bills.

Plus, they had the Featherjohn boys to worry about. The brothers had done up a Web site with a very similar URL to theirs. Sometimes when she googled "Adventure Whale Tours," the first listing to come up was Schooner Cruises. She'd have to have a good talk with their Web master about that.

In her bathroom she surveyed the countertop full of little plastic bottles: shark cartilage, omega-3, calcium, vitamin D, fish oil, glucosamine, chondroitin, vitamin B complex. The last time she was in to see the doctor, she had asked him about knee replacement. He had stood there for a long time frowning before saying that he didn't feel she was a good candidate for surgery. So she wore a brace, ate shark cartilage, got the knee massaged and acupunctured and acupressured and physical therapied. Still, she worried about ending up with that mechanized go-cart with a flag. "Paul, I draw the line there," May said aloud as she downed a handful of pills.

She grimaced as she ran a hot bath. Then she lit an aromatherapy candle. She'd bought this one from Norah, who claimed that it relieved stress and "gentled you into your morning."

Well, we'll see about that.

May thought about her work. If she allowed herself to admit it, getting up and going to work was a lot better than waking up and having nothing to do all day. Her work kept her sane and less lonely. As much as she complained, her work made her feel fulfilled. She liked researching this whole terrorism thing. She liked tracking down things on the Web, looking for clues, following leads.

It was a good life, but not a perfect life. She missed her husband. Even after six years, she missed him desperately at times. It was uncannily unfair that a marriage of thirty years should end in an instant. She missed talking to him. She missed him sitting across the breakfast table and complaining about the news. She missed the way he left the wet bath towels on the floor. She missed the look on his face when he gazed at boats and when they planned their retirement. She missed the warm, musty smell of him in bed beside her. And as much as she'd complained about it, she missed his snoring. His snoring let her know he was there. And she missed sex. Here she was, a middle-aged, slightly lumpy woman with a lame leg who missed sex.

The youth think they have the corner on sex with their thin bodies and vigor. They don't know the first thing about it. Mere children, she thought as she dried herself off and got into her clothes. *They don't have a clue. None of them do, about the brevity of life...and then it's over. No clue.*

She took her mug of coffee to the front porch. *You're doing okay, babe. I'm proud of you. I'm proud of you,* she could almost imagine her husband saying.

"Yeah, it's not so bad," she said aloud again.

She picked up her baseball cap. Paul's cap. The Squirrels was his slow-pitch softball team, a team he coached until the day he died.

It was early; no need to head to the Purple Church for an hour yet. So she drank her coffee and ate her old-person bran flakes and went through her e-mails. Nothing more from Sol. She wondered again about the death of Elise's father in prison. May was sure of her theory. It would help to know Elise's father's name and where he had been incarcerated, but so far Elise was refusing to share that bit of information.

May finished her cereal, washed out her bowl and coffee cup, put them on the sink rack to dry. She got into her SUV and drove to Elise's Creations.

It was still early, so May didn't even try to go in the front way. She

went around back and knocked, noticing the security-system sticker in the window. Rachel answered the door.

"Rachel?" May asked.

"I know you're wondering why I'm not in school yet," she said, "but I have to come down early each day now to help my mother and Jess get the place in working order. Besides, there's only one more week of school till summer."

May smiled at the explanation. "Is your mother around?"

"In her studio." The girl rolled her eyes.

"Can I ask you a couple of questions then?"

"Sure. Go ahead. I'll tell you anything. If you want to know anything about my mother, I'll tell you."

There's something going on here, May thought, something that May, who'd never had any children of her own, didn't fully understand.

"Now," Rachel said, crossing her arms across her chest. "If this is about Carl at my mother's window, yes, I saw him. It was him. My mother will say that it wasn't him, but it was him."

"You're sure about that?"

"I'm sure."

"Might it have been your next-door neighbor?"

"You mean the guy who died? No. It was Carl. I'll get my mother for you." She disappeared through the door that led to Elise's workshop and closed it behind her.

May sat down on a chair next to the computer and waited. If she was a good detective, she'd be up reading the sticky notes on the bulletin board behind her, or she'd have hacked the computer hard drive already, or at the very least, she'd be going through the stack of correspondence in the in-box. But she did none of these things; just massaged her knee and waited. After a while, though, she picked up a photo album that was sitting on the desk in front of her and looked through it. Page after page featured Elise's jewelry, a picture for each piece. May supposed that this is what artists did; they took pictures like this of their work.

She was still looking through the album when Elise came out in an apron with a set of goggles around her neck.

"May? Is everything okay?"

"Yeah, just a couple of loose ends," May said. "This is a nice book. Are these your pieces? You have some beautiful stuff. You can be quite proud."

Elise's countenance brightened, loosened, and she almost managed a smile.

"Do you take pictures of all your pieces?" May asked.

"All of them. When I design a piece, I take a picture."

"Is this something Jess does or you do?"

"I do it. Jess is good with the business aspects of things, but when it comes to the art, I don't trust anyone but myself to get the pictures right."

May closed the book and thought about that. She didn't say anything for a while.

"You said you had to clear up some loose ends?" Elise ventured.

"Right. Jake and I are thinking that Wesley Stoller may have been in contact with your father. In prison, perhaps."

Elise put her hand to her mouth. "That's not possible. That's simply not possible."

"How did your father die? Was he murdered? in prison?

"That's not important."

"Elise, who was your father? What was his name?"

Elise turned to go. "My father had nothing to do with Wesley Stoller. He died way before…before Wesley even went to prison."

"There could be a connection, though." May was insistent. "A mutual acquaintance in prison, perhaps."

Elise backed away from her. "I can't go into this."

"Elise, don't be afraid. We can help."

But Elise had backed into her office and closed the door. There wasn't anything to do but leave.

When May got back to the Purple Church, she had a message from Carrie.

"Please call. Please, please call me. I tried you at home, but you'd already left. This is important. It's Stuart again." Carrie's voice sounded breathless.

40

M y church is going to help pay for this," Cain said. "That's why I invited Lyle to come meet you."

Moon sat there, nodding. They were all sitting on metal chairs around Cain's kitchen table. Cain sat across from Moon; Lyle next to Cain. Lyle was Cain's AA sponsor, Moon had just learned. How nice and cozy.

There was something faintly old-fashioned about Lyle, something Moon couldn't quite put his finger on, until the man bent his head. His brown hair had a knife-edge part on the side and was combed over to one side. Moon hadn't seen hair like that since he was ten. Lyle also had a chin like one of those wooden ventriloquist dolls, two lines on either side of his mouth going down to his chin.

"You can understand why we're a little reticent," Lyle said. "It's not every day that a Bible-study group hires a private investigator."

Moon just kept trying to look serious, hands on his knees.

"We have a police officer in our congregation, and he says it might be a good idea to hire a private detective. The police just aren't equipped to do this work."

Moon said, "I told Wesley I'd be glad to work pro bono because I consider him a friend."

Lyle put up his hand. "A workman is worthy of his hire. We wouldn't consider not paying you."

"Well, I'm certainly not going to charge you the full amount."

"A workman is worthy of his hire. Absolutely not. We'll pay you. Not a penny less than what you would ordinarily get. We just want to make sure everything's on the up and up. That's what the police officer said. He just said to make sure we examine your investigator's license and get some references." Moon liked watching the guy's jaw when he talked.

Moon dug out the card he'd just printed off his computer, licensing him to practice detection, complete with the state seal he'd lifted from the state's official Web site.

"No problem," Moon said. "Here it is. You can call the state bureau of licensing if you wish. I'll get you their number."

"I'm sure that won't be necessary. I'm sure your word is good. What about references?"

Moon made a deprecating noise and shook his head. "That might be a bit tricky. I guarantee confidentiality. If you'd like, I could call several of my old clients to see if they'd be willing to have you phone them. I could set that up tomorrow."

Lyle nodded. "Fine."

Woodjaw—Moon's nickname for Lyle—plainly had never hired a PI. Here he was trying to come across as all suave and knowing the ways of the world. It would be too simple to get a phone number for one day and have him call it. Moon could do that sort of thing on the Internet in about five minutes.

"What is it, then, that you'd like me to do for you?" Moon asked.

Cain answered, "I've got some people I want to find; some people I lost track of when I was in prison."

"Why do you want to find them?" He folded his hands on his knees. "The reason I ask is that if it's for nefarious purposes, then I can't be involved."

Nefarious. He'd just learned that word in *Reader's Digest.*

It pays to increase your word power when you want to impress.

"No, no," Cain said. "That's not what I want at all. I want to find these people to apologize. Step nine." He glanced over at Lyle.

Moon smiled in a way he hoped would urge him on.

"Here's the list. Plus, what I know about them is on there too."

Moon looked down at the piece of paper. There were four names on the list, and Sarah and Fiona were two of them.

"I've been working through the twelve steps in AA," Cain explained. "I need to make it right with people. I don't want a relationship with any of these people. I just need to say I'm sorry and to ask forgiveness."

"You found Jesus in prison."

"Yes, I did," Cain said.

Lyle smiled for all three of them.

Sorry, Moon thought, *finding Jesus, that doesn't cut it in my book.* The thing of it was, Moon knew exactly where all of these people were. He'd kept track of them all these years. All of them. He raised his eyebrows and said, "Hmm…well, this might prove a bit tricky. You haven't seen these people in more than ten years? That's a long time in PI years. It might require a bit more of an expense." He put up his hand. "Now, I said this was pro bono and I meant it. You're a friend and I won't charge a friend. What I'm saying is that it's going to be a bit trickier than I thought."

"We'll pay," Lyle said. "We've taken a collection."

41

I 'm so upset, May. I'm so upset I don't know what to do," Carrie said.

May navigated the steep steps to Stuart's bedroom with her cane. Pop, Carrie, and Stuart lived in the big, old house behind the marina, and the small front bedroom under the eaves attic had been Stuart's room since he was a child.

Stuart liked the feeling of being surrounded and cozy, and he kept the curtains closed. It seemed that his paranoia didn't extend to claustrophobia.

It's a fairly neat room, May thought, *neater than the Featherjohn cellar.* A faded red spread covered the single bed. Books topped a chest of drawers and a desk with a computer. More books on the floor: Tom Clancy, Robert Ludlum, and stacks and stacks of old dog-eared Ian Flemings.

"This is what I wanted to show you," Carrie said and dumped some magazines on the bed. "These were underneath his bed. I was up here..." She was close to tears and swallowed several times before going on. "I came up here to maybe find clues to where Stuart had gone. And I find these!"

There were magazine articles on terrorism and computer printouts on the making of bombs. The collection included several military-type magazines and photos of terrorists wanted by the FBI. May sat on the bed. The room felt cold.

"I logged on to his computer"—Carrie sat down on Stuart's bed—"to see who he might be corresponding with, if anyone. He's on these chat rooms where they talk about blowing up things! What should I do, May?"

"Have you told Pop?"

Carrie shook her head, then looked down at the magazines. "But I know what he would say, that it's no big deal. Just like everyone else around here. You know what? Colin Nation told me he thought that the guy who died, who killed himself—Neil Watts?—that he might be responsible for Stuart's disappearance."

"Neil Watts?"

"Because he was a stranger. No one trusted him."

Stuart was known for wandering, yet when he went off, someone else had to be blamed. He was a Maynard, after all, a Fog Pointer of the first order, so he was forgiven little indiscretions and allowed to be eccentric. That's what they called it when it was one of their own; he was an eccentric, not a seriously ill paranoid schizophrenic who read magazines and articles about terrorism and wandered off without his meds.

A stranger like Neil Watts would be blamed for all the ills that had ever befallen the town.

May sat down in front of Stuart's computer and got online. The Web history revealed Web sites devoted to terrorists and terrorism activities. There were Web sites on bomb building, on bomb placements in buildings for maximum efficiency, chat rooms where the subject was people with an anti-American bent. The more May read, the sicker she felt.

Stuart, Stuart, what have you gotten yourself into?

Then she closed the Web browser and opened his word-processing program. He had marked a number of files as poetry. May opened them and read a few. Dark poems about what it feels like to be different. She scanned through the poems, then she clicked on a document titled simply "My Town." She opened it and read a few sentences. And what she read shocked her to the core.

"Carrie, I think we better find him," May said. "I think we better move heaven and earth to find him."

42

I n the early evening Jake gathered together bits and pieces of his
dirty laundry. Like a lot of Fog Point residents, he'd spent most of
the day looking for Stuart. Jake was convinced that Stuart was on the
streets in Ridley, so he left the capable search party to head home. He
was worried about something else. Elise wasn't answering her phone
again. *Why does she do this?* he wondered. *Act all friendly one day and
then distant the next.*

If they found Stuart, or if anyone needed Jake, he could be there
in an instant. But they had Search and Rescue out now, and the police
and the FBI and Homeland Security. Jake thought it was overkill, but
what did he know? They had sent him home. And Carrie, too.

"Get some sleep," they told her.

He drove Carrie home. She offered him a cup of coffee; he
declined. He was worried about Elise but couldn't tell Carrie that.

Back at his apartment he answered an e-mail from Jana and wrote
another one to Alex, wondering if he would ever make it right with
his younger daughter. He gathered up laundry, a couple of kitchen
dishtowels here and there, stuffed everything in the washer, and got it
going. While his laundry contentedly swirled around in the machine,
Jake made himself a cup of instant coffee and, feeling restless, called

Ben. He was still at church, Amy told him. She asked about Stuart, and Jake said they were still looking.

"I don't quite understand this," she said. "He's gone missing before, hasn't he? I heard they had the FBI looking for him this time."

"It looks like that's happening, yes."

"But why? And the police? They're all over the wharf. Do you know what that's about? I was down there earlier. What's going on?"

Jake said he didn't know.

"The whole town's crazy these days."

Jake had to agree with that.

"Is there anything in particular you wanted to talk to Ben about?"

"Nothing. I was just wondering if he wanted to get together. That's all. Cup of coffee maybe."

"We've got home Bible study here tonight," Amy said.

"Okay, then. Sorry."

"Why don't you come along, Jake? Why not come for supper, too, if you haven't eaten? We're just having hamburgers on the grill. Nothing special."

"I don't know…"

"Okay, how about this? You come for supper. And then after supper you don't have to stay. You can go home."

"Okay." Jake wondered why he was saying yes to Amy and no to Carrie. What was the matter with him lately?

An hour later he was sitting on the McLarens' back deck, eating burgers and chips and potato salad with Amy and Ben and their two children, and talking about Stuart and what could and should be done about him. Jake had set his cell phone to vibrate and hooked it to his hip in case anyone needed him. But he was really waiting for Elise to call. He needed Elise to call.

"Is anyone checking Ridley?" Amy asked. "He could be on the streets again, living there."

"Yes, they're looking everywhere," Jake said. "They have Search and Rescue out now. It's in their hands."

"Well, that's good," Ben said.

"Do you happen to know Rachel St. Dennis?" Amy asked Jake.

He looked up sharply. "Elise's daughter?"

"That's precisely the one. The reason I ask is because she's working on a whales project. I told her to contact you. That you know lots about whales."

"She e-mailed us. I have a couple of posters put away for her if I ever connect with her."

Amy nodded. "She's a very bright little girl."

Jake nodded.

"I'm hoping I can convince Elise to allow her to travel. I think it would do her a world of good. They've both been through a lot, and the opportunity for Rachel is second to none."

"What's that?"

"Rachel has been accepted into a special science program for girls, but it involves some travel. This fall is a biggie. It's to London. But Elise won't let her go."

"Why not?"

"She's afraid, I think. She's very protective of her. I heard there was a deadbeat dad in the picture."

"I don't think so," Jake said. "He's dead."

"Is he? I was under the impression, and I don't know where I heard this, that he is alive somewhere."

"It was before Rachel was born. Car accident."

During supper Jake kept checking his phone, seeing if he'd missed any calls, until Amy said, "You expecting a call?"

"This thing with Stuart," he mumbled.

He ended up staying for Bible study. He hadn't meant to, but they took their coffee into the living room, and people started arriving and sitting down. Even a boat bum like Jake knew it would be impolite to leave. So he stayed. Buzz and Nootie came to the Bible study, which surprised Jake. He had no idea that Buzz and Nootie went to Stone Church. There was a lot he didn't know about his good friend's church. He heard all Ben's sermons during their morning runs, but he didn't know anything about the church or who went there, other than it was made entirely of large gray stones and that people from all over North America came to photograph it.

Jake didn't have a Bible with him, of course, but the man next to him on the couch, a round bespectacled man named Ernest, helped Jake find the right chapter and verse in a Bible that Ben loaned him. Jake let the man help him, noting the irony. Probably no one there besides Ben and Amy knew that Jake had been to a year of Bible college.

"You were always too controlling. I felt stifled," Connie had said to him when he learned of her affair. "I need someone who makes me feel like me, like the me I'm meant to be." That's when he first moved to the couch and then out of the house entirely.

After it all blew apart, Keith's ex-wife and their three kids moved hastily to her parents' home in Indianapolis, and Jake got arrested for assaulting Keith, fled to his boat, and quit police work before they could fire him. That was six years ago, and sometimes he felt as if it had just happened.

Jake looked around him at all of the people who knew him only as the scruffy boat guy who'd painted a perfectly good church bright purple with a whale mural on the side. Just wait, he wanted to tell them. Don't be so smug in your happiness. It can happen to you. Look at me. Look at May. Look at Elise. Look at all of us. All of us schmucks hanging on by the skin of our teeth. It can happen to anyone.

He put his hands on his knees and watched them. When they bowed their heads in prayer, he unhooked the phone from his belt and looked at it. No calls. No messages. Where was she? And why was he suddenly so fearful?

43

H*ow do you plan a murder?* Elise wondered. *Do you make notes? Do you make an outline listing all the things that could go wrong? Do you need to be that methodical? Are there spreadsheets that can help? An Excel program where you can type in all the variables and come out with the best plan?*

The whole thing was in the hands of the police now. They had the letter and were running it through their tests or whatever they did. They wouldn't find anything. Plus, she knew how slowly things worked. It'd be months before it even made it to the forensics lab.

During the week Jess had fielded phone calls from various actors' assistants wanting information about Elise's Creations and her designs. Several had asked for private viewings and wondered where the nearest private airport to Fog Point was. The day before Jess had been fairly brimming. "They all want to come here!" Jess had said. "Elise. It's happening."

Yes, it's happening, Elise thought as she pulled her jewelry goggles over her face.

"I like those stones." Jess wandered through the shop, touching things, talking in that animated way of hers. "I like these blues. What are they, sapphires? I think you should concentrate on these blues. Like the sea."

Elise didn't say anything.

"You know something else?" Jess said. "I also think you should concentrate on the barrettes that Loren Hayes wore on TV. That's what people are going to want this year. You may have started a whole new trend. We have to get the thing patented; I'm working on that. I also think we should consider hiring more people. We're going to have to be open all the time now. None of this putting out the clock sign that we'll be back in an hour while we go to the bank. No, we're going to have to be open more. All the time."

"Maybe." Elise picked up a small emerald to fasten onto a snake brooch.

"Also, Elise, I found a diamond distributor on the Web where we can buy them wholesale for less than we've been paying."

"That's great." It would all come tumbling down, this house of gold and gemstones, this glittering world she'd made for herself.

How do you plan a murder? Maybe she should set up the Web site herself—*PlanaMurder.com*. Complete with various links.

Motive? (1) revenge, (2) control, (3) fear, (4) all of the above

Opportunity? (1) work, (2) live with them, (3) social connection

Weapon of choice? (1) gun, (2) knife, (3) poison

"So what do you think?" Jess was asking. "You think it might work?"

Elise looked at her. She had no idea what Jess had been talking about.

Jess said, "So we buy this studio instead of renting. That'll save in the long run. And then we get Mags and Hermans to move, and we expand into their place. They might be better off closer to the public wharf anyway."

"Jess, write down all of your plans in a report and present it to our banker."

When Jess left, Elise stayed in her workshop. Some of the silver jewelry needed cleaning. She didn't call Jake. He was a good man, a good and gentle man. He shouldn't have been brought into this.

Last night Sarah had called. Elise told her about the letter from Stoller and about the face at the window. Sarah was the only one she told everything to. Ever since their father had died, it had been her and Sarah. And Sarah always looked out for her.

"You're my little sister," Sarah had said.

"You're my big sister," Elise had answered.

"You know I will do anything for you."

"I know."

"I would die for you."

"We'd die for each other."

44

That night May waited in her SUV at the bottom of the cliff path for Carrie, Bill, and Jake. Earlier, May had been eating a supper of pot roast at Noonan's when the call came that Colin Nation and Farley James had seen Stuart. They'd been out in their fishing boat and saw someone on the path beyond the gazebo. Knowing that none of the summer people had arrived yet, they maneuvered as close as they could to the shore without hitting the rocks. Farley looked through his binoculars. Even though it was night, the moon was just off being full, so they had pretty good light. The man moved like Stuart, with his unusual gait. They called Pop, who got ahold of Carrie, who called Jake, who called May, who was now waiting in her SUV in the parking lot behind the boardwalk. When May had showed Carrie what she'd found on Stuart's computer, Carrie had sat on his bed and put her head in her hands. Then they printed it off and took the pages to the police. That's when the search intensified.

May lamented that Mags and Hermans was closed, so she couldn't even get herself a cup of coffee. She turned on the heater. It was chilly outside. It always cooled off at night in Fog Point. Even during the hottest part of the summer, they could be assured of a cool night. She'd parked her SUV behind Elise's Creations, which was quiet, like all the businesses this late at night.

Poor Carrie. Such panic in her voice. "If something happens, if something awful happens, it will be my fault. He was telling me he was hearing the voices… The voices were terrible voices. They wanted him to do terrible things. I ignored it. Stuart has been hearing voices for years. I had no idea he was involved in…in this!"

"It can't possibly be your fault," May soothed Carrie. "What he does is not your fault. He's a grown man who has to take *some* responsibility for his actions. There are thousands of mentally ill people who take responsibility for themselves and their own health by taking their meds. It's not your fault. And we'll find him. Everyone's looking." Including the FBI and Homeland Security, she wanted to add.

May had been with Carrie on numerous episodes just like this one. Once she had driven Carrie and Jake over to Thunder Island in her Boston Whaler to find Stuart camping out under a lean-to he'd made out of fir boughs and sticks. It was quite an ornate little structure, very well put together, and May remembered being impressed with it. He'd gone out there to work on his poetry, he said. He liked the quiet of the place. Carrie, however, was in tears, huddling her little brother into a gray wool blanket she'd brought as she led him toward the open boat and then back home again.

That was one time. Another time Stuart was found sleeping in the bottom of Johnny Browngreen's fishing boat. He'd also been found holed up underneath the porch of the CurLiCue Beauty Salon. This was just another time. She was sure they'd find him camping quite happily in the gazebo or something.

An hour passed, and the search team hadn't returned. May increased the heat and turned on the radio to pass the time. A dim light burned behind a barred, shaded window in Elise's shop. After a few minutes it went off. When no one emerged from the back door,

May assumed that, like a lot of business owners, Elise had her lights on a timer. All was dark now, so she went back to listening to a late-night radio talk show from a distant location on the other side of the country. The show's host wanted people to call in if they'd met the Antichrist, actually met him. Surprisingly, not a few seconds went by before someone was on the line claiming not only to have met the Antichrist but to *be* the Antichrist and insisting that he had a following. *Oh, brother,* May thought, but she kept listening. The idiocy of it all would keep her awake.

"Okay, Bryce from Houston, how do you know you're the Antichrist?"

"Joe, it was like this. Ever since I was a child…a little kid…my aunt, she told me I was different."

"Well, I'm sure you're different, Bryce from Houston. You sound to me like you're *very* different. Let's move on to Jill from Tulsa…"

As Jill from Tulsa rambled on, a dim light at the back of Elise's Creations turned on again. Then off again. Odd for a timer to do that.

Curious, May left the Antichrist groupies, climbed out of her SUV, and walked over to the back door of Elise's Creations. She knew Elise had a sophisticated alarm system, so there was no way May was going to try the door. Around the edge of the curtain she tried to get a peek inside through the barred windows.

Through the thin column of light, she could see Elise. She sat high on a stool, wearing goggles and a smock, bent over her work.

May went back to her SUV and waited some more. Later she got back out, stretched her legs, and made her way to the public rest rooms at the end of the parking lot. So Elise was in her shop working late. But why would she work in the dark with those flickering lights? So what? Jake said he'd been there earlier looking for her. Funny that she hadn't answered the door. May shrugged. Maybe she wasn't there then. Maybe she'd just come in the front way.

The rest rooms would be locked at this hour, but because she launched her boat nearby, she had her own key. On the way back to her SUV, she saw that the lights at Elise's were now off. Then she saw Elise running down the boardwalk.

Something was wrong.

She called after her, but Elise was too far away to hear. May took off, hobbling with her cane. But by the time she reached the board-walk, Elise was already gone. May returned to her vehicle.

Shortly after, Carrie, Bill, and Jake came down the path with Stuart. He was walking between Carrie and Jake with his head down, mumbling something. Bill walked behind him, his hand on Stuart's back. At least Stuart wasn't handcuffed.

When the entourage got closer, May could hear what Stuart was saying. "I told them it was Carl I told them it was Carl I told them it was Carl I told them it was Carl."

The three of them had searched the entire cliff path, Jake told her quietly. They had feared the worst, but they found Stuart hiding in a garden shed of a mansion that belonged, curiously enough, to one of the writers of the TV program *CSI*. The place was locked up, no one there, but somehow Stuart had found a way to get over the high fence and into the garden shed.

While they helped Stuart into Bill's police car, in a rush of words May told Jake about spotting Elise. Pop would go with Stuart, and May would follow in her vehicle.

"Carrie, come with me," May called. "Jake, you coming too?"

Jake hesitated, looking at Carrie, who turned to him, waiting.

"I'd better stay," he said. "I'll head back to the church."

Go with Carrie or look for Elise. Go with Carrie or look for Elise.

The scene replayed in Jake's mind. May had asked, "Jake, you coming too?" and Carrie in that moment had turned to him expectantly. While the question hung in the air, Carrie had opened her mouth as if she was going to say something. But at that moment Jake's thoughts had been with Elise, and he had said, "I'd better stay. I'll head back to the church."

No, this was stupid. They needed him. At least he should be there for Pop, who looked so small and huddled into himself. This man who had done so much for Jake through the years. He should be there for Pop. If not for Carrie, then for Pop.

But when he turned around to follow them, they were already gone. Maybe there would come a time in his crazy life, he thought, when he would actually start making good and right choices.

Jake got into his truck and drove toward Elise's. He pulled into her driveway. Her car was there, as it had been all day, but she didn't answer the door. Were they meditating over candles again? He went around to the back and knocked. Still no answer. And where was Rachel?

He got into his pickup and drove back to the Purple Church, keeping an eye on the roadside just in case Elise hadn't been heading for home when May saw her running down the boardwalk. As he made his way down the main hall in the church basement, he heard a series of bumps and thumps. And then whimpering. An animal? A cat somewhere? One of the summer students?

He stood still for a moment in the darkness, holding his keys. He should probably remind the summer students of the rules again: no smoking, no drinking, no partying, be in by midnight unless you make prior arrangements. No guests overnight. Keep the place clean, especially the kitchen. Label all your food and don't eat anything that's not yours. And no pets.

He knew his rules were stricter than most of the students experienced at home, but he didn't care. Getting an apartment as part of your salary was a privilege, not a right, and if the summer workers didn't like it, they could move elsewhere. Sometimes they did. During the summer Fog Point had many party houses. His wasn't one of them.

He knocked on Lyndsey's door. No answer. He knocked on the other two doors. Ethan and Matt were still out too. No lights from under the doors. He went to the far wall in the kitchen to get his clothes from the dryer. It was one of his own rules that he habitually broke: Don't leave your stuff in the washer or dryer.

A high-keening whispery wail right beside him made him jump, then turn. It came again.

And then he saw her. Crouched down beside the stove, a tiny thing, holding her knees to her chest, whimpering and rocking. One of her boots had come off and lay on its side next to her.

"Elise!"

She didn't look up but kept her face hidden between her knees, rocking, rocking. Her sweater was torn, brambles poked out along the bottom edges of her jeans, and mud caked her boots. Her hair was in disarray, and she wore only one earring, which was askew in her ear, the dangly part facing sideways, as if she'd caught it on something. The other was missing.

"Elise!" He knelt beside her on the floor, and she fell into his arms, sobbing.

"It's okay. It's okay, Elise." She even smelled like a child.

Finally spent, she moved away from him slightly. Her eye makeup had smeared, leaving black tracks down her cheeks. On another woman it would have looked messy; on her it looked endearing. He stroked her head. Her remaining earring came off, and he held it out to her.

"Your earring," he said. "One is missing."

"It probably got lost on the way over here. I don't know. I ran and ran. There was mud. I remember falling. I think I remember catching it on something."

"What happened, Elise? What are you doing here?"

"I'm so sorry. I shouldn't have come. This whole thing is stupid. What you must think of me. I don't know what else to do. I'm so scared."

"Elise, tell me what happened."

"He was in my studio! He…"

Stoller? "Who was in your studio, Elise?"

"Wesley! He's here now. He was in my studio… I ran here. I… He's here!"

"He's there now? He's in your studio now? You saw him?"

"He stole the emeralds, and then he ran."

"Tell me what happened."

She explained that Rachel was at Ashley's for the night, so she decided to go to work. She had a lot to do to get ready for summer.

"Your car…"

"I walked. It was a nice night for a walk—"

Jake interrupted her here. "Elise, I've been phoning you all day."

"Sometimes when I'm working, I turn off my phone."

He thought about that.

When she got to the studio, she discovered that the alarm was off. She thought that Jess might have gotten careless, but Jess was never careless. And when she went in, she saw all her snakes lined up and their emerald eyes removed. "And there was a knife there! And there was blood. He took the eyes out of the snakes and put blood there and a knife. As soon as I saw that, I ran here. This was the only place I could think of to come."

She was crying now. "I bought that gun so I could use it. I've been practicing. But I'm too afraid to use it now. He was here. I didn't want you to know. I didn't want you to know. You don't approve of me having a gun. But I couldn't use it." She was crying now. "When it came down to it, I just couldn't do it."

"Have you called the police yet?"

"I was waiting for you, Jake."

She clung to him like a tired child as they made their way to his truck.

I'm being hassled by my parole officer, and I don't even know this person they say I'm supposedly harassing."

Moon made sympathetic sounds while Cain went on and on about his situation. Secretly, Moon laughed. The whole thing was really funny when he thought about it.

Moon and Cain sat across from each other at the Starbucks around the corner from Aybeez. Woodjaw wasn't with them, which made Moon happy. He didn't quite trust that guy. A few times he'd caught Lyle looking at him funny, as if Lyle didn't quite trust *him*.

Well, Mr. Woodjaw, AA sponsor from the trailer park, we'll see who wins this round.

Moon hated Starbucks. He would've preferred the bar down the street, but when a paying customer is a card-carrying AA member, he'd go to Starbucks. Trade one addiction for another, alcohol for caffeine.

"What's all this about a restraining order?" Moon asked.

"They think I've been hassling some woman I never even heard of. Elise St. Dennis. I don't know anyone by that name. I tried to tell my parole officer that. I never even heard of her. She lives in some Podunk little place called Fog Point. I've never been there. Don't even know where it is. They say I've been writing e-mails and letters to a person I never heard of who lives in a place I've never been. I tried to explain that it must be a different Wesley Stoller."

"Hmm," Moon said, setting down his coffee cup. "So they got a restraining order against you?"

"Yeah." Cain looked around, shaking his head. "This is so bizarre. Finally I said, 'Fine, okay, fine, I've got a restraining order. Which will be easy for me to abide by, since I'll never go there, and since I don't know that person.'"

"You told them that?"

"Yup."

"Good for you." Moon took a drink of his coffee. Strong. He swallowed it hot, and it burned going down. "Cops are dumb. They get things wrong sometimes. They get things wrong a lot of the time." In the background Sarah McLachlan was singing, "How stupid could I be?" while other customers in small groups leaned toward one another and talked or worked on laptops. A real yuppie paradise, this was.

"So," Moon said, "You said you have a picture of this Fiona person?"

"Yup." He reached into his pocket. "It's the only one I have, so I'd like you to be careful with it."

"You can trust me. As soon as I make a copy, I'll get it back to you." Cain took the photo and laid it out carefully on a napkin. It was her all right. Just as he remembered her. Oh, this would be fun.

As they were leaving, Cain said, "I have a question. Do you have an eye problem? Is that why you always wear those sunglasses?"

"Yeah," Moon said, putting the picture in the inside pocket of his leather jacket. "Something like that."

E lise was still shivering when Jake drove her back to her studio. He would forgive her for not answering the phone, of course. He was beginning to figure out that artisans were a very different sort of people. Elise tried to explain that to him on the way to the studio. Sometimes they didn't answer phones. Sometimes they retreated into worlds of their own.

Jake kept his arm around her as they waited in the car for the police to arrive.

"Why don't we go in?" Elise suggested. "I could show you what he did."

"Not without the police."

"Will it be Bill? The one who talked to us before?"

"He's not around. There was a situation with Carrie's brother. But whoever it is, they know about Stoller, and they know about the restraining order. It'll be okay."

They waited silently in the dark. He could feel her breathe next to him.

Five minutes later a police car pulled up. Jake and Elise got out. At the door he met two officers he didn't know. One was a tall, big-boned, wide-hipped woman who introduced herself as Officer Angela

Matliano. The other was a compact, mustached police detective named Robert Hitchens, who was carrying his case of crime-scene paraphernalia.

"Has the building been checked out? Is anyone inside?"

Elise shook her head. "I saw him running. I was in here when I saw him go. I don't think anyone's in there now."

"You wait here while we secure the place," Hitchens said.

Jake and Elise waited in the parking lot. She was more than shivering now; she was shaking uncontrollably. A few minutes later Officer Matliano came back. "Okay. We're fine. No one's there. Come on in."

Jake could feel Elise steel herself beneath his grasp, the deep sigh, the straightening of the body. And indeed, she seemed remarkably calm as she walked them through her studio. On a table next to her workbench, about a dozen gemless silver snakes were arranged in a semicircle. Blood, or something red, dripped from each empty eye socket. By now, clear fluid surrounded each drop. Clearly the stuff had started to break down, so it obviously wasn't real blood. In front of them lay a large meat cleaver, blade side out. It looked like some bizarre religious ritual. For some reason it made Jake think of Norah and her candles.

The detective photographed the entire scene from many angles and then put the tip of a gloved finger to the liquid, then to his nose. "I could be mistaken, but I think this is ordinary ketchup." He put a small sample in a clear plastic bottle.

Meanwhile, Officer Matliano had taken out a notebook and was questioning Elise. When had she come back to the shop? What did she see? Was anything else taken? Elise nodded and answered as best she could.

"How would someone take out these gemstones?" Hitchens asked her.

"Easy if you have the right tools," she said.

He plunked the snakes into a plastic baggie.

"You have to take them?" she asked.

"I'm afraid so. Do you recognize that knife?" he asked.

"I've never seen it before."

While Hitchens photographed the scene and picked at pieces of stuff with his tweezers and Officer Matliano continued questioning Elise, Jake looked around. This was the first time he'd ever been in her studio, and it surprised him. It looked more like a mechanic's workshop than a place to make jewelry. It was larger than he imagined too, about the size of a single-car garage with a terrazzo floor and various worktables. Tools and goggles hung from hooks, along with an apron and even a headset, for hearing protection, Jake supposed.

A long wooden workbench sat to the left of the door, with a small vise attached, as well as a couple of adjustable gooseneck lights. Against the wall behind the table were columns and rows of hundreds of plastic pullout boxes, the kind hardware stores carry for storing nails and screws. They weren't labeled, so obviously Elise's filing system was in her head.

Assorted tools lined the table, recognizable things like hammers, pliers, mallets, picks, and files, but all in miniature. He also saw other accoutrements of her trade whose function he could only guess: a small square box with hundreds of nail-like objects protruding from it, an odd square saw. He could only guess what direction to hold the saw.

Across from the worktable were more shelves and drawers and a glass box with velvet access sleeves that allowed Elise to work on things she placed inside it. The box reminded him of a hospital bassinet for premature babies.

Other tables held pieces of jewelry in various stages of completion. Jake saw earrings and necklaces and chains of gold.

"Show us around," Officer Matliano said. "What else is missing?"

"Nothing."

"Nothing else is missing?"

She nodded.

Detective Matliano asked to see the whole studio, and Elise toured them through the second room, which housed a kiln, a trim saw, a hydraulic press, and a rock tumbler.

"You use all of these things?" Jake asked.

"Yes."

"I'm impressed."

She kept her chemicals in a locked cupboard below the sinks. Her supply consisted of containers of muriatic, nitric, and sulfuric acids, and aqua regia.

"Aqua what?" Matliano asked.

"For dissolving gold. I'm a jewelry maker. I use all of these in my trade."

"Can you check your supplies? Has anything gone missing?"

Elise knelt, went through her bags and boxes and jars, and said, "I don't think anything is missing." She looked at Matliano, then at Jake.

"What tools would you need to remove those stones?" Hitchens asked.

Elise pointed.

"We're going to need to take those as evidence."

"But I need them in my work!"

"This is a crime scene. And there might be fingerprints. We'll get them back to you as soon as we can."

"And they took nothing else?" Matliano looked.

"It was meant to be a warning," Elise said.

"A warning?"

"If it was a regular burglary, they would've taken everything. I know it was a warning from Wesley Stoller that he's coming for me."

Matliano frowned as she wrote more notes. Detective Hitchens kept up his brushing and tweezing and spreading powder everywhere.

It wasn't until Jake was back in his apartment at the Purple Church that he realized he still had Elise's silver earring. He'd forgotten that she hadn't taken it back when he'd held it out to her. He took it out of his pocket, palmed it, and placed it on his dresser.

48

E lise was alone. She couldn't sleep, so she sat by her bedroom window and looked out into the darkness.

She hadn't realized how much the eye sockets would bother her, until she saw them. She was a child again, and she and Sarah had gone to their fort in the woods, the secret place where Elise kept her Barbie dolls. They weren't allowed to have dolls, not that kind of doll, anyway. Barbies have breasts, and they weren't allowed dolls with breasts. Only baby dolls. But Elise had Barbies because she had stolen two from Kmart, placing the oblong boxes under her jacket each time and walking out. Who would think that this tiny girl with the long yellow hair and wearing a church dress would steal anything? Western Barbie was first; Golden Dream Barbie, the second.

She remembered the sight of them that day, their arms and legs out of their sockets, and their eyes blackened as if they had been gouged out. She and Sarah screamed when they saw them, and Elise gathered up the body parts and carried them home in the folds of her long skirt. She locked herself in the bathroom and set about repairing them, putting the legs and arms back where they were supposed to be, brushing out their long hair with her mother's hairbrush, using soap to try to wash the eyes. But it was Magic Marker, and it wouldn't come out. She washed the dirt stains out of their clothes and put them back on wet. A doll wouldn't mind wet clothes.

Later that night she took the Barbies to show Sarah. "See, Sarah. See, I fixed them. See? See?"

"You shouldn't have them," Sarah said. "They're evil dolls. I told you."

For a long time she thought one of the boys across the street had ruined her dolls—the littlest boy, the one everyone said was crazy. It was only in recent years that she'd come to understand that Sarah had done that to the dolls. It had been Sarah all along. It was Sarah who, even now, was a faithful member of the church of their dead father, carrying on the tradition. Even after all they'd been through.

"I would die for you."

"We'd die for each other."

49

T he house where Neil Watts had lived was no longer a crime scene, and the yellow police tape that lay abandoned on the lawn reminded Jake of that fact. Even though Jake and May knew the crime unit had been through this place with tweezers and toothpicks, they still had to see if they could find out whether Watts's murder had anything to do with the threats against Elise. Was Elise in danger? Jake worried about her. There was something wrong, something bubbling just under the surface, something that he couldn't name, couldn't define.

Plus, there was Stuart to think about now. Where had he gotten the information he had on his computer and in his room? He was still sedated at the hospital, and the police still hadn't been able to talk with him to find out what he knew. The only thing he kept saying was, "I told them it was Carl."

Before coming here they'd stopped in at the police station and talked with Bill.

"Any headway on the B and E last night at Elise's?" Jake asked him.

"If that's what you want to call it," Bill answered.

"What would you call it?"

"I don't know what I'd call it," Bill said. "Maybe 'woman trying to get attention.' First of all, Elise has probably one of the most sophisti-cated security systems in all of Fog Point." Bill moved his glasses up to his forehead and continued. "So a person manages to get through this system and gets in. Okay, so he's in. There are all these gems and dia-monds lying all around. You saw them. So did my officers. So this thief, whoever he is, takes the trouble to get one of the tools to remove the gemstones from these little snake pins. Why not take everything? Why the theatrics? And what's with the knife and the ketchup?"

"Maybe the whole thing was meant as a warning. To frighten her, like she said?"

"Then it's not your standard robbery. Here's problem number two." He held up two chubby fingers. "It takes some skill to remove those stones. You just don't go in there and willy-nilly start breaking things apart. Think of it this way: Have you ever tried to remove a diamond or a stone from a piece of jewelry? Like from a ring, for example. It's not that easy."

Bill held up three fingers. "Problem number three is that earlier in the evening, May saw Elise through the window, working."

"That's not a problem," Jake said. "Elise said she went there to work. And then she noticed the eyes."

But May frowned. "Jake, she was there a good hour before she went running out."

"What about Stoller's restraining order?"

"That's problem number four. We've been in touch with the police out in Buffalo as well as his parole officer. The guy hasn't left the city. He's practically not even left the two-block radius where he lives and works and goes to church. That's right, goes to church. He claims he's never heard of Elise St. Dennis, never heard of Fog Point, and doesn't know why *she's* harassing *him*."

Now, as they stood in the driveway of the house where Neil Watts had been murdered, Jake glanced over at Elise's house. He didn't see her, didn't expect to see her. She'd be at work, in her own little world again. She was maddening. Yet when he saw her, there was something about her that was so needy and vulnerable.

"So how do we get in, Mr. Bright Idea?" May asked.

"We break in. We go around back. We find an open window. I don't care. But we do it. I have to find out what's going on. What the connection is between Elise and this guy. None of it makes any sense. We need the link to Stoller and to Stuart and to Elise."

May sighed. "Jake, I wasn't going to say anything, but I think you need to rethink Elise. She has you totally wrapped around her finger."

Jake angrily stepped over the yellow tape that lay across the lawn. He'd been a cop. He knew what genuine fear looked like. And Elise was genuinely afraid. You can't fake something like that. He turned the door handle and opened the door wide.

"It's unlocked?" May asked. "All this time and it's unlocked?"

"Apparently."

They entered. May planned to look for something that would help Stuart—and, ultimately, Carrie—out of his mess, but Jake was there to vindicate Elise.

The house was much like Elise's, old but not huge, not like some of the other old places on this street. The furniture was shabby and old. Faded chintz spreads on chairs and couches, dusty thick drapes, an Oriental rug, ragged around the edges. The police had obviously been here. Fingerprint powder coated everything.

They weren't alone. A woman stepped out of a back room, holding a box. "Hello?" She put the box down, adjusted her glasses. "Who are you?" she asked.

"More important," May said, "who are you?"

"Neil's sister." She spoke quietly. Her eyes were red; she kept blinking. "I'm…"—she sighed, looked down—"I'm just here collecting a few things."

She pushed her hair behind her ears and peered at them through thick glasses. Underneath them her eyes looked oversized, protruding. Like eggs. "I need to sit down," she said. "My head." She sat on the nearest surface that would hold her, the edge of a box. "I'm prone to migraines. This has been so hard on the family." She looked up at them. "They think he's some sort of terrorist. That's the part that's so confusing. That's the part no one understands. They keep asking about his chemicals. Over and over."

"Chemicals?" Jake asked.

"Like for his darkroom. For developing pictures. He was just setting up one in the basement here. They tore everything apart down there. Took everything."

"Why was he here in Fog Point?" May asked. "Why was he here at this time of year?"

She shook her head. "I don't know. I don't think there was any specific reason." She bent her head forward, her elbows on her knees, and pressed the fingers of both hands into her temples. "I'll be okay in a minute. I just took a pill before you came. It should kick in soon." She sighed. "To answer your question, no, I don't know why he came specifically to this little town now, other than he said he'd figured something out and needed to come here."

"Figured something out?" Jake asked.

"That's what he said. That's all I know. I told the police that."

Jake knelt beside her. "Neil took pictures of terrorists. That's why they're so concerned."

"That was so stupid. That was for a documentary book he was working on. He's a journalist."

"A coffee-table book of terrorists," May said. "How charming." She walked through the house, looking around. A Westminster chime clock on the mantle and a couple of framed photographs of flowers were all that remained. All the good stuff had been taken by the police.

"He also took pictures many years ago at a trial," May said.

"He took pictures at a lot of trials. He used to be with a newspaper until he went freelance."

"The trial was Wesley Stoller's, who was convicted of killing his brother."

With her fingers still pressed to her temples, she said, "Oh, *that* one. He was obsessed with that trial." She looked up at them. "He talked to so many people about that. You would've thought he was the journalist and not just the photographer. He took so many pictures and read everything he could about it."

"Do you know why he was so obsessed with that particular trial?"

She shook her head.

"Had he talked to you about it recently?"

"Just to say that the guy who was convicted of the crime is now out of prison. He'd kept tabs on him all this time."

"Why would he do that?" Jake asked.

"Because he never believed the guy did it. He had his own theory about the whole thing. A theory no one wanted to talk with him about."

"What was his theory?" May asked, walking over to the woman.

"Only Neil knew that. Or you'd have to read his notes or possibly look at his pictures, all of which are missing, I might add."

"Does Neil have any boots here?"

The woman stood up. She hugged her arms as she stood there. "Boots? Why are you asking about boots? He had boots for the marsh. He was taking pictures of the marsh."

"Could we see them?"

"Well, that's a new one. The one thing the police didn't ask about were his boots." She motioned with her hand. "Sure, I don't care. I've been packing up his stuff. The Browngreens, or whoever it is that owns this place, have been on my back to get his stuff out of here. You'd think they'd give us some slack. People in these small towns are just so unfriendly. I tried to get a cup of coffee at this diner place, Noonan's or something? The old man was nice enough because I was a paying customer, but everyone else just stared at me. I just want to get Neil's stuff and get out of here. His boots would probably be on the back porch. Out through the kitchen. If he had any, that's where they'd be."

Two pairs of boots sat next to each other on the porch. Jake and May compared them to the photo Jake had printed from his digital camera. Neither pair matched the photo. They were too small, far too small. Neil Watts was a small man.

Jake snapped a couple of photos of the soles anyway.

"If you don't mind my asking, who are you people?"

"May Williams and Jake Rikker," May said. "We're private investigators, and you are?"

"Private investigators? Hmm…well, I hope you find what you're looking for."

"Do you mind if we look around for a while?" May asked.

"Tear the place apart. I don't care. As you can see, it's kind of a dump anyway. Which is why I can't understand why he rented it. Such a dumpy old place. Why wouldn't he rent something closer to the water? He wanted to take pictures of the marsh. Why wouldn't he get one of those apartments right on the water? Those condos? Neil was doing okay for himself. He'd made some money. Not me. I live in a trailer park. But Neil was such a good brother. He visited so often and helped out."

May and Jake spent the next hour looking through closets, behind dressers, in basement cubbyholes, in drawers, and behind furniture. They didn't find much. It was like picking over a garage sale two hours after the sale began. If Watts kept notes about the Wesley Stoller trial, they weren't here.

Deciding it was time to leave, May and Jake made their way toward the door. Neil's sister, who was sitting quietly on the living-room couch, said, "Can you please let me know if you find something? Here, I'll give you my card. I know this doesn't have anything to do with terrorism. Neil was a good person. He would never have been involved in terrorism. He would never..."

50

Outside, the sun contrasted blindingly with the darkly carpeted and heavily draped house they had just left. May pulled her Squirrels cap more firmly down over her eyes and squinted at Jake, who was taking yet another furtive glance in the direction of Elise's.

"She's not there, Jake," May said. "Keep in mind what I said, okay? I don't trust her."

"You never did, May."

May nodded toward Lenore Featherjohn's. "Hey, you want to try that place for boots? You feeling lucky?"

"Sure."

Lenore seemed pleased to see them, invited them in, told them to come back to the kitchen and out onto the deck for tea. "I'm making tea for my guests, my first guests of the season," she whispered. "And tomorrow they're going out on the *Freesia*."

"Hope it doesn't sink," May muttered to Jake.

"What we really want," Jake said, "is to look at Carl's or Earl's boots."

She squinted at them. "Carl keeps his boots on the boat, May. I already told you that. What do you need to see their boots for anyway?"

"We're measuring something," May said.

"We're *measuring* something?" Jake whispered to May when they were alone in the mud room.

"Sure. We're measuring the tread. To see if it matches the tread in the picture you took."

"You know we have to stay for tea," Jake said.

"No, we don't. We get these pictures, and we just leave. If I have to spend another afternoon making cinnamon swirls, I'll turn into a vampire and suddenly want to kill something."

"No. We stay. She is an absolute repository for gossip. She knows things. She looks out her windows. She may not know that she knows things, but she does. I vote we stay for tea."

About half a dozen boots belonging to either Carl or Earl littered the mud-room floor. Jake turned over each one and lined them up.

"Anything?" May asked.

"Close, but no cigar."

"What about these?" May grabbed an extremely muddy pair next to Lenore's washing machine.

Jake turned them over and placed the photo next to them.

He said, "Houston, we have liftoff."

May bent closer. "So do we take this to the police now or later?"

"I don't know. All this tells us is that one of the Featherjohn brothers stood in Elise's garden underneath the eaves. It doesn't mean that either one of them was there that morning."

"Still, two witnesses saw Carl."

Jake took more pictures, then they went back inside for tea. May chose green tea again out of the wicker basket, and Jake chose peppermint. They drank tea and ate cinnamon swirls while Lenore talked about the *Freesia* and her boys and all the preparations they were making. "But you know that cook they hired? JoMarie?"

Jake raised an eyebrow and May shrugged.

"That little fling between JoMarie and my Carl didn't last very long. Truth be told, I don't think that girl was very stable. I hope she works out somewhere else, but I have my doubts. Carl could see through her, and I'm glad he was able to before the summer began. But it looks like Carl may have a new flame—Elise. Those two have been spending more and more time together. But I wish Earl would find himself a nice lady friend. He just stays down in that basement day after day, working on those projects of his."

Carl and Elise? Jake blinked. A little smirk formed at the corner of May's mouth.

51

M oon and Cain were flying down the back roads on Moon's Harley. That's what it always felt like to Moon, flying. He could almost forget that he was carrying a passenger, something he'd swore he'd never do. This was the one exception.

"I've found Sarah McCarthy," Moon had told Cain yesterday.

"That was quick."

"I'm a professional. When you hire a professional, you get professional work."

"Did you find the others yet?" Cain asked.

"Not yet, but I'm working on it. I should have something by the end of the week."

"But you found Sarah?"

"I did, and I'll take you to her. She's not that far from here."

"No. I think I'd just like the address," Cain said. "I can get there myself."

"How?"

"Bus, maybe. Something." Cain shrugged.

"I have some vacation saved up. I don't mind going. We can go on my Harley," Moon offered.

"Oh, I don't know."

"Really, it's no problem. It's only four hours from here. It's no problem at all. I can wait in a bar while you go and apologize or whatever it is you want to go there for. I've got an extra helmet, extra leathers, and extra boots. What size shoe do you wear?"

Cain paused. "Ten."

"Good, got 'em. We're in business. You ever been on a Harley?"

"Not a Harley. A friend I knew once had a Kawasaki ZX-12R."

Moon shook his head. "If you've never been on a Harley, you've never been on a motorcycle."

And now the two of them happened to be on the back roads on the way to Sarah McCarthy's. It wasn't as if Moon hadn't been there before, though. He'd been there plenty of times. Just like he'd been down to see Fiona. Lots of times, but not on his Harley. Never on his Harley before this trip. Too recognizable. He usually drove his truck. If he didn't want to be recognized, he didn't drive a Harley into a town like Sarah's.

Usually when he came, he'd just park outside her house and watch her come and go. Waiting, waiting.

Moon had made a photocopy of the picture Cain gave him and tacked it up above his computer. Just to remind him. A time long ago Moon had been in love with her—until she, too, betrayed him. Like everyone else. Like his parents and his brothers. Like everyone.

Moon felt the bulge of his Glock on his hip, next to it his Spyderco knife. Two things he always carried. Two things he felt naked without.

Halfway there they pulled into a McDonald's, their one and only stop. Cain ordered a coffee and a Big Mac and fries, and Moon ordered a Coke, a couple of Quarter Pounders, some McNuggets, and super-sized fries. They sat inside, and Moon watched people look at his bike. He liked watching people look at his bike.

"You seem familiar with the roads," Cain said.

"I'm familiar with all roads," he said.

"You like your Hog, don't you?" Cain asked.

"Yeah."

"I keep wondering how can you afford a Harley like that, all customized and everything...if you don't mind my asking."

"I inherited some money. Rich father. He died. Rich Mother. She died. Just call me lucky."

"My father died when he was the age I am now."

"No joke."

"Bar fight."

"Tough break." Moon stared at Cain through his mirrored glasses and wondered if Cain remembered any of that night.

"My mother died when I was sixteen," Moon said. Another lie, of course.

"Your rich mother?"

"Yeah, my rich mother."

Outside, a car cruised by, trailing the rumbling bass of music. "I used to drink a lot. Went to AA in prison," Cain said.

"No kidding. They got AA in prison?"

"They have everything in prison: AA, Bible studies, college classes, even Toastmasters. Everything."

"Toastmasters? What do you want Toastmasters for there?"

Cain shrugged and chuckled quietly. "I don't know. I was in for ten years for something I did when I was so dead drunk I can't remember a thing about it. Whole day's a blank. Next thing I know, they're telling me I shot my own brother."

"Didn't they hypnotize you? Lie detector? Find out what really happened?" Moon leaned forward in his seat. How could Cain not remember anything of that day when Moon remembered every second as if it had just occurred?

Cain shook his head, gulped down his coffee, and wiped his mouth with the back of his hand.

"Your brother's dead, then?" Moon said.

"Yeah."

"My brother's dead too. We got a lot in common."

Cain nodded and pounded a fist gently on the table a few times as if he were leading a board meeting. "I remember being mad at him that day. I can remember that. He was coming on to my wife, the way he always did." He paused, shaking his head. "Sometimes I hated my brother, but I never would have killed him. That's what alcohol does. Makes you do things you wouldn't normally do. That's why I don't touch the stuff anymore."

"Smart move."

Moon finished his Coke, slurped up the bottom through the straw. "Now it's my turn to be curious. Why's it so important that you apologize to this Sarah person?"

"I need to make it right. Step nine—forgiveness."

"Forgiveness," Moon scoffed. "For what?"

"For how I treated her."

"How did you treat her?"

Cain didn't answer. When they got outside, a few people were eyeing Moon's bike.

"This yours?" some guy in a puke-yellow Windbreaker asked him.

"Yup," Moon said. "She's mine."

"Nice."

"Yup."

Even though he always acted like it annoyed him, he loved it when he got to say, "Yep, this is mine. I'm twenty-three and already I own a Harley. And it's paid for, and I got money in the bank and more where that came from."

Back on the road, the scenery sped by them. At a little after two in the afternoon, they made the turn into Sarah's town. And ten minutes later, they were parked in front of Sarah's house.

Cain looked up at it. "So she lives here?"

"Yep, this is the place." It was a big white house with a porch across the entire front with lots of flowers in landscape beds.

"It looks big," Cain said. "It's nice."

"It is. Looks like this Sarah is doing all right for herself," Moon said.

"She's married, isn't she? Do you have that kind of information?"

"She was. Husband died. Car accident. Four years ago."

"Does she have children?" Cain asked.

"No, my sources say no children. She lives here alone now and works for a church. A secretary or something."

"A church."

Moon watched Stoller's face. Cain seemed pensive, nervous. Good. "If you're feeling, you know, a little nervous, I'll walk up there with you."

"That won't be necessary."

"I know it won't be necessary, but I don't mind, really I don't. I know you must be feeling kind of weird right now. I don't mind helping out. That's what friends are for."

Cain walked toward the house, up the flower-lined sidewalk, and Moon stepped in beside him. He laughed when he thought about

Sarah, what she would do, two young hunks at her door, although he had forty pounds of muscle on Cain. Still, Cain was a good-looking guy. Cain had one of those *cute* faces. Moon saw the way some of those young girls at McDonald's looked at him.

"I wonder if anyone's home," Cain said.

"Well, only one way to find out. Ring the bell." And Moon proceeded to do just that.

After a couple of minutes, the sound of feet echoed from inside, and finally the door opened. A woman in a long denim dress and hair in a bun leaned her head out. Whenever Moon saw her, he wondered why she didn't do something to make herself look better, a nice outfit or something. Shorter, for one, lower cut for another.

"Yes?"

She was thirty-two, but she dressed like an old woman. She was still a part of that church her father had started. That's what Moon had found out. Funny the whole thing hadn't shut down by now.

Cain seemed tongue-tied. His eyes were wide, and he just stared. He opened his mouth to say something and then closed it. Then finally he said, "I came to apologize. I want to say I'm sorry, Sarah."

Then she leaned her head forward a bit. "You!" She went to slam the door, but Moon's foot blocked it.

"Please, Sarah. I just want to apologize."

"You can apologize all you want. It doesn't change what you did."

"No, it doesn't. I'm a Christian now, Sarah. I've made a commitment to God to try to make things right. I've served my time and paid for my crime."

Moon found this whole exchange hilarious. He actually had to cough a little to cover up the laughter bubbling up. Sarah was standing there in a denim dress and white socks and Keds, her finger wag-

gling while she repeated, "No, no, no!" Good thing she had no children; he could imagine her waggling that finger in front of them. She
was thin and small and would be pretty, really, if she took her hair out
of that old-lady bun. Wayward frizzes stuck out around her face, as if
she'd been mopping the floor before they came.

Moon also knew that her mother lived with her. She would be
somewhere in a back room, probably, on a hospital bed with a com-
mode across the room and a little color television on a table in the
corner. Maybe Sarah had just come from emptying her bedpan.
Maybe that's why she looked so frazzled.

Moon always wondered how the mother managed to stay alive.
But maybe staying alive was a kind of torture.

"There's nothing," she said, now pointing, "*nothing* you can say
that will make it better. You say you're a Christian. Well, I'm sorry, but
God's grace does not extend to people like you. It does *not!*" Then she
turned to Moon. "And who are you?"

"Just a friend. I came to give him moral support."

"And look at the two of you in your gang clothes. If you don't get
off my property, I'm going to call the police."

She kicked Moon's foot out of the way and slammed the door so
hard that he thought the glass in the front window would shatter.

On the way back to the Harley, Moon said, "Well, that went
well."

Cain hung his head.

Moon slapped him on the back. "Let it go, bro. Leave her. You
tried."

Jake stood at Elise's door and rang her bell while holding a tube of whale posters in one hand and a bouquet of flowers in the other. It'd been a long time since he'd stood at a woman's door with flowers in his hand. He stood there feeling rather foolish, wondering if he was being totally inappropriate and if, perhaps, he had misunderstood. It wouldn't be the first time he'd read the signals wrong in this whole adult dating game or whatever the heck this was.

When he and May had gotten back to the Purple Church, a phone message was waiting for him. From Elise.

She told him that she was really bad with people, especially men. She was so sorry she was being so on-again, off-again, but so much troubled her now. Maybe that was why she was so devoted to her work and art. Maybe that's why she wrote to prisoners. She'd wanted a relationship that wasn't face to face. Face to face scared her. Or maybe she felt she didn't deserve anyone else. It was a long message.

Would Jake forgive her and come for supper?

"I love to cook," she said, "and I don't get the opportunity very often, not with my busy schedule. Plus, Rachel would love to meet with you. She talks about you all the time. She calls you Jake the

Whale Guy. And I do need to clarify some business issues with you too. I have one more check for you."

So what was it, a date where he should bring flowers or wine or a business meeting where he'd bring a notebook and a pen? When he asked May, she only shrugged and said, "How should I know, hot shot?"

Elise met him at the door smiling and exclaimed over the flowers. She led him down the hallway to the kitchen. The kitchen smelled of seafood, and there were three places set at the table. She wore a long dress made of what looked like colorful neck scarves. They draped in different lengths around her calves. She wore long, delicate earrings and high-heeled platform sandals with lace-up ribbons, higher heels than he'd ever seen on her.

Rachel sat at a computer in a small room off the kitchen.

"Rachel," Elise said, "this is Jake."

"We met," the girl said, "when you broke the dish, Mom."

"Hi, Rachel," Jake said.

"If you'll excuse me," Rachel said, "the whales are calling me. You might be interested in this, Jake."

"I'm sure I will be," Jake said as he entered the computer room.

"I plan to be a marine biologist," Rachel said.

"That's a wonderful profession. If I had to do it all over again, that's what I'd be."

"Really?" She looked up at him, obviously surprised.

"Absolutely."

Rachel wore pink corduroy pants and a T-shirt with a butterfly on it. Her red hair was falling out of an unkempt ponytail, more outside the elastic than inside. Although Jake saw some mother-daughter resemblance, Rachel was taller and more solid looking than Elise, and she must have had her father's eyes. Dark and brooding, they were nothing like her mother's.

"I brought a couple of whale posters for you." He laid the tube beside her computer.

"Thank you. If you're interested in whales, look at this Web site."

"Rache, Jake's not interested," Elise called from the kitchen.

"I beg to differ. Of course I am." He looked over Rachel's shoulder. "Whales are my business. I'm always interested in whale information."

"You should link your *Purple Whale* site to this one," she said. "On this site you can click here and listen to whale sounds. Did you know that each clan has a distinctive voice?"

"Can I hear some?"

She clicked on a few links, and for the next ten minutes the two of them listened to whale music.

"Isn't it pretty?" she said.

"It's beautiful. You know a lot about whales. I should hire you for the summer when you're older."

"Do you promise? How old do I have to be?"

"I usually get college kids."

"Well, you remember that, because I'm going to study marine biology. And I'm pretty smart. I might be going to these science Olympics in England. If I can talk my mother into letting me go."

"Rachel," Elise had joined them and now looked at her young daughter. "We've already talked about this."

"I *know,* Mom. You're afraid of me flying all by myself. But I won't be by myself. There's, like, a gazillion chaperones."

"I just…" Elise bit her lip. "I don't trust them with you, darling."

"I'm going to talk you into it," Rachel said. "That's my mission in life now…to talk you into it."

Elise moved toward the computer-room door. She seemed to wear a forced calm when she said, "Jake, how about a glass of wine on the patio?" He said fine.

She led him out to the patio and brought a bottle of wine and two glasses. She'd set a vase on the deck coffee table, his flowers wonderfully and wildly arranged in it. She said, "I got my furniture moved out here."

"I see that." The previously vacant deck now had slatted chairs, a table with an umbrella, and a cushioned two-person swing. "This is nice."

"I like it out here. I come out here at night when the mosquitoes aren't too bad." She gave Jake the wine bottle. "Would you do the honors?"

He uncorked it and poured two glasses.

"I'm so glad Rachel likes you. She doesn't take to people easily. She's a very precocious child."

"She's a nice kid."

"She has trouble making friends sometimes."

"That trip to England sounds interesting, though."

Elise looked past him. "That's a sore spot between us now."

"Oh?"

"The flowers you brought are beautiful," Elise said, effectively changing the subject.

"Thank you."

She jumped up. "I almost forgot. I've got appetizers." He watched her go through the open french doors into her kitchen, the scarves swishing around her calves.

Even out here on the patio, he had the same feeling he had the first time he was here, that the house was vacant, that nobody actually lived here. Oh, there were things around, various interesting sculptures, but nothing that made the place look really lived in.

She returned with a plate of scallops wrapped in bacon, a hunk of Brie cheese, crackers, and a knife.

He picked up a scallop with a toothpick and popped it in his mouth. "You made these? They're wonderful."

"Thanks."

Dinner itself was a seafood casserole with plenty of lobster meat, salad, and french bread. Rachel sat with them and said little, but Jake got the impression that she was watching and listening carefully to everything her mother said. Seeing the two of them together, he noted more differences between them. Elise was fair with pale eyes, as if the artist hadn't quite finished filling in the color when he was called away. Instead, the artist used all the leftover color on his palette on the daughter, endowing her with flaming hair and dark eyes.

Elise and Jake talked about the summer and his sailboat that he promised to take them out on if they were interested. Rachel's eyes brightened at that. Elise told him about the course she was teaching at the craft college in Ridley and about some new whale brooches she was making for the summer tourists. They carefully avoided the subject of the snake eyes. Jake didn't know if this was in deference to Rachel or to Elise.

Rachel excused herself before dessert, saying she had homework to do.

"A kid who *wants* to do homework," Jake commented. "And on a Saturday night."

"Oh, she's a good kid. Just not speaking to me now, that's all."

"Get used to it. She's only eleven. Wait until she's a teenager."

"I just can't allow her to go to England," she said when Rachel left.

"Why not? If Amy's involved, I'm sure it's well chaperoned."

"You know Amy McLaren?"

"She's the wife of one of my best friends, Ben, the minister at Stone Church."

"I can't explain it, but I can't let her go."

Jake said nothing. In many ways it was safer to hop on a plane to England than it was to drive through Ridley Harbor during rush hour. They took their coffee and went out onto the patio again. It was dark by now, and they sat together on the swing. He remembered how her hand felt in his. Across the backyard, through a filigree of trees and underbrush, a few people sat out on the lawn at Feather-john's B&B. The patio lights were on, and their voices tinkled across the trees like coins dropping.

"I still have your earring. I meant to bring it."

"What an awful night."

Jake nodded. He didn't tell her that he had spent some time looking at the earring. He didn't know much about how jewelry was made, but this little piece with its intersecting gold wires and tiny jewels seemed to him to represent Elise herself—tiny, delicate, and easily lost and broken. "Did you find the other one?" he asked her.

She shook her head. "And it was one of a kind. All my jewelry is."

He nodded.

"Are the police any closer to finding the guy who broke into my place?" she asked.

"Not really. Elise, there's something else. We sort of have proof that it was really Carl Featherjohn at your window last week."

"Proof?"

"That boot print belongs to one of Carl's boots."

"Are you sure? Are you absolutely sure?"

"We've taken it to the police."

"Well, I really don't know what to make of that, then." She looked away from him. "I've made such a fool of myself over this whole thing, constantly blubbering."

"You're frightened, Elise. It's nothing to be ashamed of. We all get scared." Jake stopped, then asked, "Elise, does the name Sarah McCarthy mean anything to you?"

Her eyes flickered.

"You know someone by that name, don't you?"

"Where did you hear that name?" she asked.

"The building superintendent where Stoller lives talked about a Sarah McCarthy. Said to ask you about her."

Elise took a long drink of her coffee, then said, "A long time ago I knew someone named Sarah. But Sarah is a common name. It just startled me, your saying that name. The surname McCarthy is unfamiliar to me."

"You're sure?"

They were quiet for a long time, rocking gently in the swing, before she said, "My sister's name was Sarah." She paused. "I need to tell you some things, some things about myself. I think of you not only as a detective but also as my friend. This should help you understand me and Rachel. My father..." Her voice broke and she paused again. "He began this church. His own version of how men and women should relate to one another, which meant women were trodden upon. My father hit my mother on a regular basis. I never told you that part. He beat her if things weren't perfect. If Sunday dinner wasn't perfect. Plus, he had affairs with all the beautiful young things at church. It was his right, as head of this church he made up. So if I act a little crazy sometimes, that's why."

He took her hand. "Norah told me there was abuse in your life."

"You don't know the half of it. My father finally ended up in prison, where he died. I was glad when he died. My sister and I, we learned to get out of his way. For whatever reasons, my mother did not. Sometimes we'd play games. My sister was always playing them. She had this idea that she needed to take care of me. I've always been little, and all my life people have felt they needed to take care of me. I've had to fight to be independent, to have people feel they don't always have to take care of me."

The squeaking noise of the rocking swing was hypnotic to Jake.

She continued, "I grew up in this home where my father beat my mother because it was his God-given right. And then here's the stupid thing. I went out and got married when I was seventeen to the same kind of guy. He beat me. Not because it was his God-given right but because he was usually drunk.

"Next door to us lived this family, and they had these sons who were so cool. I especially liked the middle one. He was beautiful, and I fell in love with him and he with me, or so I thought. Long story short, I got pregnant. My father said I had deeply shamed him and so he kicked me out, told me never to come back home again. Never. So I never did. My boyfriend and I got married. I jumped from the frying pan into the fire and ended up in a more abusive situation than my family home. Yeah, my father was abusive, but my husband was abusive *and* an alcoholic. One of life's little ironies."

"Do you have any contact with your sister or mother now?"

"My father died of cancer. In prison. Which is quite fitting, since his whole life was a cancer. My husband died too. A car accident before Rachel was born. Dead drunk. It was just fortunate he didn't take anyone out with him when he drove into that tree. I've lost track of my mother and my sister. Rachel doesn't know about the kind of man her father was. But I'm sure she wonders why she's never seen a picture of him."

Elise crossed one leg over the other. In the evening chill she drew a throw around her shoulders, one of several blankets she had draped on the porch furniture.

"Is St. Dennis your father's name?"

"I kept my married name. I would never keep his name. I had two choices: keep the last name of a man who beat the crap out of my mother on a daily basis or keep the name of a man who beat me and threatened his own daughter."

"I thought you said he died before Rachel was born."

"She was a baby when he died."

Jake's narrowed his eyes. Hadn't she just told him that Rachel's father had died before she was born? He tried hard to remember.

After a while she sighed, played with a corner of the throw with her fingers. Finally she looked up at him. "Okay, I've told you my sad story. Why don't you tell me your sad story?"

"My story is very boring, and how do you know it's sad?"

"There is a sadness about you, Jake. I can see it in your eyes."

Someone over at Featherjohn's laughed.

He shrugged and told her about Connie and Deacon Keith. He even told her about their little kid, Mickey, his two daughters, how he almost killed Keith, and how sometimes he wished he had.

"You almost killed him because you still love your wife."

He was quiet for a while, then said, "I loved her once. It was a long time ago." He thought about the picture and the redwood trees and how he had loved his funny, little brown-haired pixie who played the flute in their college orchestra. How he had loved watching her play. He had once loved her with everything in him. "Then she left. And I left."

"But now you're here."

"Now I'm here."

53

Late that night, after Jake had gone, Elise put the dishes in the dishwasher and tidied up the kitchen. He'd wanted to kiss her good-night. She knew that. But she couldn't. She had backed away. And she would keep backing away until this whole thing was over and she was free to begin again. She filled the casserole dish with water and set it in the sink to soak.

When she finished cleaning up, she took her cigarettes outside to the patio with a glass of wine. Her dear father should see her now. Cigarettes, a glass of wine, earrings, and don't forget the shorn hair.

What was that whole dinner thing tonight about, anyway? Who did she think she was, leading him on like this?

That she should grow up to make jewelry in a home where jewelry was forbidden was the ultimate irony. Elise had always liked glittery things. When she was a little girl, she liked the way the sunlight came in through the bedroom window and made patterns of color on the walls. Sometimes she would crumple up a piece of plastic wrap and tape it to the window in such a way that it reflected and diffused the light all over the room. She would lay with her head over the edge of her bed and watch it. The boy next door had a kaleidoscope that she looked through for hours.

Elise made her first piece of jewelry when she was eleven, Rachel's age now. On top of someone's garbage can on the street where they lived, Elise had found a pair of gaudy gold earrings with stones missing. She grabbed them and put them in the pocket of her long skirt. At home in their bedroom she put them on, clipping them to her earlobes. Sarah looked at her, horrified, and gasped, both hands to her mouth. The funny thing was, the earrings didn't feel foreign or strange to her. They felt natural, like her ears had been expecting them all along.

As a child, sometimes she would take them out from under her bed at night. The gold paint was flecking off. If she stuck her fingernail underneath the paint, whole patches came away. Underneath was a kind of hard plastic, pale blue and ugly. She got some of her father's white paint from the shed in the back and painted them carefully with a Q-tip. She discovered that when the paint was still wet, all kinds of things adhered to it. Tiny shells, pieces of sand, colored paper from magazines.

One day she found a whole box of jewelry for a quarter at a garage sale. She and Sarah were biking past, their long skirts whipping against the bike frames, and there it was, the forbidden fruit—a shoe box full of costume jewelry. A whole box for a quarter. Elise had dipped her hands into the box, loving the cool feel of the jewels.

"I'm going to get these."

"You can't!" Sarah said.

"Sure I can. Here's my quarter that I found."

"But…"

"Halloween party?" the woman asked as she took Elise's quarter and handed her the box.

Elise nodded while Sarah stood open-mouthed. That was another thing they weren't allowed to participate in. Never Halloween, that most sinful of holidays. "No," Sarah said. "Not Halloween! A dress-up party."

"Same difference," the woman said going back to her lawn chair and thermos.

Elise kept the jewelry in a box under the bed. Sometimes when her parents were out, she would put on all the necklaces, every single one. Then she'd tie up her hair, pretending it was short, and prance around like a fancy lady.

Sometimes she would take apart the strands and redo them, stealing thread from her mother's sewing box to make new designs.

She made little necklaces for her Barbie dolls. And cut their hair. Her mother found the jewelry and the dolls under her bed and told her to get rid of them at once. The threat was there; it was unmistakable. *I'll tell your father.*

So she moved them to the secret fort. A place only she and Sarah knew about. But then their father found the jewels and the earrings, and all were taken from her. She cried and cried while Sarah hugged her under the covers.

"At least it's not snowing…"

"At least there isn't a hole in our roof and it's raining on us…"

"At least there aren't bugs in our bed…"

"I would die for you…"

"We'd die for each other…"

"I would kill for you…"

"We'd kill for each other…"

54

Q uestions about Elise persisted, despite Jake's wonderful evening with her. It was Monday at noon, and Jake and Ben
were eating lunch at Noonan's Café when Nootie came over and asked
Jake if he liked the lobster casserole.

He grinned up at her. "I'm sure it's fine, Nootie, but today I feel
more like a hamburger."

"We're going for two Buzz Burgers," Ben said.

"With the works," Jake added.

"No, silly!" She chuckled. "I *know* you boys ordered hamburgers.
They're on the grill as we speak. I'm talking about Saturday night,
Jake—the lobster casserole."

"Pardon?"

"For Elise. I don't cook big meals the weekends. I kind of take it
as my day off, but Elise said she needed it for a special guest. You. So I
made the casserole."

Jake stared at her, and his world, already shifting sideways, shifted
a bit more. First the earring and now Nootie was asking about lobster
casserole. Did he like it?

"Yes," he responded. "It was fine." But his voice was barely au-
dible. But why was this even a problem? Elise never actually said she

made the casserole from scratch, had she? It was just implied. Or maybe it wasn't. And what did it matter? Why should that matter?

"Jake?" Ben waved a hand in front of Jake's face. "Hello? You okay, buddy?"

"Fine."

"For a moment there I thought we were going to have to call the paramedics."

"Something just came over me, that's all. It's nothing."

How could he share with his good friend about Elise? When he was with her, there was nothing he wanted to do more than listen to her, understand her pain. He wanted to protect her. But when he was away from her, he doubted everything she said. Her husband died when Rachel was a baby by driving into a tree. Her husband died before Rachel was born by driving off a bridge. She said she never spoke to Neil Watts, yet he'd seen her doing just that.

Plus, there was a little matter of her earring. The so-called one-of-a-kind earring she'd lost. He'd seen its match only that morning at her studio.

Earlier Jake had stopped by Elise's Creations to say hello. Jess greeted him.

"How was the jewelry conference?" she asked him with a grin.

"Oh, just peachy."

She laughed. "And you saw Elise. I know that because she told me all about it. Come on back and wait. She should be in shortly."

"I could come back."

But she had grabbed his arm and started dragging him toward the office in the back. "Have a cup of coffee and wait."

Jake sat and waited. Five minutes. He really needed to get to the Purple Church. May would have his head if she knew he was sitting waiting in Elise's office just to say good morning, especially when they had a kayak trip in the morning and a whale-watching trip that afternoon. Plus, with all this Elise business, he hadn't taken the *Purple Whale* out to look for the whales himself.

He got up, walked around, stuffed his hands in his pockets, took them out. Jewelry rested in boxes, some on shelves waiting to be boxed. Pretty stuff. She was really quite talented. Maybe it was just her artistic temperament. Artists were a different breed, weren't they?

And there, sitting by itself on a shelf, was the match of the earring on his dresser. The one she said she lost. The one she lost in the bramble bushes as she raced to his apartment and sat crouched next to the stove. Again, so what? She must've retraced her steps and found it. Maybe. He picked it up and looked at it.

Then there was her photo album. May had told him about that. "She takes pictures of all her stuff, and then she goes and exposes film when she takes it out of the camera? Think about it, Jake."

"... daughters arrive?" Ben was asking now.

Jake regarded his friend blankly.

"You really are on another planet. Are you sure you're okay?"

"I'm fine." *Snap out of it.* "What were you asking about my daughters?"

"I wondered when they're coming."

"Jana comes in a couple of weeks. Alex later."

"We'll have them over when they come. I think Jana is pretty close to Blaine's age." Blaine was Ben's daughter.

"That'll be nice."

Halfway through Jake's Buzz Burger, Amy arrived, breezy and blustery. Her blousy jacket had a sailboat on it. "Hey," she called. "I'm glad you guys are still here. Wanted to show you something, Jake. You remember at our house when you said you thought that Elise's husband was dead?"

He nodded.

"Well, I don't think he is."

Jake closed his eyes just for a second.

She sat down across from them and laid a file folder in front of Jake. "At least I don't think he was dead when Rachel was registered for school six years ago. So I thought you might be interested to see this." She spoke quietly and quickly. "This is her registration questionnaire, plus a letter Elise wrote to the school. Photocopies. I'd get in major trouble if they knew I copied these. But let me get coffee. I'm dying for coffee."

There were two sheets of paper in the file. Jake read the top one:

> To Whom It May Concern:
> A lot of my papers and personal documents,
> including Rachel's immunization records and her
> birth certificate, were destroyed in a house fire when
> Rachel was a baby. I have written the public-
> health unit in the city where she was born, plus the
> state government for her birth certificate, and will
> get these to you as soon as they come in. They told
> me it might take six weeks to six months to get
> these replaced. I hope Rachel can attend school
> while we wait for the documents to arrive.
> Elise St. Dennis

When Amy returned, coffee in hand, she said, "Last night I was lying in bed, and I got to thinking about Elise. She seemed so pleased that Rachel had been chosen for this special science Olympics for girls until I mentioned that Rachel would need a passport. And to get a passport, you need a birth certificate. I got to thinking, *that's* really what this is all about.

"So I looked in the school records, and there is nothing on Rachel St. Dennis. No birth certificate. Not even a place of birth. You notice in her letter that Elise carefully maneuvered around a place of birth. Rachel's gone to school here for her entire school career, and yet we have no birth certificate. There is nothing to indicate where or when she was born."

Jake looked at the note. "Maybe that's what really happened. A house fire." But even as he said it, doubts niggled at his mind.

"Yeah, and if you believe that, I've got a bridge for sale… We have nothing here. For all new students, we require an immunization record and birth certificate, some form of ID. We received nothing."

"How did they let her in school, then?" Ben asked.

"Fog Point is a small town. You probably couldn't get away with this in a big city. I would even say you couldn't get away with this in Ridley Harbor. It was one of those things that seemed of little importance after a while. Rachel is bright and she does well in school. Elise is part of this community. All those things. The school forgot about it, and eventually it became unimportant."

"You said you think that Rachel's father is still alive," Jake said.

"Page two," Amy said. "The questionnaire. There are major gaps in it."

Jake skimmed through it. There were questions like family dynamics, divorce, ages of siblings. Elise had checked single parent but had left blank the question asking if it was divorce or death. There were a number of questions requiring essay responses as well as statements on discipline and what she deemed the child's strengths or weaknesses. Whole sections were left blank.

Amy said, "I guess this is where I got the idea that her husband is still alive. She checked divorced rather than widow. Plus, I remember a conversation she and I had a number of years ago. Maybe six years ago now. We were fairly new in the community. I was at the school, not Rachel's teacher, but there just the same. And I remember seeing this very small woman with her beautiful red-haired daughter. And I think I made some comment about Rachel's red hair and how she must take after her father, and Elise said that thinking about Rachel's father was a pastime she didn't often engage in. They were here because he was abusive, and they needed to get away from him. In other words, I got the impression they were hiding out here. I think I made some comment then that this would be a good place because Fog Point is really off the beaten path. I think at the time I was kind of stunned. First that she would share this with me and, thinking about it now, if that's what she told the principal or the school officials, they would've been more lenient in letting Rachel in."

Jake lined up the papers, put them back in the file, and handed it to Amy.

To my mother, who hangs around totally geek Carl too much,
I'm glad you invited Jake the Whale Guy over for dinner the
other night. He's kind of a cool guy, and I want to get a summer job with him when I get to be in college, because you
know I want to study to be a marine biologist, and he could
use a good marine biologist for his whale-boat operation. And
can you imagine how fun that would be? To be out there
telling people about whales?

But that's not what I want to write about here. I want to
write about Carl, because no sooner had Jake the Whale Guy
gone home and you cleaned up, you went out on the deck with
your cigarette. And after a while sleaze-face Carl Featherjohn
comes over. From my window I see him sauntering over, duck-
ing through the break in the hedges along the back. I could
see him come, but I can't hear what you guys are talking about.
That's one bummer about my bedroom being up here. I can
see people down there, but I can't hear exactly what they're
saying.

I can hear this soft murmuring. Sometimes I hear a laugh.

It's like you're old buddies, the two of you sitting down there and talking away for a long time. I watched you pour a glass of wine for him. I saw the smoke from your cigarette, a little dancing ghost shape. I watched you go in and get the leftover fish thingy we ate. I heard the microwave ding, so I guess you must've heated it up. Then I watched you put the rest on a plate for Carl.

I think this is weird. Jake the Whale Guy comes over, and then after he goes, you're sitting on the patio smoking with slimy Carl?

The thing that is like the weirdest is that you never go out with any guys. You told me once that it was because you were so in love with my father, that when he died, you just couldn't think of anyone else. If that's true, then how come I've never even seen a picture of him? My own father.

Oh, I forgot. You went out once with Colin Nation. This was a long time ago, when I was little. I even had a baby-sitter. Now the only person who ever baby-sits me is Jess. Or if you know you have to be somewhere, you ask me to see if I can go to Ashley's. So anyway, this one time I get a baby-sitter, and you're getting all dressed up. And then Colin comes to the door, and he's all dressed up, and like Jake, he's carrying flowers. (I think when guys show up with flowers, it's kind of dorky.)

So you went out, but here's the weird thing: You were back like before I was even asleep! And you never went out with him again. You never went out with anyone again. Until Jake the Whale Guy.

Colin Nation is married now, and they live right behind us,

and they even have a baby. See, I could've had a baby brother. Weird!

Last week I saw you do something really funny. You had your good boots, the suede ones with the really high heels, and you're out in the back where there's dirt along the house, and you're sitting on the deck and putting mud on your boots with a rag.

I was in the kitchen drinking milk. I go out and say, "What're you doing?"

You got all flustered and said, "I'm cleaning them! They got dirty!"

But to me, it looks like you're putting mud on them. Why are you doing that, Mom? I don't understand how you can hang around Geek Carl when that nice Jake is there? I love you, but sometimes I just don't understand you.

Your daughter,

Rachel St. Dennis

~

Whale Ears
By Rachel St. Dennis

To help them find their prey and to help them find each other, whales have the ability to do something called echolocation. Think of the two words echo and location. Their heads make these sounds that bounce off objects. Sometimes the sound is a clicking sound. This lets them know where they are and what's out there to eat.

This helps whales find their way through the black and choppy waters of the ocean. They just swim right through and know exactly where they are. I think it's neat that whales can do this. We have the lights of the sun and the moon to guide us, but sometimes at night it would be nice to be able to do this, to have our own built-in radar system. If I could do this, I could hear anyone who came to the patio below my window.

56

I am going to blow up my own small town. I have already set bombs in locations known only to me—under the public wharf, at the bus stop, in the basement of city hall.

It is quite a brilliant plan, really, doing this. Getting back at all of them. Those teachers, all of them who paid no attention to this dying, sick...

Jake put the papers down on the closest surface, an upside-down barrel, and looked over at Carrie. "So this is what he wrote."

She nodded but didn't look at him. "So you can see why the police were all over him, can't you?"

He nodded.

"But," she sighed, "I should have believed him. I should've understood that none of this was real. All of us, the police, all of us, should have believed him. We jumped to the wrong conclusions. All of us did."

They were in Pop's shop, standing among the discarded engine parts and boards and containers of oil. It was where she chose to meet, possibly, according to May, because she didn't want to bump into the FBI men who were still wandering around Fog Point.

"You'd think that bus stop would've tipped them off," Jake said.

"I didn't see that, Jake, and I'm his sister!"

The sun filtered through the grimy panes, flecking her skin, the frown, the marks around her eyes. He wondered if she had slept at all since this whole thing started.

"There are no bus stops in Fog Point," Jake said. "Unless you count the Greyhound stop out on the highway."

"And," she pointed out, "there is no city hall."

"There's only a town office, which hardly qualifies as a city hall." Jake picked up the two sheets of paper and read them in their entirety. It was a master plan for blowing up a town, complete with where to put the bombs. But more than that, it was a cry for help from a young man who had always been on the fringes of society. It talked about a group called The Edges, who were planning this. Just at the part where Stuart was being coerced by members of The Edges, the writing stopped. "Is this all we have?" Jake asked.

Carrie nodded. "That's all any of us had, but it was enough for the police, the FBI, Homeland Security. Did you see the mess they made of the wharf looking for the so-called bomb? And with the tourists arriving any minute now."

"The police have to check everything. That's their job."

"But to jump to such horrific conclusions." Carrie brushed a hand through her hair, fiddled with a strand before tucking it behind her ear. "My brother and that Neil Watts involved in some sort of terrorist sleeper cell? It's crazy."

"When in actuality you should be quite proud of him." Jake tapped his fingers on the papers. "This is quite good writing."

Stuart had been writing a novel. All along he was writing a novel. Safely in the hospital and back on his medications, he'd called Carrie in. He had something to tell her. "Tell them, Carrie," he had said. "Tell them how much I read spy novels. Tell them I'm writing one."

Slowly, slowly, as she sat beside him in his confined hospital room, with the guard out in the hallway, what he said began to make sense. She listened to him and then called Jake. A fanciful dreamer, Stuart had been merely working on a piece of fiction.

She picked up the paper now and skimmed through it. Jake watched the furrow of her brow, the way her thin lips pursed, the way she kept fiddling absently with her hair, a finger twirling the ends of it. He remembered that. That's what she always did when she was nervous.

"May told me to call you, Jake," she had said. "Otherwise I wouldn't have bothered. I know you're busy."

"Carrie, I'm not too busy for you. I'm never too busy for you."

She didn't say anything to that because, of course, that had not been entirely true.

"He says all the books and magazines and Web sites were for research."

"Do you believe him?"

She nodded. "And I've tried to persuade the police of this, but they're still holding him. I don't know how to make them understand that he was writing a book. I showed them all his poetry. I even found a chat room where he was getting online critiques of it. May said that you might have some connection with the police, that you might be able to persuade them."

"I'll try, Carrie. I'll see where they are with this."

"Thank you, Jake."

~

57

According to the report May was reading, Wesley Stoller was the second of three sons, David, Wesley, and Warren. His mother worked two jobs to support them. His father went from job to job and was often away. Every month or so he would come home for a couple of weeks. The report noted that these were never pleasant times for the family.

Hospital records indicate that Wesley's mother was admitted on seven separate occasions for injuries ranging from a broken nose to a broken wrist to general cuts and bruises. Wesley's father was arrested, but no charges ever stuck. Wesley's upbringing also included a parade of men who lived with his mother when his father was away.

Neighbors at the time pointed out that the father directed much of his rage at the youngest son, Warren. Wesley told a psychologist at the time that he wanted to stand up for his younger, smaller brother but was afraid his father's wrath might fall on him instead.

Psychologist: Why did your father pick on him?

Wesley: Because he could. Warren was small.

Psychologist: Did your mother ever stick up for Warren?

Wesley: No. She never stuck up for any of us.

Psychologist: How did you get along with David?

Wesley: We got along fine. We were closer in age. It was just Warren that no one liked. David was my best friend when I was little. He was my only friend.

Psychologist: What about Warren?

Wesley: He always wanted to butt in. We hated him.

May adjusted her glasses. *Interesting.*

When Wesley was twenty-two, he married the girl next door, a pretty girl named Fiona Beechim. In that short-lived marriage, Wesley found himself mirroring his father's behavior. Whenever Fiona did or said something that upset him, he would hit her. She became like his mother to him. In a vicious cycle, the more he hit her, the more she became like his mother. And the more she personified his mother, the more he hit her.

At the time of David's death, Wesley, Fiona, and David were living in a trailer at the Golden Spruce Mobile Home Park. They were in business together and were hoping to start a lawn-care service, which met with only spotty success—literally—at best. Wesley and Fiona had a daughter, Ruthie, who was a year old at the time of David's death.

May was reminded of the Featherjohn brothers, going into one failed business venture after another. She kept reading.

According to neighbors, Wesley and David disagreed about everything to do with the lawn-care business. They often fought over money. Neighbors reported hearing late-night arguments.

May put the report down and took off her glasses.

One of these arguments escalated one night when Wesley took a gun and aimed it at his brother. He always maintained that he was too drunk to remember anything. All the evidence collected at the scene pointed to Wesley as the killer.

He served ten years of a life sentence and was now out on parole.

58

There are some things you need to know about Sarah," Moon said. "Things I just learned. My research has uncovered certain, shall we say, character flaws."

"I already know her."

"No, you don't. Not everything. Not about her husband. Not about her father."

They were sitting in Cain's favorite Starbucks again, but what the hey; at least Cain was talking to him. One of his rules: When marks felt comfortable, he got more out of them.

"What about Sarah's husband?"

"Well"—Moon dunked his almond biscotti into his latte with the extra shot of espresso, extra hot—"this is something you're going to be interested in."

"Okay, tell me."

"I know meeting Sarah to try to *apologize* to her"—Moon tried to keep the sarcasm out of his voice when he said the word—"didn't go so well."

"So much for step nine."

"Okay, anyway." He pointed his biscotti at Cain. "Around ten years ago her father dies in a car accident…"

"Yeah, I already know that. So?"

"And six years ago her husband dies in a car accident."

"So?"

"It was the same sort of car accident, bro. Her father, well, his car was so totaled that they couldn't figure out what caused it, but it may have been that the brakes were tampered with. Now Sarah's husband, well, the brakes were definitely tampered with. So the police were screaming murder. It's been six years, and it's still under investigation. What's interesting is that Sarah's husband was a recent convert to the Church of Power and Fire. He was the one who took over the ministerial duties after Sarah's father died. And so when Papa died, all the church money went to Sarah's mother."

"There was never very much money in that church. Not from what I remember."

Moon grinned. "You're wrong there, buddy. This McCarthy character? He came to the church with a whole lot of ideas about raising money. The two of them—this McCarthy fellow and Sarah's father— well, they ended up profiting from McCarthy's know-how. The two of them were like this." Moon crossed his fingers. "So what I'm saying is this. Sarah's mother inherited a nice little nest egg when her husband conveniently died. But not long after that, Sarah's mother conveniently gets sick. So who takes over the church? You guessed it—Sarah. And she marries this McCarthy fellow. That Sarah, she is good."

Cain stared at Moon.

"I'm just saying"—Moon took the last bite of his biscotti—"that if I were you, I'd steer clear of that family. They are not nice people."

"No." Cain was shaking his head. "You don't understand. I need to see Fiona."

"Why?"

"At my trial she testified against me. My own wife. I've had a long time to think about this, but I know now that that was the only thing she could've done. That she did the right thing, the honest thing. She reported what she saw. And I want to apologize for hating her for doing the right thing. For ten years a vision has haunted me. And as soon as I became a Christian, I knew I had to find her and apologize."

"A vision has haunted you? You mean like a ghost?" Moon waved his arms and said, "Woo, woo."

"No." Cain smiled. "A vision, like a memory. I remember the last time I saw her. It's something I'll never forget. She was standing there. She had this really long, whitish blond hair, and when they led me out of the courthouse at the end, I was stumbling in those leg irons…"

"Oh, tough break."

"And I looked back and said really loud, 'I'll get you for this, Fiona. I'll come back and kill you if it's the last thing I do.' That's what I said to her. I need to find her now, to tell her I'm sorry. That I would never do that. I would never kill her."

"You're a changed man." Again Moon tried to keep the sarcasm disguised.

"Right."

"And you want to live happily ever after with Fiona."

"I can't expect that. I don't expect that. She's probably remarried by now. We were divorced when I was in prison. A lawyer brought me the papers, and I signed them. I assume she did that because she wanted to get married. I really can't blame her. I wasn't a very good husband."

"Okay, then, I've saved the best news for last. I have Fiona's phone number."

"You do? Why didn't you tell me this sooner?"

"This is sooner. I've only had it since this afternoon."

"No, I meant like first thing instead of telling me about Sarah? Do you have her address?"

"No can do. At least not yet. It's not like the old days when if you had a telephone number, you went into a crisscross and got an address. Not in this day and age of cell phones." Moon was always impressed how he could schmooze his way out of anything. Because now, with the Internet, it was actually easier to get an address than in the old days. But Cain was nodding, idiot that he was, and actually believing this shovel full of crap.

Moon placed on the table a piece of paper with ten digits on it. "Her phone number."

"Thank you," Cain said.

"So now you can call her. Maybe she'll give you her address. Maybe she'll tell you to hit the road. Who knows?"

Moon unhooked his cell phone from his belt and placed it on the table. "Here, call her from here while I take a trip to the little boys' room. Use my phone."

"You sure?"

"Sure I'm sure. My long-distance calls cost me practically nothing. I get a special plan because I'm a building super."

The transcripts of Stoller's trial had come as an e-mail attachment, and May skimmed through them. The trial had taken place in New Brunswick, New Jersey.

Fiona Stoller, having been called as a witness, being duly sworn, testified as follows…

May had gotten past all the preliminaries and came to this testimony by Wesley Stoller's wife.

She looked at her address. The Golden Spruce Mobile Home Park in New Brunswick. There was that New Jersey connection again.

Q: Mrs. Stoller, can you tell the court what you saw on the date in question, September 14, 1995.

A: I was feeding Ruthie. We were in the corner of the living room. I heard this commotion outside. It was Wesley coming home with Dave. They were arguing. I…[indistinguishable words].

Q: Speak up, Mrs. Stoller, so the jury can hear you. What did you hear?

A: I got scared. They fought so often. So I put Ruthie back in her playpen and waited. I was so afraid.

Q: What were you afraid of?

A: That he would kill me. You have no idea what he was like.
I thought he would kill me. He beat me. All the time he beat
me. I was so afraid of him, and Dave, too. And after Dave
came to live with us, it only got worse. Dave didn't hit me, but
he belittled me all the time. Made fun of me. And…"

Q: And what?

A: He raped me.

There were a couple of objections here. May skimmed and got back
to the story.

Q: Go back to the night in question, Mrs. Stoller.

A: I was setting the table. That's another thing. If supper wasn't
ready, Wesley would hit me. So I was setting the table, and
when they came in, I saw that Dave had a gun.

Q: Had you seen this gun before?

A: No. I had never seen a gun before. We never had a gun. Both
of them were drunk and on drugs, I think. I got really afraid
because they were fighting. Wes said Dave owed him rent,
then Wesley punched him, and they started fighting, fist fighting. I mean they'd gotten into scuffles before, but nothing like
this. And then Dave aimed the gun at Ruthie. She was in her
playpen laughing, and Dave was aiming the gun at her. I
screamed. He called me stupid and a coward.

There were a few more objections by the defense counsel that May
passed over, like skipping the boring parts of a novel.

Q: What did you do then, Mrs. Stoller?

A: I grabbed Ruthie and ran. I heard a shot when I was down at
the end of the driveway, holding her.

Q: Did you actually see Wesley pull the trigger and shoot his
brother?

A: No, but I heard it. I heard the shot. I came back, looked in the doorway, and saw Dave on the floor.

Q: Where was Wesley at this time?

A: Passed out on the couch. The gun was still in his hand.

Q: What did you do then, Mrs. Stoller?

A: I called my sister.

Q: Why did you call your sister instead of calling the police?

Another objection. May moved on…

A: I was afraid. My sister would know what to do. She's always taken care of me. I didn't know what I was doing. So she came and calmed me down and then we called the police.

May took off her glasses and rubbed her eyes. Most neighbors claimed they heard one shot, but one neighbor said there were two shots, and he maintained this position throughout the trial. According to forensics, only one shot was fired.

May got out the pictures she'd printed from the trial, the ones Neil Watts had taken. One of Wesley, one of David. But it was the crowd scenes she was most interested in. She put her glasses back on and stared at the images. The picture of the mother and the baby and the little girl caught her attention. She studied it. The one she assumed was the mother looked too young now to be a mother, especially of a teenage girl. Sisters? They had to be sisters; an older sister and a younger sister, perhaps?

She focused on the older sister. She held the baby in one arm, and the other arm was up trying to shield the younger girl from the camera. Her mouth was shaped like an *O*. At first glance the younger girl looked about twelve or thirteen. May studied her. Her hair was blond and hung long and tangled down her back. She was in profile to the camera, the two of them captured in that moment by Neil Watts.

A moment later, and her head would've been turned. May looked at that young girl, the pale eyebrows, the nose, slightly down turned at the end. Yes, she looked young and probably always looked younger than she was, somehow. Neil Watts knew. And he had come to Fog Point. He had moved in beside her.

She punched in Jake's cell number. "Jake, call me immediately; I've got something here. Call me right away."

Sarah sent her another article today. In this one, a woman in a cult group had shot and killed her abusive husband. The courts were being lenient. She added it to the shoe box.

Elise was quite proud of herself. Carl had put up some man-sized targets at the stone quarry, and she was getting quite good at hitting them. Right in the center, right in the chest. *That's where you aim, darlin', the biggest mass. Not the head, unless you're right up close, but the chest, and you'll bring the bad guy down.*

She practiced with her gun just about every other day now. Sometimes she drove out to the quarry by herself, driving up and down around the ruts like Carl did. It was getting easier. It hadn't rained in a few days, so the spring puddles were drying up. She would stand back and aim at the man-sized targets. She gave her targets names—Wesley, Wesley, and Wesley. And she shot them all right in the heart. She was getting really good at it.

The sun fought to come out as Jake maneuvered the *Constant* past the moorings. A gentle ten-knot breeze was blowing, perfect for someone like Elise who'd never been sailing before. It was a breeze that would ruffle past her hair and take the heat off a warm day, but it wasn't enough to send the crew scrambling. It was the sort of breeze to set the sail and sit back and really enjoy the day. It was the sort of breeze to set the autopilot and then confront a passenger about a lie in her past.

Elise sat in the cockpit and smiled up at Jake as he stood behind the wheel. She had no idea why she was here, and that was fine with Jake.

"It's a gorgeous day," he'd told her on the phone. "Take two hours off and come away with me."

"I can't possibly," she said. "I've got jewelry to make and a shop to run. How can I take time off with a shop to run and summer almost here?"

"I can't believe you've never played hooky. I'm sure Jess can manage."

"Can May manage?"

"May can more than manage. She'll kill me for sneaking off, but she'll manage."

Truth was, he was out there with May's blessing. And truth was, he was dead tired, and as much as he loved sailing, today it was the last thing on earth he felt like doing with Elise.

He and May had spent an entire day looking at pictures and confirming facts on the phone. He was reluctant, but yes, he had to agree with May. Elise St. Dennis was indeed Fiona Stoller, wife of Wesley Stoller, and formerly Fiona Beechim, daughter of Lester Beechim, who was the leader of a quasi-religious group known as the Church of Power and Fire. Not quite a cult, but the next closest thing. Rachel St. Dennis was Ruth Stoller, daughter of Fiona and Wesley, and a baby at the time of Wesley's incarceration. Sarah McCarthy was formerly Sarah Beechim, sister of Fiona and sister-in-law of Wesley Stoller.

Elise, or Fiona, or whoever she was, had testified against her husband and then disappeared.

At first Jake said, "So what? Her husband is an abuser and a convicted killer, and she wants to disappear? Let her. That's her right."

"Okay, then, Jake," May said, pouring him coffee from the second pot she'd made, while they sat on her screened-in porch. "Then why bring us into the mix? If you want to stay hidden, why make up some cockamamie story about him being an e-mail pen pal? Just go about your business and hope that he doesn't find you."

They'd gone back and forth, adding things to the mix: the face at the window, Elise's seeming friendship with Carl, the murder of Neil Watts, who was, according to his sister, obsessed with the case, and the letter postmarked Buffalo, where Wesley lived.

"We need to find out what's going on," May said, "and why we were hired. Why she's using us. And you should do it. Take her sailing. Make her a captive audience. Get Nootie to pack up one of her picnic coolers with sandwiches and cold drinks. Take her out into the bay where she can't run off, confront her with it, and find out what's going on."

"Yes, boss."

With the breeze blowing lightly and the mainsail up, Jake guided the *Constant* past lobster boats while Elise sat with her face to the breeze, the sun playing games with the planes of her face. She looked extraordinarily beautiful to him at that moment. Beautiful. Such a clichéd word, yet he could think of none other to describe the way she looked in her shawl and lace-up sandals, one foot under the other.

"This is nice," she said as she leaned her head back to catch the rays of the sun. He watched her and remembered May's words to him before he left to pick up Nootie's cooler. "Jake, this is business. Get over your feelings for her. Now! She's using you, Jake."

But was she? No, she wasn't. She couldn't be. Not with the way she was looking at him now. Maybe it started off that way, but surely not now!

If he followed May's plan, he would take her out, hold her upside down over the edge of the boat, and shake the truth out of her. Yes, he planned to talk to her. But not like May would. He'd tell her that he knew she was Fiona, but that he also knew why she had to keep hidden, and how he would help her keep that secret. He would offer shelter.

"I've never been on a boat before," she told him now. "So tell me if I'm about to do anything stupid, like stand when I'm not supposed to or sit where I'm not supposed to sit."

"You're fine. The boat is big; the water is perfect. You just sit back and enjoy the scenery."

"Can you teach me how to sail? I'd like to learn."

"Really?"

She nodded eagerly, like a child. And so while they made their way out to the island, he told her all about his boat. It was a sloop, he said, which meant it had one mast and two sails; one in the front and a mainsail that went up the mast. "Some boats have two masts. They're either ketches or yawls. This one's a sloop."

"'We came on the Sloop John B.'"

"Right. The song." He then explained that each sail had sheets and halyards. The halyards controlled the vertical movement of the sail, and the sheets controlled the horizontal movement. He told her that there were no ropes on a boat. Instead, they were all called lines, and they each had specific names. He showed her the various winches and devices for manipulating the lines and sails.

Right now the mainsail was up, and the engine was still running. He explained that the mainsail gave the boat stability. "Now, I'm going to unfurl the jib, and the boat will start moving a bit faster. The foresail, or front sail, is the boat's powerhouse."

He turned off the engine and unfurled the jib. The boat heeled slightly.

"Wow. This is cool," she said.

"And this is barely a breeze."

The only other boats on the water were lobster boats. Jake and Elise waved as they passed.

"It's so quiet without the engine running," she said.

"That's why I like it."

Okay, Jake, talk to her. Now's your chance. And he was just about to when she asked about whales. He told her that when they'd gone out yesterday, they'd seen a school of humpbacks, which pleased the tourists.

"They got their money's worth," she said.

It was an easy beam reach, so he set the sails, engaged the auto-pilot, and sat down beside Elise in the cockpit.

"Don't you have to steer the boat?"

"Otto's doing it. Autopilot. Otto for short. My faithful crew member. I don't leave home without him."

"You lived on this boat?"

Jake smiled. "I did. This was home for me."

"Where did you come up with the name *Constant?*"

"Oh, that. Way back when I was young and innocent and thought things like love were constant."

"And now?"

"Now I'm not so sure. Now I'm not so sure about a lot of things."

"Neither am I."

He asked her how business was shaping up for her this summer, and she told him it was going to be busier than ever, which is why she really needed to be back in her studio making more dragon pins and not out sailing. He laughed. She laughed. She told him that now that school was out, Rachel had left for summer camp this morning and wouldn't be home for a week. She didn't know how she felt about that. She didn't want Rachel coming back home with a lot of weird ideas.

"If it's the camp with Stone Church, I'm sure it'll be fine."

"It's her first time away for such a long time. A week is a long time."

"She's a sweet kid."

"I would do anything for her," Elise said.

"I know."

"Anything."

Why did she say that? Jake wondered. *Does she have an inkling that I know about her?*

Neither said anything for a while. Far out at sea, a freighter moved slowly across the horizon.

Elise said, "It's nice to play hooky."

Talk to her, Jake! Talk to her now!

They were probably three miles offshore and sailing south. If they kept this course, they could be at Ridley Harbor in about three hours. Two sailboats bobbed in the distance.

"Yes, it is nice to take off work every so often," he said. "Puts things in perspective."

They had rounded the point now, and to the right stood the houses of the summer people. Some were lovely beach cottages, and some were many-storied mansions perched high on rocks. "Look at those places," she said. "You never see them from their fronts."

"That's why it's so much fun to go out in a boat." He pointed to the mansion belonging to the *CSI* writer. "And that, my dear, is what a cool twelve million gets you."

She took the binoculars he offered her and looked through them. "Wow. Where is Loren Hayes's?"

"Hers is around the corner; it faces south. We'll be coming to it soon."

In a few minutes he found Loren's mansion and told Elise where to look. It was several stories, painted blue, and set up high.

"Wow! That is absolutely gorgeous. How do you know all this?"

"Believe it or not, it's part of my whale-watching tour, pointing out the summer homes of the rich and famous. Do you want to know where G. G. Gun lives?"

"The rapper? He's got a place here?"

"He bought a house, but I don't think he's ever been here. It's that one with all the skylights, hidden in the trees over there."

"I see it. This makes sailing more fun. Can you imagine having money to buy a house like that and then only come like one week a year?"

"That'll be you, Elise. If people like Loren Hayes keep wearing your jewelry on television."

She looked at him, looked down, didn't say anything, folded her hands in her lap. "I came from such poverty. It's something I can't imagine. Something I can't even dream about."

Talk to her, Jake! Tell her what you know.

"You are very talented, Elise."

"When I was a child, we lived in this crummy little house," she said. "We didn't even have the whole house. The church was in the basement, and part of that was the school. People would traipse through our kitchen all the time..."

Jake already knew this. May had found this out, pointed it out to him on the Web.

"And then when I got married, we lived in a trailer park. And we were so poor because my husband was such a drunk that he couldn't keep a job. We had to...um...take in a boarder. In a trailer!"

That would've been David Stoller. Tell her you know who she is. Call her Fiona. Just say the name. Fiona. Fiona!

"Elise!" he said, "I..."

She turned to him. "Yes?"

"Would you like some lunch?"

She laughed then. "You had such a serious expression on your face just now, and all you want to do is offer me lunch?"

"Right. Lunch." He set the autopilot five degrees to starboard, went below, and brought up Nootie's cooler. Nootie made lunches for tourists—sandwiches, cakes, fruit, and drinks, all packed in returnable coolers for a small deposit. They were a hit with the summer crowd. He opened up the cooler. It was a joke that one of Nootie's sandwiches could feed a family in a third-world country for a week. They were piled high with roast beef, ham, and all manner of veggies.

He handed a sandwich to Elise. "I used to make these, you know," she said biting into one. "Way back when I worked for Buzz and Nootie."

"I heard," Jake said.

"They've always been good to me, like family. Here, take half. I'll never eat all this. I know what she packs in here. And carrot cake! You got the package with the carrot cake! I love you!"

Said in jest, of course, but the words pained him nevertheless.

She reached hungrily for it. "I love her carrot cake, and Nootie makes this cream-cheese icing with real butter. Well, everything's real butter with Nootie. This is *so* great. Can we eat dessert first?"

"Sure." He kept his voice light.

So they ate dessert first, and Jake didn't tell her, not then.

They tacked, and Jake explained to her that meant moving the sails to the other side of the boat so they could head back.

"Ah, do we have to?"

He looked down at her sitting there. And sighed.

"This has been so fun, Jake." She smiled up at him. Her eyes seemed to linger.

"Yeah." He was very close to her now. He could smell the sweet scent of her hair and something else, a kind of floral perfume. Jake looked down and noticed for the first time that she had freckles across her nose. He turned to her, touched the side of her face with his hand, then brought her face to his and kissed her. He hadn't meant to. Not today. Not with all he knew about her. Whatever she did, she did it because she had no choice. All the lies she'd told him, they all had logical explanations. She tasted of sun and salt and smelled of flowers and pain and tears and yearning. It had been a long time since he had kissed a woman like this.

He forgot about the missing gemstones and the murder of Neil Watts and about Wesley Stoller and the earring he had found that hadn't been lost. He forgot that the woman he was now kissing was Fiona Stoller. Proving what? Nothing. He forgot about Nootie's lobster casserole and the film Elise ruined and all the other things that didn't make sense. She was real and she was in trouble and she needed him. And he needed her. This is what made sense. When she moved away from him, tears glistened on her eyelashes. She blinked them away.

"What's wrong?" he asked.

"I can't…" She shook her head.

"You can't what?"

"This. You. I can't. It's just me. I'm not a good person, Jake."

"Elise." They were still very close. "No one's good. We, all of us, bumble along as best we can."

She leaned against him, stayed that way. "If we stayed on this boat and if we never got off, where would we end up?"

"The direction we're headed now? Nova Scotia."

"I would like to go there. I would like to get away from everything."

Jake felt the same way. He kept his arm around her as Otto steered the boat. Occasionally he tweaked the sails, but the breeze was light and didn't require a lot of work on his part. *It would be nice,* he thought, *to escape with Elise. Even for just a little while. Pretend that the rest of the world doesn't exist.*

Her cell phone rang. She dug through her pocket. "I'm so sorry," she said. "I keep this on when Rachel's away, in case she calls."

"No worries. Family's important."

She answered the phone and gasped. Literally gasped. Then she tried to cover it up by coughing, but he'd seen the look of fear on her face. She bent her head into her hand and turned away from him. Then she got up and moved to the other side of the cockpit, as far away as she could get from him and still be on the boat. She was at the stern, facing away. She was on the phone for maybe ten minutes.

Something kicked in, and Jake the love struck became Jake the PI, former police officer. He pretended to adjust something in the autopilot, bending down to check screws underneath. He grabbed a screwdriver that he kept in a small toolbox, and pretended to work. He heard "I was just afraid. That's all." Pause. "Of course you can see her. Ruthie will be there."

Ruthie!

And then he thought he heard "Monday night," but he couldn't be sure. "Yes, there's a bus," he thought she said. Then mumbling. "Okay, then, nine thirty" and then a hasty good-bye. She stayed facing away from him for a moment or two before she turned back. When she did, her expression was bland, impersonal.

"Business," she said, snapping her cell phone closed. "It never ends."

"Hope everything's all right."

"Everything's all right," she said quietly. "Everything will finally be all right."

Later, when they arrived back at the Fog Point wharf, he realized he was going to have to come up with something to tell May, because he never told Elise that he knew she was Fiona Stoller.

~

62

While May waited for Jake, she puzzled over Stoller's trial. There was the little matter of the two shots. One neighbor claimed to have heard two shots. She picked up the phone. The chance of neighbors still being there was slim to none, but she had to try.

She was able to reach Simon Summerstein. *The gods must be looking down with favor on me.* Ten years later, and he was still living in the trailer behind where Fiona, Wesley, and Dave had lived.

When May introduced herself as a private investigator and asked him about the two shots, he said, "What, are they reopening the case now?"

"A few things have come up that we're looking into. You reported hearing two shots that night."

"I did. Yes."

"None of the other neighbors did."

"Well, I can't speak for the other neighbors now, can I? I heard one shot clear as day. Then, maybe ten, maybe fifteen minutes later, I hear another one, but sorta muffled."

"You didn't call 911?"

"Look, I told them at the time. I thought it was a car. Or someone's TV. I was watching TV. My son had the other one on, and I thought it was from a TV show. But when I heard what happened, I can't say as I was surprised. Those brothers were trouble from the get-go. You didn't need a rocket scientist to figure out that you put three no-goods together, and you get fire. Especially that youngest."

"You mean Wesley."

"I mean Warren. The youngest. Just a boy at the time. There was something about him that was scary. I mean really scary. He used to pull the wings off dragonflies. Seemed to enjoy it. Of course the father was no help on that score. Used to beat the snot out of him. They all picked on him. He was one of those kids who seem to invite bullies."

May's brows furrowed. Warren, the youngest son. He was living there too? She asked Summerstein about that.

"Well, I don't know as he was living there, but he was sure there a lot. I don't know where he lived, truth be told. He was just a kid, maybe thirteen, fourteen then. I think, though, that when the kid had enough, he'd go set up his tent in the woods next to the trailer park."

"And those three brothers didn't get along?"

"You ask me, it was the younger's fault. I said it at the time, but no one believed me. They all thought I had a bug up my butt because that Warren killed my cat."

"Warren killed your cat?"

"Nothing's for sure, but it's something I've always suspected."

"So what you're suggesting is that Warren killed David and Wesley didn't?"

"That's what I think."

"Are you familiar with the Church of Power and Fire?"

"That crazy bunch?" And then Summerstein told her more of what he remembered. While he talked, May cradled the phone in her ear and googled the church. Her search led her to two links. The first was a news article from New Brunswick, New Jersey, an obituary on the death of Lester Beechim, founder of the church, who died in a single-vehicle accident when his car skidded on a slippery road, went through a guardrail, and tumbled down a cliff. He was on his way to "special meetings" in Pennsylvania when it happened. The article went on to say that he was survived by his wife, Olivia Beechim, and two daughters, Sarah and Fiona. She also learned that the forty-member church had a school.

The information on the next link was dated five years ago and announced the end of the Church of Power and Fire. Someone named McCarthy had taken over the church after the death of Elise's father. He had disbanded the church and moved his family to Upstate New York. No city was given.

"Thank you, Mr. Summerstein," she said.

"No problem. Glad to be of assistance."

She made several other calls, found out that other people who had lived near the Stollers were dead or had moved. She didn't have much more luck. She did talk to a woman who'd lived down the street from the house where Fiona and Sarah grew up. She said she "always felt sorry for those girls."

"Why?"

"Never being allowed to play with other kids, always having to wear skirts, not allowed to go to school. That young one, Fiona. She was sure spunky. I always liked her. But that Sarah, now Sarah was a strange one."

Another strange one? "You knew her?"

"I did until a few years ago. She married a man in the cult; someone with money, I think. I think he passed away. In some ways she seemed to be like the mother, but really, I think she grew up to be more like her father."

"Would you happen to know where she lives now?"

"I heard that after she and that McCarthy fellow got married, they moved upstate."

"Any other neighbors you remember? Friends of the family?"

"Not really. Well…"—the woman paused—"there was that guy who always took pictures."

May was instantly alert. "That guy who took pictures; do you know his name?"

"Can't remember offhand."

May remembered a bit of something. *I lived in a trailer park. Neil was such a good brother. He visited so often and helped me.*

"Does the name Neil Watts ring any bells?"

"That's him! That's the one. It was his sister lived there. He was around her place a lot."

Next on her list was Neil Watts's sister.

"Did you find anything?" she asked.

"Did you happen to live in the Golden Spruce Mobile Home Park in New Jersey?"

"I did. I don't anymore."

"But you did when David Stoller was murdered down the street from where you lived."

"I did."

"And you didn't think this was important when we were asking about Neil's connection with Wesley Stoller?"

Neil's sister was quiet.

May continued, "You said that he was obsessed with that trial. Yet you never mentioned that you just happened to live down the street from the Stollers, the very people involved in the murder trial."

Shallow breathing sounds came through the phone receiver. "No, I didn't connect the two. I didn't see a relationship with the murder here."

Another fly in the pie, May thought, shaking her head.

63

M oon had a recording device in his own phone. That afternoon, with Cain at work, Moon sat at his table, ate a Big Mac, and listened.

Well blow me down, the two of them, Elise and Cain are going to meet!

Plan A: Drive to Fog Point and pay little Elise a visit. Things were moving fast.

Elise would remember Moon. She of all people would remember him. He remembered that night like it had just happened. His father was home, so he'd left the house and set up his tent on the edge of the trailer park. He'd been on Fiona's back step, reading through a stack of Popular Mechanics he'd bought at a used bookstore for a dollar a bundle. Old technology, but some of that old stuff worked just as well or better than the newfangled stuff. And besides, he couldn't afford the newfangled stuff. Not then, anyway. He was there because Fiona was the only person who paid him any kind of attention. She was kind to him, and he was under the mistaken notion that she was in love with him, and he with her. He was also under the mistaken notion that he could protect her. On this particular afternoon he'd taken up his perch outside the window and read his magazines. Something he could do for hours. And then Wesley and Dave came home drunk or high or both. He heard shouting from inside.

Fiona ran outside with a gun. She told him that Wes had passed out in the bedroom and Dave was yelling. As much as he loved Fiona, Warren hated his brothers more. He saw his chance, a chance he'd been waiting for his whole life.

He could barely make sense of what she was saying. She waved the gun wildly and said that Dave had been aiming it at Ruthie and saying he was going to shoot her. Dave had put the gun down on the table for a second, and she grabbed it and ran outside.

"Go shoot them, then," Warren had said calmly, looking up from his magazine. "Go back in and shoot them in the head. Just do it. Both of them."

"I can't. I can't."

"Of course you can." He put down his Popular Mechanics. "Go do it, Fiona. Do it. Nobody will blame you when they're both dead. Where are they now?"

"Wes is passed out in the bedroom, and Dave is drunk in front of the television."

"Go do it." He said it calmly. He was surprised at his own calmness.

"I have to get my baby!"

"Do it!"

"I can't."

"Do it, Fiona!"

"I can't!"

"DO IT!"

She went back inside. He heard a shot. He waited. No second shot. He looked in the kitchen window in time to see Fiona grab

Ruthie from her crib and run out the door. Dave had fallen forward and was cursing.

"Die, you stupid moron, die," Warren had said aloud. Eventually, Dave did.

He decided then that except when it was absolutely necessary, as in the case of Neil Watts, he would get other people to do his dirty work for him. Which is why he'd been sending Fiona articles from all over the world about women who'd killed their abusive husbands and gotten away with it. He also e-mailed her once a week, pretending to be Wesley threatening her. Moon was a patient man. All good things come to those who wait, and half the fun is the chase. Just to see if he could do it.

Neil Watts, that nosy journalist, had guessed and guessed right. He'd been there right from the start, asking his questions, taking his pictures. And since he'd found out the truth, Watts had to go. So Moon had driven to Fog Point one night, taken care of the problem, and then left.

And now he was listening to a taped conversation between Cain and Fiona. Cain tried to sound so apologetic, and he expressed such surprise about her being in Fog Point, and of course asked her about someone named Elise St. Dennis.

"That's me. It's the name I've taken."

"But why?"

"I needed to start over. For Rachel's—Ruthie's—sake. It was for her."

He asked about the restraining order, and she said she'd call the cops right away and have it lifted.

"Why did you get it in the first place?" he asked.

"I was just afraid. That's all. I was just afraid. I had some weird things happen to me, and I thought it was you. I had to do it. I'm sorry now, because I really would like to see you."

"I just want to apologize. That's all."

"I understand."

Moon listened while they made arrangements. She told him that Monday night was fine. Around nine thirty because she had to work until nine.

"Will Ruthie be there?"

"Of course she'll be here. She's here now. Where else would she go? She'd love to see you. Her name's Rachel now."

"Rachel."

"Yes. Will I recognize you? Are you different?" she asked.

"I'll be wearing a Red Sox ball cap and a blue nylon jacket."

"I'm looking forward to it."

Monday night. This Monday night. Cain didn't know it, but Moon planned to be there with bells on.

64

M ay was furious. "So you just went out there with company money and had a nice sail? You never talked to her; you just sailed around? I wish I could do that. Maybe I should, Jake. Maybe I should get in my little Boston Whaler and get a nice little cooler from Nootie and go off and have a picnic, right in the middle of the day while e-mails come in by the dozen and Ethan's dealing with an irate customer about a compass that he claims is skewed, and he's got his blood in a knot over it, and poor Ethan…"

"May, slow down. Just slow down." Jake was mad too. She could tell by the lines around his mouth. And Jake didn't often get mad. "Just slow down." He even put up his hand. "I made an executive decision that I would not tell her."

"Oh, do tell? Tell me about this." She sat down behind the computer, and he leaned his back against the wall.

"I made an executive decision after she got a very long and intense phone call while we were out on the boat. I was going to confront her, I was about to, when her cell rang."

"That was convenient," May muttered.

He ignored her. "After listening to her half of the phone conversation, I decided to play along. The thing that tipped me off was that she told whoever it was that someone named Ruthie would be there for a meeting on Monday. I'm guessing Elise was referring to Rachel, who left for camp today, by the way. After hearing that, I decided we'd pretend we don't know everything. It gives us the upper hand, May. Think about it."

"The upper hand for what?"

"Something's happening. I don't know what, but something is up. Until her phone call, she was calm and enjoying her day. After the phone call, there was this jitteriness in her, and she kept making these cryptic little remarks like 'In a few days, everything will be all right.'"

May opened up a file on her computer. "I should show you what I found, then," she said. "Here, read this." She rolled the chair away from the computer. "Meanwhile, I'm starved. Haven't eaten all day."

"I can solve that," Jake said. "We barely made any headway into Nootie's cooler." He pulled the cooler out of his sail bag. "Half a sandwich for you and half a sandwich for me. Supper. As soon as Elise got that phone call, it was like a switch was flipped. She didn't eat any more."

"Okay," May said, hungrily biting into a Nootie Club House. "Whatever it is with Elise, it happens on Monday night. Did you happen to catch a time?"

"Yes. Nine thirty. That's p.m."

May told him about the phone calls she'd made that day, how the neighbors called both Warren, the younger Stoller brother, and Sarah dangerous and scary.

"So," Jake said scrolling down the computer screen, "you think Sarah had something to do with her father's and her husband's accidents? Her father was in prison, though."

"No, he wasn't. He was never in prison."

"I still think Elise might be an innocent in all of this. I think she's being used, and I think she's scared out of her mind. And so she has to lie to cover up."

"So what you're saying is that someone else gave her a new identity and told her to stay away. Someone else just made her take those gemstones out of the snake eyes and claim that Stoller did it."

Jake frowned. "We haven't totally established that."

"Well, you may not have established that, but go talk to Bill. The police have established that. And they're not spending a ton of time on the Peeping Tom thing, either. And it's likely that letter she probably wrote and sent to herself is sitting in some evidence locker marked 'not urgent.'"

May sighed. She intended to say more but didn't. Jake was getting angry, and they didn't need that. They didn't work well together if one of them was angry.

"I'm sorry, Jake. It's been one of those days."

"I'm sorry too."

"We're both tired. So who do you think Elise is meeting on Monday night? Sarah? It couldn't possibly be Wesley, could it?"

May looked at him. She was thinking about something then, trying to add two and two to get four, but she kept getting five or six. Nothing made any sense. She thought about it some more.

"Elise said nine thirty?" May asked.

"Yes, that's what I heard."

May quickly consulted the Internet. "And whoever it is she's meeting, Sarah or Wesley, would presumably be coming on the bus? She said bus, right?"

"Right."

"Okay, I say we meet that bus and intercept whoever it is and have a nice chat with that person."

65

To my mother, who's not like other mothers,

I wrote you a postcard yesterday from camp. Our counselor wouldn't let us go to archery until we'd written postcards to our parents and put stamps on them. We were all complaining at first, even Ashley, and she never complains about anything. One of the girls in the cabin said, "Why can't we just e-mail them?"

But our counselor, a real pretty girl named Jenny, said we had to write on regular cards with stamps. She even gave us the cards. The other girls were writing cards asking about their pets or their brothers and sisters or talking about the stuff we did here. But I didn't know what to write to you.

I found a box in your closet of magazine articles about dead people. This is totally beyond weird! You're so busy now making jewelry that you're not home a lot, so before I came to camp, I was in your closet trying on all your shoes and walking around in them. They all fit me.

Well, there were these boxes at the top of the closet. And I wondered what was in them. More shoes? I pulled them down. More shoes. And weirdness of weirdness, there were actually flat shoes. Really, really ugly tie shoes like an old lady would wear, and a pair of sneakers and flat sandals.

There was this other box behind the shoes, and I pulled it down. It didn't have shoes in it. It was filled with pages from magazines and newspapers. And every one of those was about murdering people. I read, "Wife Poisons Philandering Husband with Pesticide." It showed a picture of the lady who did this, and her hair was all wild and gray. She'd be the perfect witch in a play.

There was this other article from the newspaper about a wife who shot her husband and then hid him in the basement. She kept on living her normal life, like going to church and to work and coming home and watching television, all with this dead person in the basement. Gross!

Why do you have all these articles about dead people? About poisoning people and putting them in the basement? Why do you put mud on your boots instead of wiping it off? Why do you have a gun, and why are you hanging around Carl Featherjohn? I wanted to talk to my counselor about you, but all that came out was, "I can't write a postcard. My mother's not like other mothers."

"How so, Rachel?" she asked me.

"Well, she wears high heels all the time. And I mean all the time. Just ask Ashley."

"Rachel, let me tell you something. All mothers are not like other mothers. Every girl thinks her mother is the one who is not like other mothers."

But I said no, my mother really isn't like other mothers.

But I couldn't tell my counselor about the articles about dead people and about the gun. I couldn't. I just couldn't.

So here's what I wrote:

Dear Mom,

I love you even though you're not like other mothers.

Love, Rachel

I showed it to Jenny. She smiled. I'm sure she's thinking you will laugh about it.

But then, at least I was allowed to go to archery.

Your faithful daughter (maybe I'm not like other daughters),

Rachel St. Dennis

~~

Across the Ocean
By Rachel St. Dennis

Whales know how to swim very fast. They can actually move from place to place faster than most boats. In 1980 they put a tag on a finback whale and discovered that it had traveled more than a thousand miles in five days. A finback can swim about twenty-five miles per hour. Killer whales also swim very fast.

I think it would be neat to be able to swim that fast because you could get away from things then. You wouldn't have to stay around when strange things happened to you. You could just swim away.

Ashley and I watched a movie about a girl who rode on the back of a whale. I was thinking I'd like to ride a fast whale all the way across the ocean!

66

I *love you, Mom, even though you're not like other mothers.*

Elise taped the postcard on the refrigerator, where it stood out, the lone piece of paper on a wide expanse of clean white. Rachel was right, of course. She wasn't like other mothers. Most mothers don't plan murders. Most mothers haven't lived with a secret for ten years, a secret so profound that it destroys their souls and renders them incapable of love, of passion. Or had it? She loved her daughter with a fierce kind of love. And it hurt her, what she was doing to Jake. But even in the beginning, even long ago, everything she did was out of love.

Jake was a good man. He was a good and gentle man who didn't deserve what she was doing to him. She had chosen him. She had chosen him out of all the others. When he first walked into her shop to buy bracelets for his daughters, she had looked at him, studied him. She'd seen the way he winked at her. She'd noticed his crooked glasses, his slouchy sweater, and the way he grinned. And she knew, she *knew* he would be perfect. The fact that he was a private investigator was so much the better.

The shop had been unlocked that day, something that never happened, but it turned out to be just a simple mistake. She and Jess had their wires crossed. She thought Jess was there, and Jess thought she was there.

But that had planted the idea.

She wasn't in love with Jake. When he kissed her on the boat, she felt nothing, only a vague sense of sadness and longing.

She was a user, one of her father's gifts to her. And she was using this good and gentle man who was falling in love with her.

On the day Elise first met Jake, Sarah had called back.

"You didn't leave a message," Elise told her. "You're always supposed to leave a message."

"He's out."

"What do you mean he's out?"

"Ten years. He's out on parole."

"He can't be!"

"He is. What will you do?"

"I'll get a restraining order. A gun. I don't know. He can't be out."

"Well, he is, sweet sister, and you better think about what you plan to do."

And then Elise made her decision. No longer hiding from Wesley Stoller, she would take action. Part of the plan, the major part, involved finding a man to cry to and pretending to be stalked, so that when they did find Wesley's gunned-down body, she could claim self-defense, and that man would be her star witness. Then she changed her Web site, added her picture, all as a front and a lure.

She could imagine Jake testifying. *Yes, Your Honor, she came to me many times, very afraid. He appeared at her window; I saw the boot prints.*

The boot prints. That had been a mistake. That was Carl's idea.

"I'll do what you want. I'll look in your window and you scream. But what do you think about making boot prints?"

She should have listened to her own instincts and said no to the prints. She should have realized that people can do a lot with prints, like match them to boots. "Stupid, stupid Carl," she said aloud. She had no choice but to destroy the film and pour a bucket of water on the prints and then wreck the eaves. But that hadn't worked. There were so many things she hadn't thought of.

She'd run out of Noonan's that day because of the letter, the letter she had sent to herself because this letter set her plan in motion. And she was afraid. While Wesley was in prison, he posed no threat. She was well hidden then, but some deep instinct told her that when he got out, he would move heaven and earth to look for her.

She'd read the articles that Sarah had sent, the many other women who'd done this. Who'd been pushed this far and did what they had to do. She was just doing what she had to do. And any court could see that. It happens all the time.

Sarah had helped her out of the first situation. It was Sarah who made it right, after Fiona had run out of the trailer carrying Ruthie. She had run to Sarah's three blocks away.

Sarah made it right. Sarah came back, wiped the prints from the gun, and placed it in Wesley's hands. But Warren showed them that they had to fire the gun. Wesley's fingers had to have powder residue on them. Sarah and Fiona had fired the gun into the pillow, as a silencer.

And then Warren had turned to Fiona. "Now it's our turn. We can get married, Fiona. I'll take care of you. Now that he's gone, I'll take care of you and Ruthie."

Sarah threw back her head and laughed, but Fiona sat down on a chair, held Ruthie close to her, and turned her face away from him.

"Warren," Sarah said, "are you insane? Do you think for a minute she'd marry you *now?*"

Fiona did not turn her face to look at him. Not once. She never wanted to see him again. She couldn't see any of them again. It had to be that way. For the sake of her daughter. After the trial she left. She found someone who would give her a new identity, and she moved away. Wesley hit her. Wesley beat her. Wesley belittled her. Dave raped her. While Warren just stood looking at them. He did nothing. He never helped her. Only watched, like he enjoyed it.

She needed to kill Wesley. She had to kill him. Because what if he remembered what really happened on that day?

67

Jake hoped he would recognize Wesley. He had the ten-year-old picture folded up in his wallet. Would that be enough? He had no idea what Sarah looked like, but he thought he would have a better chance recognizing her. Plus, this whole thing was a long shot anyway. He kept checking the schedule. The bus from Buffalo was due in at the Ridley Harbor station at 7:30. The challenge would be getting Wesley to listen to him—or Sarah. Jake's hunch was that it would be Wesley and that the guy would be coming alone.

Jake sat on an orange chair and sipped old coffee from a Styrofoam cup. The bus from Buffalo would come in at this bay; that's what they told him at the counter. He looked at his watch. Ten minutes. Jake could take one of two approaches if Wesley showed: He could either strong-arm the guy or merely walk up and introduce himself. He hadn't decided yet which approach he would take. If he strong-armed Stoller, there was always the chance that he would yell, alert the authorities. But if Jake just walked up to him, Stoller could run. If Sarah showed up, he'd just walk over and calmly introduce himself.

He looked around. Everything about the bus depot was gray,

except for the orange chairs. A kiosk in the middle, manned by a tired-looking East Indian, sold old coffee and stale donuts.

He sat there and tried not to think about Elise. He tried not to remember that kiss, the way her hair smelled, the way her back felt, frail and so vulnerable as he held her, that soft place on the back of her neck. May could still have it wrong. It was possible.

Jake finished his coffee and dropped the cup into the receptacle beside him. Three seats away a large man in an unbuttoned coat was leaning back and snoring slightly. Across from him three teenaged girls draped their thin bodies over the chairs and jabbered loudly.

May always made sense, and as much as Jake didn't want it to be true, some deep part of him sensed it. He leaned back, looked at the ceiling. In its former life this place was a train station, majestic high ceilings, big octagonal windows at the top, lots of stonework. It was a place where, in days past, businessmen carried leather briefcases and went to important meetings out of town. It was a place where lovers held each other and said their long good-byes.

Now it was a bus depot where old men snored and young girls giggled. He wondered what designer's nightmare had concocted orange for the chairs.

A bus was arriving, and Jake got up.

Stoller was the fourth person to get off the bus. Jake recognized him immediately. He carried a backpack and a couple of plastic shopping bags. Jake approached him. "Wesley Stoller?"

Stoller turned, stopped. His face fell. "Oh man. I can't believe you're here. You guys are good."

"I'm not with the police or a parole officer. But I need to talk with you about Fiona."

"You're not the police? Because I can explain."

"I'm sure you can, but I need to talk with you about Fiona."

"The parole board?"

Stoller was an inch or two shorter than Jake. He had the beginnings of a beard, which was coming in red. Other than that, he had a soft baby face and freckles.

"Not that, either. I'm here because my partner and I think you might be in danger."

"In danger from who?"

"Let's go somewhere so we can talk."

But Stoller stood there. "I'm not going anywhere with anybody. Who are you?"

"I'm a private investigator. Please, Mr. Stoller. Hear me out. This is important." He had taken hold of Stoller's jacket, but Wesley shrugged away.

"Look, I don't know who you are or what you want. I just know that I have an appointment with my wife and daughter in a few hours. I've got a bus to catch."

"I know all about that. I know your ex-wife. She's going by the name of Elise St. Dennis."

"I know that. That's not news."

"Please," Jake said. "Let's go somewhere. A coffee. A public place. And if at any time you feel uncomfortable, you can get up and leave. I'll drive you to Fog Point, by the way, but if you feel more comfortable, the bus for Fog Point leaves in an hour and a half."

"Okay. Just a couple of minutes. In a public place."

They settled on a coffee shop about a block from the bus depot that advertised fresh pies and coffee. Stoller placed his backpack and shopping bags on the seat next to him. One of the bags was from Toys "R" Us.

"You've been shopping," Jake said.

"That's none of your business."

"You're right. It's not."

Wesley sighed. "I'm sorry. I don't know what you want or why you're here. I bought presents. Peace offerings, okay? I have a daughter who's eleven. I don't know what eleven-year-old girls like. Barbie dolls? That's what the lady in the store told me. So I bought a Barbie doll."

A waitress came and took their orders. Jake wanted peach pie, and Wesley ordered chocolate mousse pie. They both said coffee would be fine.

"She's really into whales," Jake said.

"How do you know that?"

"Because Elise…Fiona hired me."

"Hired you to do what?"

"To find you, actually. And to make sure you never came to see her ever again."

Wesley winced, looked down. "I don't expect anything from her. I just want the chance to apologize. I did a lot of horrible things," he said. "But God got ahold of me in prison. I owe my life to God and to AA. This is all step nine.

"I killed my own brother when I was so drunk that I can't remember that day. I put Fiona through hell. I found Sarah. I apologized to her. I need to do the same with Fiona and Ruthie. Then I have to find my brother Warren. Dave and I treated him like garbage. He was always the brunt of our jokes. He was small and skinny, and we picked on him. Everyone did. We even sicked the school bully on him once. I need his forgiveness before I can move on."

"Your daughter won't be there when you get there tonight."

"Fiona said she would be there."

"Your daughter's at camp. There are some things you need to know about Fiona. She lies…" It actually hurt Jake physically to say that. There was a choking in his throat, a feeling of hotness in his temples. He smashed at the piecrust with his fork. "Wesley, I need to tell you something, and I need you to listen very carefully."

68

E lise sat in her darkened kitchen, the gun across her lap. The french doors were open, and she felt the breeze on her face. Across the backyard some of Lenore's B&B people were laughing. The party lights strung between trees swayed slightly in the breeze. Elise's deck light was off. She'd keep it that way. Her eyes had adjusted to the dark. She was like a cat. Not a big, lumpy lap cat but something small and feral. Something that squeezes through small spaces and walks unseen from room to room. She was that cat tonight.

What had happened to turn her world inside out like this? To form her into this person, this cat, unable to love or receive love, so much so that she didn't even try anymore. She wasn't like other mothers. That was for sure. Did she even love her own daughter? She claimed to, but it might not be love. Just some instinct that said she must, she *must,* keep this child from growing up the way she did. Was that love? Was that human love? Or did she love her daughter like a cat mother—protective, instinctive, but with no real emotion?

Did her father make her like this? Her father who belittled and derided the women in his family, who beat and raped their mother, who backhanded his daughters, all in the name of religion?

Maybe it was her own mother who had turned Elise into this

stranger to herself, sitting in the dark, a gun across her lap. Her mother who stood and took it and told them to take it as well. He's the head of the house. You listen to him. Could she blame their mother who sat, even now, a babbling, drooling wheelchair-bound old woman, in the backroom at Sarah's? Could she be blamed for this? For not standing up. For not giving her daughters a sense of purpose and power.

Could Wesley be blamed for this? Her beautiful flame-haired husband who smiled at her from across the street, she in her long denim dress, so unfashionable. Yet he loved her. And she loved him, the only person she had ever loved. If love was that smiley feeling that captured her in the middle of the night and made her want to dance on her bed in her long, white nightgown.

Her father kicked her out when she got pregnant, but that was okay. She would marry Wesley. But he had turned out to be just like the rest. He drank and drank, and when he drank he hit her. He hated her for her innocence, he said. And she hated herself for being like her own mother and not leaving.

Was Warren to blame for this? Wesley's odd younger brother who stared at her and then ran when she called to him. This strange young boy who told her he would love her more than anyone could.

Or did the blame ultimately fall on her? She wasn't strong enough to rise above it all, take on the world and write books about abuse and come out as an advocate. It was her fault that she couldn't do this. Her fault again.

But she would go on. In a few minutes, maybe an hour or two, they would come and find his body, and she would claim self-defense and go on and make her jewelry. Maybe, like Jess said, she'd even become as famous as Harry Winston. Dear, sweet, innocent Jess.

Maybe Elise and Rachel would move to California, and she'd set up shop on Rodeo Drive. Never mind the high rent; she'd be making lots of money then. Rachel, with her beautiful red hair and soft skin, would take acting lessons and be a movie star someday. And in her Academy Award speech, she'd hold up her Oscar and thank her mother, her wonderful single mother who taught her that she could make it on her own. And maybe Elise would even find happiness, or a kind of happiness. Maybe she'd find someone like Jake to marry. She wouldn't love him. She didn't know what that felt like anymore, but they would have some sort of companionable life together in their mansion that Elise's Creations built. She would go on. And this day would ultimately be forgotten.

She breathed. It seemed later than nine thirty, but she dare not get up and check, if only not to lose her night vision. So she sat. But surely it was almost ten by now. She became jittery. She looked down at the gun. Picked it up, held it the way Carl had taught her. She held it in her hands and aimed it toward her patio. *Kapowee,* you're dead. Then she put the gun back on her lap. It looked funny. The bullets looked funny. But everything looked funny when she had only moonlight to see by.

Elise heard a car door slam out front, then footsteps. He would take the bus, Wesley had told her, and then a cab from the bus station. She picked up the gun and tensed. Then she stood up quietly, like the cat that she was, her feet shoulder width apart, shoulders relaxed. She held her gun hand the way Carl had showed her, holding it securely with both hands, aiming through the sights.

He was whistling. It was Wesley. He always whistled in that off-key way, the tune that was one of his favorites—"Slip Slidin' Away." It was him! She had that Paul Simon cassette tape. She almost faltered, almost put the gun down. But no. It had to be done, and it had to be done now. This was it.

He walked up the walkway like he said he would, in a Red Sox ball cap and a dark jacket that was probably blue. And out of the sides of his ball cap, his beautiful red hair. She had loved that hair once. She remembered the way if felt, soft and springy. Like Rachel's. There was so much of him in Rachel.

He stood in front of her now, maybe twenty feet away, looking at her. She couldn't see his face in the night, but she could tell that he'd grown a beard. He said nothing. Just stood there. The whistling stopped. *Wesley! Wesley! You betrayed me!*

She spoke the rehearsed words. "You were drunk when I killed your brother, and you're sober now when I will kill you." She took aim and fired two shots right into his chest.

He fell with a groan, a grunt, and a sideways clutching of his chest. She wondered if he would die right away or if he would moan and curse like his brother.

Then there were noises. And lights. And people coming out of nowhere to grab her. People in police uniforms. She saw Carl. Carl? And she saw someone who looked like May rush over to the body on the grass.

And then Wesley moaned and got up from the grass, shook his head, and took off the ball cap, which also took off all that red hair of his. Elise looked on in confusion. Jake! It was Jake, not Wesley. Jake! How could this be Jake? How could she have shot Jake? But no, he was shaking off the grass. He wasn't dead. It wasn't like last time with Dave.

Bill was there, too, and he came and put his hand on Jake's shoulder while Elise continued to look on in confusion.

She looked at Jake then, straight into his eyes, begging him to try to understand. He looked at her. Their eyes locked for a long minute. And then nothing; he just turned away. Wesley was there then, the real Wesley, and he stood to the side. Jake gave him back his ball cap, and Wesley put it on. Wesley was looking at her. His hands were at his side, and he held a bag from Toys "R" Us. Police officers were on either side of her now, and they handcuffed her and led her quietly to a police car. She heard snatches of conversation.

Jake said, "I'm glad I didn't need this Kevlar vest."

May countered, "We can thank Carl for that."

Carl! He had come to her house around nine. Said he needed to see her gun, had to fix a "manufacturer's defect" in it. It was real important, he said, that he have a look at it. What had he done to her gun? Made it so it misfired? What had he *done?*

And Jake again, "But I need my glasses. Blind as a bat without them. May, do you have them? Almost walked up the wrong driveway."

"Thanks, Carl." May now. "I apologize for all the miserable things I've said about you. You really came through in the end."

"No worries. It was the least I could do, darlin'."

They held Elise's head down as they put her into the back of the cruiser. The last thing she remembered before they closed the door on her was the unmistakable sound of a Harley retreating in the distance.

EPILOGUE

It turned out to be the best season yet for whales. Toward the end of the summer, Jake and May made two trips a day and guaranteed whale spotting every time. They had a money-back guarantee on seeing whales, and by the end of the summer, every trip paid for itself. Happy customers saw minkes and humpbacks, and one minke gave a show by blowing. And, of course, there were dolphins and plenty of seals.

They ended up hiring two more summer students, and that was in addition to Jana, who turned out to be indispensable in the sanctuary of the Purple Church. Alex took a bit more time to warm up to living in Fog Point for a month. But at Ben's urging, she joined a girls' softball team; then her summer turned out okay.

One weekend Jake took his daughters out overnight on the boat, anchoring in a cove just south of Ridley Harbor. On the way back they stopped in Ridley, and he bought them L.L.Bean sweatshirts.

All of this while Elise awaited trial. The courts were notoriously slow. For his part, Jake knew he would probably be called upon to testify at some point.

It turned out that Elise had hired Carl Featherjohn to stand at her window and look in. She'd written that letter herself and had Carl drive it to Buffalo and mail it. She'd paid him handsomely. And for his part in all of this, he'd felt ashamed. He had no idea what she was up to. But in the end, Carl had come through, removing the bullets from Elise's gun and replacing them with blanks. As a precaution, he took all of the shells away with him. Fortunately, she hadn't looked too closely at the bullets in the gun, nor had she noticed that her other bullets were missing.

As Bill suspected, Elise herself had removed the gem eyes from the snakes.

Her story was written up in *People*, and afterward, a Women's Defense League headed by none other than Loren Hayes started rallying to her cause. Everyone in town thought that Loren would probably angle for the lead when the story was made into a TV movie. All the publicity was no doubt good for Elise's jewelry business. She'd probably sell more jewelry in prison than she did in Fog Point.

As for Wesley, he was trying to make a life for himself in Buffalo, where he took on a management position at Aybeez Car Wash. He also spent the summer getting to know his daughter through court-attended visits. From all accounts, they seemed to be getting along fine.

Rachel went to live with Ashley and her family. They applied for custody, but, unbelievably, Sarah also put in a bid for full custody. Wesley accused Sarah of killing both her father and her husband and of orchestrating the cover up of Dave's murder, but Sarah procured accident documents that proved otherwise, so Wesley's claims were disregarded.

Jake only hoped that the courts would really be on the side of the child in this custody battle. But no one made any guarantees. What did Rachel want? To be with her mother. "My mother needs me," she told the judge repeatedly.

Throughout the summer May and Jake occasionally received whale-related e-mail from Rachel. And at the end of the summer, Rachel and Ashley and her family took a ride aboard the Purple

Whale. Rachel actually smiled. Ashley's mother said it was the first time Rachel had smiled since her mother was arrested.

As it turned out, the whole incident in Fog Point had nothing to do with terrorism. Stuart, they had discovered, was actually writing a novel on terrorism, a Tom Clancy type of thing. As long as Stuart stayed on his meds, he was fine. That night he had wandered through the backyards because of the face in Elise's windows. He'd seen Carl. He and Rachel had seen Carl, but no one had listened.

Jess stayed on in Fog Point and decided to open her own business-consulting firm. She was doing well. The sculpture of the hands stood proudly in her front window.

A rumor went around town that Earl Featherjohn had provided Elise with her new identity, that he had done that sort of thing for others and had done it for her. Some of the neighbors remembered seeing strangers they described as "shady characters" going in and out at Featherjohns' at all times of the day and night. The police were never able to get a search warrant, however. The shady characters and criminal types were most likely guests at the B&B. Still, the rumors persisted. But that was Fog Point.

The one remaining missing piece of the puzzle was the murder of Neil Watts. The official word from the police was that it was still under investigation. Elise had an ironclad alibi for the murder, and so did Sarah and Wesley. Police remained baffled.

Around midsummer, Jake decided to fill Moon in on what happened. After all, Moon had been quite helpful at the beginning. According to Wesley, Moon had been helpful all along, finding Sarah and leading him to Fiona. Jake wanted to say thank you, but when he called, Moon's phone was answered by Troy Davenborn, who said he was the owner of the building. When Jake asked to speak to Moon, Davenborn said, "The little SOB took off on his Harley…," and then he let out a series of epithets that made *The Sopranos* sound like *Sesame Street.* "And if I ever get my hands on that stinkin' piece of…"

At which point Jake silently closed the lid on his cell phone.

As summer day added onto summer day, he thought about Elise. He remembered the way she had sat there in the dark on her patio. He'd been used. He'd been had. But he had May, his daughters, and his friendship with Ben, who spent more than his share of time chatting and drinking coffee with Jake over the summer.

All that glitters is not gold. Elise glittered, but she was not gold. *All who wander are not lost.* Maybe there was a chance for this wandering boat bum. He'd keep talking to Ben.

Jake picked up his phone. He felt like a scoundrel, like the lowest of the low, the scummiest of the scum, and if, when he called her, she told him where to go, he would.

Nevertheless, he punched in the number. She answered on the first ring.

"Uh…Carrie? Hi, it's me, Jake. I was thinking about something. I owe you a birthday present, and I was wondering if you'd like to go out on my sailboat with me. We could look at the fall colors, and…"

"I'd love to, Jake."

ABOUT THE AUTHOR

LINDA HALL, a member of the Crime Writers of Canada, is the author of eleven novels, including *Chat Room* and the Christy-nominated *Steal Away*. She and her husband, Rik, live in New Brunswick, Canada. When she's not writing, they enjoy spending time aboard their sailboat *Gypsy Rover II*.

Linda would love to have you visit her at her Web site: *writer hall.com*.